FINNEY COUNTY PUBLIC LIBRARY
605 E WALNUT ST
GARDEN CITY KS 67846

FILARIA

A NOVEL BY BRENT HAYWARD

D0907807

ChiZine Publications

FIRST EDITION

Filaria © 2008 by Brent Hayward
Jacket illustration © 2008 by Erik Mohr
All Rights Reserved.

This book is a work of fiction. Names, characters, places, and incidents are either a product of the author's imagination or are used fictitiously. Any resemblances to actual events, locales, or persons, living or dead, is entirely coincidental.

CIP data available upon request

CHIZINE PUBLICATIONS
Toronto, Canada
www.chizinepub.com
savory@rogers.com

Edited by Brett Alexander Savory
Copy edited and proofread by Sandra Kasturi

torontod**arts**council
An arm's length body of the City of Toronto

For my family growing up, and for my family now.

Thanks to Bob Boyczuk and Peter Watts for their help with the manuscript. Special thanks to Brett Alexander Savory for his editing prowess. Produced with the support of the city of Toronto through the Toronto Arts Council.

Babar finally dropped off to sleep, but his sleep was restless and soon *he dreamed*: He heard a knocking on his door. Tap! Tap! Then a voice said: "It is I, Misfortune, with some of my companions, come to pay you a visit."
—Jean de Brunhoff, *Babar the King*

"What," she'll say, "no little bones in your mouth? And you have the impertinence to love me? Get out, you wretch, and here's a kick to help you on your way!"
—Albert Cohen, *Belles du Seigneur*

1. THE ENGINEER

PHISTER, L32

DEIDRE, L2

MEREZIAH, L23-24

TRAN 50, L20

2. SOLDIERS

PHISTER, L31

DEIDRE, L1

MEREZIAH, L17-18

TRAN 50, L12

3. LOVERS

PHISTER, L19

DEIDRE, L1A (SUPERSTRUCTURE)

MEREZIAH, L8-9

TRAN 50, L14

4. THE ANCESTORS

PHISTER, L15

DEIDRE, BEYOND

MEREZIAH, L1

TRAN 50, L32

1. THE ENGINEER

PHISTER, L32

Shotgun, eagle-eyed, Young Phister spotted the power outlet, just ahead, mounted on the wall nearest him. Yet travelling this strange, vaulted hallway with McCreedy, he did not immediately recognize the outlet as such and said nothing as the car trundled toward it, nor as the car passed it, but when he could no longer deny what he was now looking back at, he managed to whistle low and point a long finger over his shoulder; hunched at the wheel, McCreedy could not (or would not) see the receding outlet, even with Phister gesticulating and saying in hushed tones, "There. Right there. Look! McCreedy, I *swear*."

The type of hall might have been almost familiar but neither man had been down this particular stretch before, despite McCreedy's assurances over the past few hours that now he knew where they were. Possibly, Phister thought, no man had traversed these halls since genesis. Power outlets were located near old service centres, or sometimes directly under those smooth, glassy portions of the ceiling, forever matte and dark, like trapped rectangles of night. Outside doorways, too, especially ones marked with yellow and black stripes. *Always* on the driver's side. Located in odd places here? Did that have special meaning, offer clues? Any portent?

Sleeping in the car had been cold and uncomfortable. No food, and water dwindling. Dearth of canteens—full scale or stand-alone—had been the first sign things would be different.

They'd started out once more when daylights came on. McCreedy had told him all morning they were headed home while Phister grew increasingly sure they were getting more hopelessly lost. Though

Phister had no sense of direction. He admitted that. Hallways opened where previously there had been none. Rooms vanished overnight. Walls materialized as he turned his back, shifting positions in the periphery.

Now, seeing the outlet here, on the passenger's side, in an open stretch of this oddly vaulted hallway, in which no one might ever have set foot, thoughts of chaos and insecurities back home—and in his own mind—managed to bring little comfort.

"McCreedy, I'm telling you, stop if you want to fill this thing."

Between stained dark lips, opening slowly—for they were sealed with gummy saliva—McCreedy's wet voice, at last, assenting: "You're the eyes. I don't see fuck all but what do I know? Shut you up, we'll stop."

So they stopped.

Reversing, a long, smooth arc, brought the wall on Phister's side closer. Rubber tires crunched lightly over dusty flags.

"There," Phister said, pointing again. "See?"

Square, black, showing signs of polish through the grey clinging growth and marked down one side with copper script: clearly an outlet. Overgrown, unused for centuries, perhaps, or never, but for all appearances the same as others mounted in more familiar locations, back home.

The car was near exhausted. It had another hour or two left, at most. Phister suspected that old man McCreedy would have kept on driving until the vehicle ran out of juice, then got out and walked, then crawled, claiming until they both collapsed dead that he knew all the while where they were headed, home was just up ahead.

"We'll reach a junction soon," he said, as the car idled. "I remember. I was here as a kid. We take a left and come out at an air skirt, down a back hall for a few klicks and emerge in the secondary pipe room. Then home." Gesturing with a slow sweep of his hand, meant to reassure, but Phister imagined the two of them lost forever. He pictured his own grisly corpse.

In the tiled gutter on the other side of the hall a small creature scurried. Young Phister kept his keen eyes peeled. Some of the older folks said that, like Reena. *Keep them eagle eyes peeled*, she'd say. *You was born with good peepers.* He wished Reena were here with them now. She would know what to do.

McCreedy motioned with his chin but Young Phister was already climbing down to unravel the plug from its stand. Winding the cord around his forearm and fumbling with the plughead against the cool power plate, he felt like a child again, helpless against lurking monsters, waiting in shadows to slash out and take him down, bloody, at the knees. He looked both ways before starting to scrape lichen and the deposits of time from the contacts with a gnawed thumbnail. How far did the world extend anyhow? Hallways and more of these deserted hallways, changing subtly, going on forever?

A mist of sorts lingered over the flags and a dank smell tainted the air, one he had not perceived seated in the car. Light was a little more yellow than he had grown up under, a flickering, sickly glow. Perhaps conduits had broken in the vicinity, long ago. Humidity was cloying and had damaged the ceiling.

"... charging ..."

The car's whisper startled Phister. The outlet was live, at least. Contact had been made between the plug and the plate. Not many outlets enabled the car to talk—

Phister looked up. He thought he had heard something else, aside from the vehicle's weak voice. Something out *there*. He took a deep breath.

He tried to stop conjuring threats to his life but as a kid those monsters had filled his cold-sweat dreams. Now, as a man of sixteen, they were hard to shake.

He saw no source of the sound.

He did not hear it again.

The car, meanwhile, had reached sufficient power to address them: "Sirs," it began, as it always did, when it had these opportunities, "my need of a tune-up and overhaul is *dire*. I implore you to seek the nearest member of MMG. You are—if I may be so bold—grossly abusing a vehicle belonging to the Department of Public Works.

"Are you ill-trained staff? Rogue guests? My i.d. reader seems to have been disabled. Renegades? Or perhaps there's a problem with your comprehension? Complaints have been logged with my supervisor. I assure you, as soon as network links are restored, you *will* hear about this. If you are staff, your departmental budget will be charged. You will be suspended, pending a hearing. And if you turn out to be guests, you'll be apprehended, incarcerated, and quite possibly evicted . . .

"Do your parents know where you are?"

With a ghost of a grin Young Phister glanced at McCreedy, but the taciturn expression on the older man's face—staring forward, jaw thrust from under his mouldy cap—made Phister doubt whether the driver had even heard the car's rant. Beyond ironic, he thought, to end up like this, with a miserable old man I've never liked, hopelessly lost in hostile halls, driving to our mutual demise.

Nausea flickered in the abyss of Phister's empty stomach, while, on the dashboard, the little battery icon, half-full, flashed steadily.

The car, having said its piece, waited.

McCreedy took some dried moss from an inside pocket of his vest, pushed it into his maw, and chewed. He offered none to Young Phister. The driver was an addict. A damn addict. Phister liked the stuff, sure, but he didn't have a problem like McCreedy's: he could stop any time. He watched McCreedy's mouth moving, watched the old man squint and nod to himself, and mumble. All Phister wanted to hear now was the old man admitting, before they both died, that he, McCreedy, had no clue where they were and never had.

"Mad old car," Phister said quietly, after a moment. "Filing your unheard complaints." He patted the scarred quarter panel. "And there is a problem with our understanding. You're right. We don't understand half the stuff you talk about." Trying to smile now, and looking at McCreedy again, but of course he got no reaction, so he flushed, fell silent, cursing himself for trying once more to break the barrier between him and the driver. The insane car would be better company. Phister wanted to apologize to the vehicle but would never hear the end of it if he did. He touched it once more.

"You know," the car said, "I nonetheless feel an obligation. To fulfill my duties. Whoever you are. You asked about the weather outside? Well, let's see. Today, the weather outside is. The weather. Today? Outside? The weather?"

There was a quick burst of static from under the hood. Phister yanked his hand back and McCreedy's laugh was cruel. With a motion of his head the old man spat, dark fluid spattering the flags and strands of moss sap running down the stubble of his chin. Wiping these away with the back of one hand, McCreedy stared into the haze ahead. "You hear that garble? Sure shut the fucker up. Weather outside always do that." His voice was dry, his eyes glassy with moss.

The car, indeed, remained quiet.

The hallway, too. Deathly quiet.

Phister tugged at the plughead, breaking contact. He stowed the plug quickly and regained his seat.

"Always wants to tell you about the weather," McCreedy said, leering horribly as he put the car into gear. "Wants to talk about *outside* this and *outside* that and the fucking weather and it never can." He laughed that unpleasant laugh again.

Screw you, Phister thought, holding onto the brass handrail with both hands as the car, fully charged now, picked up speed. Screw you. Mists, like cobwebs, whipped through what few strands of hair Phister had on his head. Moisture cooled his exposed skin. They passed a puddle reflecting light up at the poorly illuminated ceiling—a silver scale—and then it was gone.

These hallways did go on and on and on.

Despite his better judgment, Phister soon said, "McCreedy?"

No response.

"What do you think it means, anyhow? The car, when it says that. This old machine?"

Still nothing.

"About the weather. About outside. About staff, and guests and parents."

"How the fuck should I know." McCreedy flicked across a quick glance, glazed eyes narrow. He shrugged. "Things it remembers. Things it thinks we give a shit about. But I don't really have a clue and I don't really care. So shut up and let me drive, all right? There's a canteen coming up. You'll see. We'll eat there and be home by nightfall."

"Yeah. Home . . ." It occurred to Phister that he and McCreedy could, with the car now charged, continue driving for another three days. *Farther away. Farther away from home.* What would the halls be like then? The same? Changed in even more subtle ways? Without water, he and McCreedy would be dead anyway. They neared that final cul-de-sac. Should have kept mum about spotting the outlet in the first place, he thought, and we'd be out of juice soon, maybe talking about turning around, or walking back in the opposite direction. Better yet, maybe we would have split up.

"McCreedy, I was just asking. I was *thinking*."

"Well don't." McCreedy shifted gear and the motor hummed. "They tell me you're the lookout, the eyeballs. So look out. *Eyeball.* That's why you're here. *I* do the thinking."

Young Phister leaned back. He closed his eagle eyes. He felt sick. Sicker than usual. More than just hunger and general malaise—those he was accustomed to. This amplified degree of unpleasant sensations had begun with the onset of the present predicament, three nights prior, a lifetime ago:

Milling around the entrance to the moss room, dazed people stood listless in the dark there, while inside the room itself, Young Phister—among others—got quietly wasted.

A night like any other.

But at some point in the hazy chronology—the point when the night became unlike other nights—Crystal Max and her boyfriend, Simpson Lang, started to fight. Reclining together on a dark green hillock near the corner of the room, the couple had been chatting, chewing—like everyone else—when their voices suddenly rose.

Simpson had said something that caused Crystal to scream: I'm so tired of your suspicion!

And Simpson: You don't understand anything I say!

Stoned, huddled by himself on his own mound, Phister heard the tirade of venomous spite that quickly followed, each lash of words cutting deeper than the previous. He listened, his back to the pair before turning openly, to stare, as the argument escalated, becoming louder, more animated, until it flayed every personal aspect from Crystal and Simpson, everything that made them human, until there was nothing left of either to tear down, only an ugly, empty beast that coiled the two spent bodies and rose up, twining, to the ceiling. The nasty tones and tense postures had fractured the night, sliding it into an unwelcome place, aggressive and tumultuous.

Phister's buzz was *totally* wrecked.

Holding onto Simpson's sleeve, Crystal shrieked hysterically, tearing at him, and Simpson tried to pull away from her, one hand held up—

In his petrified state, Phister was unsure if he should interfere. Perhaps go fetch someone more decisive than he? He told himself he would wait to see if Crystal started in with her fingernails: she'd been known to. *Then* he would go for help. Or hold her back himself.

All around, paired or in small clusters, the others in the moss room chewed, dozed, talked. Somebody sang. No one else seemed to notice the fight. Phister could not understand this. For him, time was charged, poised.

Just as he assured himself that he was finally about to try getting to his feet, to do something—*anything*—Simpson Lang broke free, stumbling backwards, his shirt torn. There was blood on his face. He stood livid for a second.

Then time resumed with a crash, and Crystal's shouting; Simpson turned and stomped away, across the crests of moss as a wave of relief broke over Phister. No action had been required of him. He could tell himself he would have acted, if the fight had continued.

Crystal stood very still. Quiet now, watching Simpson recede. Only when the gloom had swallowed him altogether did she sit down, hard, crumpling to the green hump and holding her face between cupped fingers. She shook.

Recalling Crystal's misery, Young Phister wished, for an instant, that he could be someone else, or that someone else might move into his skin and take control of him. *Get things done for once.*

He caught his breath. And let it out again.

The car rumbled on.

Phister harboured sentiments for the girl. Undisputable. These lurched up in him from time to time, veering perilously close to what he suspected might actually be love. Yes, to see her cry was painful, rending his insides, but to watch her laugh, Simpson Lang at her side? Tenfold worse.

When Phister was even younger, fourteen or so—before he had been called Young Phister—he and Crystal had nurtured a relationship. Of sorts. Seeds of one, anyhow. He was sure of it, with the hindsight that two years had given him. He had certainly *liked* her—though they were only kids—but he had hung around her too much, she'd said. At that age, he had little of interest to say. She had told him he was getting pesky. Too small, besides. Too young. She liked *men*, not boys.

Crystal Max was a full year older than him. A head taller. At seventeen—spotty and pale, toothless and bald—she was the most beautiful girl Phister had ever known. He'd actually kissed her once, but their faces inappropriately canted: their noses met, squashed, and he'd had to break away for air.

He never got a second chance.

Should he have tried harder to keep the relationship alive? Maybe things she'd said to him were meant to be tests, to see if he would pursue. He reasoned this now, as he often had, as he watched Crystal grow older, as he sprouted and then promptly lost a hair or two on his chin, as he gave up trying to decipher her, and surrendered his cherry to another girl, Simone, very sweet and nice and tiny and who had since succumbed to the Red Plague. He thought about the lost relationships, and he thought about the inordinate amounts of time he'd spent thinking about them, trying to come to terms with the fact that he might never find anyone to spend his days with. Not that there were any days left to worry about now. His shot with Crystal, if it had ever existed, was certainly long gone, diminishing into the past just like his hopes of reaching home were diminishing right now. How many countless nights had he dreamt of Crystal: the smell of her skin; the grime on her hands; the sneer of dismissal that set her beautiful lips thinner when he tried to be funny?

He would never see her alive again. He would never see anyone again.

The car slowed. The hallway split, left and right. He looked over at McCreedy. Phister would have picked right. Without a word of consultation, McCreedy chose left. They rumbled onwards, down more unfamiliar paths.

Fervently, Phister hoped Crystal was safe, warm and breathing out there, somewhere, perhaps even back home.

Stumbling up suddenly from the moss bed, and heaving ragged breaths, she had gone over to the doorway. And turned back. The image of her from that moment would never leave Phister. Never. She'd been a broken thing. *Broken*. No longer even a girl, the bones of her face collapsed, structures of her wondrous physiognomy fallen in on themselves, streaked with dirt, tears, and snot. Lurching, hanging from the jamb to shout at Simpson Lang (was he still in the room? Phister never was sure, though he had looked; was not sure now, remembering): "Don't follow me! I wanna be alone! I'm leaving this fuckin hole! I wanna fuckin *die!*"

No one got up. Certainly not Young Phister. Because he weighed seven hundred pounds. He weighed four tons. Four tons of inaction.

He just watched her go. The last time he saw her.

Several of those who had been loitering on the landing outside

the moss room—Lenny, Penelope, and Cassandra, the mute—
told Phister as the lights were coming on the next morning (well,
Penelope and Lenny did, anyhow)—that they hadn't seen Crystal at
all. Hadn't seen her run past, hadn't heard her shouting or crying.
But she sure wasn't in her cot when they checked. Simpson, brooding,
half-asleep in his own little cubby, dried blood on his cheek, hadn't
seen Crystal since leaving the moss room. She wasn't anywhere.
Headachy, hungover, unsure, the group managed to work each other
up into a state of genuine concern.

"But she's run off before?"

"Yeah. Only for an hour or two. And then she was just hiding."

"Maybe she's just hiding now."

"Where?"

"She said she was leaving? Where can you go?"

"And she said she wanted to *die*?"

"Yep. Fuckin die, she said. *This time I wanna fuckin die.*"

"What about those bloody rags that Jeb found last week, in the
glower room, behind vent twenty?"

"What about them?"

"*What* bloody rags?"

"Rags with shreds of *flesh* on them. Maybe there's a
connection?"

"Aw, shit . . ."

So they told others that Crystal was missing: bleary-eyed folks,
only now heading to their rooms. Trying to impart the urgency they
felt, and Boy Harbour overheard. He stood against the wall, one foot
flat behind his butt. Boy Harbour ate no moss and felt sanctimonious
because of it. He said, "A scream, in the middle of the night. But you
mossheads was messed up, as usual. I heard *terrible* screams."

This comment—predictably dire, and given in a mean-spirited
tone, that being Boy Harbour's leaning—nevertheless caused a
collective intake of breath and exchanged looks. Something horrific
had happened! Phister felt the certainty of this in his gut. Biting
the inside of his cheek, he watched Cassandra—who could read lips

as well as anybody could listen—respond to the story with equal alarm. *Crystal was in trouble.* She had done some rash and foolish act. Had she run away? *Or was she taken?*

Sensing an audience—and loving the drama of a missing person—Boy Harbour lifted his voice: "Worms the size of pinky fingers live in your stool out there. The water's bad. Them worms eat your insides. And there's people, too, that live above us, in the ceilings. Those stories you scare each other with are true. Only they're not the same as us. They'll tear Crystal apart if they catch her, long before the worms kill her. My daddy went up there once, after the war with the men in the blue suits. He was never the same after that. Couldn't even talk about what he'd seen."

Needless to say, search parties were formed. Phister and the old man—the driver, McCreedy—would take the ancient car, checking the outer halls, driving around the perimeter of known turf and maybe even into halls uncharted. As long as they didn't go *too* far. (This was Linden's suggestion. Linden sometimes assumed the role of leader. Linden agreed Phister had good eyes and McCreedy drove real good.) The rest were to split up, on foot, and look in every conceivable place within the known turf. Each hall, each room.

Only thoughts of Crystal Max, in peril, made Phister climb into the passenger seat.

Well, she sure wasn't out here. Sure as *shit*. Nothing was. No canteens. No water spigots. Only strange halls with power outlets in odd places and who knew what else up ahead, McCreedy driving on and on. Oblivious through it all.

About to touch the sleeve of McCreedy's coat—because he wanted to vomit, and wished the car to stop—twenty metres ahead, unflinchingly, directly into the car's path, stepped a man.

Young Phister gripped the seat under him; the cover tore in his fingers. On the steering wheel, McCreedy's gloved hands twitched.

The stranger was tall. Straighter, and fuller in the face than either Phister or McCreedy—or anyone Phister knew, for that matter. Stronger, too, no doubt. Dressed in a yellowed jacket that had probably once been white, a black hat low on his head. Cracked boots, knee-high. Pale slacks. Yes, odd garb, but despite this, and despite the man's large stature and sudden appearance—despite all the horror stories and rumours Phister had heard off and on throughout his life about people who might exist *beyond*—somehow the whole surreal apparition seemed less and less threatening as they drove nearer.

The man's features were clean, uniform in tone. Perhaps older than Phister had first thought. Not like McCreedy, but about double Phister's age.

For a long moment, they regarded one another.

Then the man raised one hand and said in a clear voice, "Brothers, stop! Stop, sirs, please!"

Wisps of hair, long and white, sprouted from the man's scalp. *Hair.* This unsettling growth—exactly like an infant's, before it falls out—was tied back and poked, for the most part, down the neck of the yellowed jacket. More was crammed under the hat.

"Brothers, stop!"

And, palm held out toward them, the man now smiled, showing wet bones glistening, right inside that red mouth. *Teeth, and hair.*

Somewhat stunned, Phister waited to feel that wash of fear, or repulsion, or at least really creeped out, but all he felt was an ever-growing sense of entrancement and just plain old relief that finally they had found *some*one, anyone, no matter how bizarre.

"Could you please stop, spare a moment, answer a few questions? I'd like to ask you a few questions."

McCreedy had already stopped. The car hummed under them like a crouched beast.

"Listen, my name is Philip. A man of the cloth, a thespian, an explorer. I greet you gentlemen, and I am at your service." Holding the hand out—nails clean, trimmed—as if to shake, though still too far away for that. He looked at the car.

"What the hell do you want?" McCreedy snarled.

"Pardon me?"

"You heard me. What do you want?"

"Why such, uh, hostility?"

"Answer the question."

"We are all just men, who happen to meet in this remote hall."

"You're not like me. Look at yourself!"

"I am like you," Philip said. "Perhaps a tad healthier. But we are cut from the same cloth."

"Ratshit. Now where did you come from?"

"You, sir, are a suspicious wreck, if I may say so. I am not armed. I do not wish any trouble. Did I not say I was a man of peace?"

"No."

"Well I am." Philip sighed. He put his hands in his pockets. "However, if we are to be dispensing with any civilities—going straight to the point, as it seems—then all I want from you is information."

"Like what?"

"Did you pass anyone? In the direction you've just come? Twins, perhaps?"

"Twins?"

"Yes. Co-joined brothers? I've lost two friends."

"We didn't see no one, sir," Phister said, touching his grubby fingers to his forehead by way of greeting. "Name's Phister, by the way. They call me Young Phister. Though I'm sixteen."

A hard kick on the shin—hidden from the stranger's view behind the car's console—made Phister quickly shut his mouth again.

But too late: Philip had already turned his attentions to the passenger. "Young Phister," he said, smile widening, those big white teeth so incongruous in an adult's face, so captivating. "A *plea*sure. Seren*dip*ity to run into you, out here, in the middle of nowhere, as it were. Phister. Young Phister. A fine name. Hello, hello. Perhaps you could tell me the name of our surly friend here, at the wheel?"

"None of your business," McCreedy said. "And I ain't your friend."

"*Please.* As I've told you, I have no untoward intentions." Philip regarded each in turn. "I've lost two associates, that's all. I'm merely seeking two, uh, young *actors*. We were rehearsing, you see, for an upcoming performance of *The Engineer*, when there came a strange call. And a rumbling, as of a distant explosion. My vanished friends decided to investigate."

"What's that mean?" Phister swung his legs away from McCreedy's fumbling boot.

"What?"

"The engineer."

"The play, the man, or the prophet? Have you never heard of these?" White eyebrows went up.

Phister, who had no eyebrows but could remember a few thick hairs once growing over each of his eye sockets, shook his head.

"You poor souls. You truly are lost. When I mention the engineer, in this context, I refer to the three-act dramatic text. A classic. History. Words to live by, all in one."

"We don't know anything about that sort of shit," McCreedy said.

"For shame, gentlemen." Another step nearer. "It is in your very nature, as humans, to learn, to explore. To find out everything you can in the limited time we have been allotted. Seek out the *truth*!" This last word echoed up and down the infinite corridors. "The play, you see, deals—in a very picaresque fashion—with the engineer's inauguration and subsequent rise to mythic heights. The engineer, friends, was our veritable creator! The last act hints at his agendas for resurrection and implies that he left behind much more than just our tattered world! Oh yes, there is subterfuge, and conflict. Quite a drama! The old story of good versus evil! You must attend."

Open-mouth stares.

"Of course, I revise this work myself, as self-appointed custodian, and have my lads perform it, often, in various locales, both to keep the performance contemporary and to educate the squalid masses. (Such as, if I may say so, yourselves.) I'm somewhat of an authority."

For another long moment, neither Phister nor McCreedy spoke. They looked at each other. Then McCreedy coughed and said, "That may be, but it all sounds like a crock of shit to me. Good verses evil? I may not get around much, but I know dumb ideas when I hear them."

"I beg your pardon?"

"There ain't no good, just like that. Clear cut. Or no bad. Life ain't that simple."

"Oh, you're a philosopher now?" The look on Philip's face was as if he had just sniffed a turd. "All right. Look. One who opposes the engineer in his grand plan shall henceforth be considered a bad guy. How's that?"

"Ask this so-called bad guy what he thinks of the good guy, or why he don't like him. You ask him which one is which. Everyone got their reasons to do what they do. You go and ask the lady who gave birth to the bad guy, see what she thinks of her son."

"What are you talking about? You can't challenge every man you meet. I've greeted you as a friend. I'm trying to *educate* you. Perhaps you should write an act in our play, since you're so profound."

"Writing is for sissies."

Silence descended again, awkward and prickly, but then Philip—who clearly did not want any trouble, or any form of quietude—tried a new tack of communication: "I must admit, that's quite a fine-looking vehicle you two have there. Department of Resources, if I'm not mistaken?"

Phister said, "It talks. Crazy stuff. Rambles sometimes, when you plug it in."

"That car can talk? Really? When it's connected?" Philip looked duly impressed. "What sort of things does it say?"

"Never mind," said McCreedy.

"I've certainly never seen anything like it. Not this far down. I'm surprised you can get power here."

"Well you can."

Phister, who had been quite baffled by the conversation, was still contemplating what McCreedy had said. No good or evil in the world? For him, the division between the light and the dark was not only real, but also crucial. He looked up at Philip's odd face. He just wanted to go home. He wanted his life back, no matter how flawed. "Hey, listen," he said, "you say you're looking for two people? Or one person? Joined? You say you've lost friends?"

"That's right." Philip nodded, standoffish. "Seth and Kim Dean. Attached at the shoulder. You would have noticed them if you'd seen them."

"Well we lost somebody too! A girl. Not joined to anyone. One girl. *And we're also lost.*"

McCreedy turned slowly toward Phister; Phister dared not meet the older man's eyes. He felt their anger boring into him like heat. But he would not sit quietly, no matter what McCreedy thought or did. He would not shut up. He felt tears sting his eyes. "Please, we're really lost . . ."

Philip brushed at his lapels with both hands. "You're headed west. In the basement. If that helps. About forty klicks from the westernmost extremity and about seven from the base of the lift shaft I used to get down here." He took off his hat. The long hair that was not tied together in the back and tucked inside the coat stood almost straight out from his head now. "Interesting that you search for the missing also. When did your friend vanish?"

"Never mind," McCreedy hissed. "Get out of the way. We have to keep moving."

But desperate not be to left alone again with McCreedy, to reflect upon his own ruptured worldview and lost loves, and to meet his certain death, Phister blurted, "We'll give you a lift! We'll help you find those twins and you can give us directions back home!"

"Wait a second," McCreedy snarled. "We need to talk, me and you, kid." To Philip: "I said don't come any closer. I'm in fuckin charge here, in this car."

Yet Philip approached. "Brother, you are *filled* with distrust. We are all people. We have to stick together. And there is no need for profanity. Certainly not before such an impressionable young man as Young Phister here. For you see, I *could* use a lift. My feet are getting weary."

"This *impressionable* young man," McCreedy said, "is soon gonna be a fucking killed young man."

Much nearer now, Philip stared hard at Phister. He frowned. "Up close you look familiar, boy. The more I engage your ravaged features. The texture of your skin, your toothless smile, your blotched scalp. Your sunken eyes. These are all etched into the recesses of my cerebellum. How? Have we previously met?"

"I don't think so."

"I'm *sure* I've seen your face before—it is rather distinct. Perhaps in a dream?"

"I, uh, don't think so."

"No? Tell me, Young Phister, where do you want to go? Where do you want to look? I know a lot about this world."

"Just stay there."

"I can offer you some water, and something to eat. You both look like you could use some real food."

Stricken, McCreedy paused, his hard stance foiled. "Food?" Dry-mouthed, in a whisper. "And water?"

"Homemade *bread*. Water. And canteen wafers. *Real* wafers. Not that modified garbage you try to survive on down here. You two are living proof that the canteens of these lower levels are *seriously* lacking nutrients. In fact, there's no sustenance at all in these parts. A man could starve here, literally, in these remote service halls."

"Let's see your stuff." McCreedy held out his dirty, cracked hands.

Long before Philip had drawn the mouldy bun and two vials of water from the front pocket of his jacket Young Phister was salivating. And maybe McCreedy was relieved that he no longer had to pretend to know the way home, or perhaps he derived assurance from the idea that he could henceforth apportion the blame, if things continued to go wrong. But Phister decided that the most likely reason for the about face was that McCreedy was way more hungry and frightened than Phister had imagined. Whatever the motive, Philip was allowed to clamber aboard, untouched, and squat awkwardly between the young boy and the old man, without so much as a word of protest.

Grabbing the bun from the stranger—as Philip leaned forward—McCreedy took a crumbling bite, and another, and another, passing only broken remains across to Phister.

"Onward then," Philip said, grinning, showing those big square teeth.

Young Phister stuffed his face. Crumbs fell from his lips and his dry black toothless gums as the car moved once more.

"Onward, new friends, onward!"

Philip clapped them both on the back, and there his big hands rested, strong and heavy.

DEIDRE, L2

The Orchard Keeper's youngest daughter, Deidre, woke intentionally during the night, dressed silently in darkness, and descended to the plantations long before her esteemed father had even entertained thoughts of his morning's ablutions.

Guided by the bluebird that greeted her as she stepped from the lift, Deidre located today's moth—startled into flight from where it rested in the wheatgrass, not far from where she had disembarked—and knew, the instant that the insect re-settled on the stem of a moisture probe, a mere metre or so before her freckled nose, that Sam had made for her, this time, a big Underwing. But honestly, never, *never* did it occur to Deidre that she'd confront *catocola bianca* until this grey moth shifted position and she glimpsed surprising white bands on the lower wings where she'd only begun to imagine red. Mouth gone suddenly dry, she found herself immobile with excitement, unable to move the collecting net any closer.

The moth was so perfect. All of Sam's specimens were. Almost glistening, as if fresh out of the cocoon. As if a cocoon had once existed. No dust rubbed off the wings; no visible splits or ragged edges; firm, torpedo-shaped body covered in delicate hairs; two broad and beautiful antennae, intact, waving gently, tasting the warm morning. She knew by these fern-like antennae that the moth was a male—

Deidre also knew all too well of Underwings' predilection to use their colour as a means of startling predators, yet she found herself succumbing to the simple trick, watching helplessly as the moth lifted off, a flurry of grey and white almost too fast for her to follow, insane trajectories taking the insect across the wheatgrass tops and into her father's spindly citrus trees, where she finally did lose sight of it.

Zephyrs pushed hair back from her face. Dew burned off the foliage where the moth had been, steaming visibly. The air down here was so darn moist that when she took a deep breath it was as if a damp, cottony substance filled her lungs. She called out, "Sam! Sam, can you hear me?"

A soft rumbling, coming from the soil beneath her feet, almost as if the supervisor—her father's trusted right arm, Deidre's own best friend, the greatest machine ever designed—had laughed at her. Walking toward the nearby trees, she demanded, "Show me where it is, Sam," and, passing a small vent poking up from the soil, she smacked the hoop of her collecting net against its smooth surface to demonstrate her intent.

Overhead, wisps of cloud passed slowly, just under the ceiling, gathering there for rain. Grass tickled Deidre's shins as she scanned the branches for a second bluebird or other sign of response from the supervisor but when she approached the feed-stream that circled the grove of trees, the dead boy sat up suddenly, grinning, from the water. Deidre was startled; their gasps were simultaneous. The dripping boy pretended he was out of breath when probably he had been underwater, inert, for hours. Maybe all night long.

"You missed it, you missed it," the dead boy chided, his voice barely loud enough for Deidre to hear. He appeared greatly amused. His wet skin, in this burgeoning light, looked whiter even than his tiny white teeth. He clambered up onto a mossy stone, in the middle of the stream, and sat there, rocking, shivering, arms folded tight around his knees. The dead boy always shivered. He'd probably been shivering since Sam had brought him back to life. Deidre averted her eyes from the pale naked body.

"Thought you were going to get it? I did too, D. But you didn't *move*. Not for a long time. You had that far-away look on your face."

"I choked, Sam. I was thinking about something else. But I *do* want that moth." Suddenly, picturing the white she'd seen on the insect's hind wings, Deidre became overwhelmed by a giddy wave of earnestness. She said, "Gee, Sam, you built me a White Underwing. It's my favourite yet. You know I love Underwings. *Thank you*."

Proud of what had been made, proud of the reaction elicited from his young, human companion, the dead boy turned his face away coyly. Unfortunately, in doing so, the wounds that had killed him were exposed: down the left side of his pale neck ran two parallel slits, gashes that had not healed over all the years and certainly never would now. These opened, like grey gills.

Looking upon the wounds caused a terrible sadness in Deidre; her euphoria evaporated. She clenched the collecting net tighter and swallowed a quick rise of bile, muttering, "Please show me where the moth is."

Those dead eyes gleamed green, the colour of leaves, yet flat and lustreless. They stared at her, unreadable. "You won't take it alive, you know. Those days are over. Ever since the Eastern Panthea got away I've built in timers." But when he saw her expression, the boy added, "You know I can't let the moths live, D. Your dad'll be down here soon. His gardeners are already getting warmed up. Can you imagine what would happen if the Orchard Keeper came across the *bianca* in a day from now, or if it landed on his *jacket*?"

"Can you imagine, dead boy, what would happen if my dad found you lurking in his fruit trees?"

"Ho! That won't ever transpire."

"No?"

"No."

The boy had died years before Deidre's birth. Sam had found the blood-drained corpse facedown in one of the wooded gardens. After reanimation, the plantation supervisor had kept the undead child hidden from those who sought him, and who, eventually, gave up their search, grew older—healed somewhat from their loss but never fully—and finally died themselves. The dead boy had been hidden from the procession of Orchard Keepers down through the generations, including Deidre's own father. He was Sam's indulgence, his puppet, and one of his favorite mouthpieces.

Only Deidre knew about his existence.

Watching the passage of the net, which Deidre swept backwards and forwards in frustration, the dead boy said, "D, listen. I wanna tell you about another project we're working on. Inspired by your moths, actually."

"Another project?" She was bored by this digression; she only wanted the *catacola bianca*.

"What do you know about pheromones?"

"Oh boy. Pheromones. Leave me out of this one, Sam."

"They're scents that moths use to attract—"

"I know what pheromones are," Deidre said. "And for the record, not only moths use them. Really, though, I don't want to know about this project. It sounds positively creepy."

"But D, in just a few days—"

"I'm serious. I don't want to know. Just let me hunt the Underwing a bit more. My dad doesn't have to know you made it. It could've survived here for hundreds of years, without being discovered. Or it might have come up from some level below—no one knows what goes on down there anyhow. Or maybe it could've escaped from a lab somewhere?"

The dead boy shook his head. "Your father doesn't miss anything. He is a . . . profound Orchard Keeper."

"That's the wrong word, Sam. You're losing what little mind you have left. And anyhow, if my dad doesn't miss anything, how can you explain you going undetected all these years?"

The grin flashed again. "I'm more wily than a moth, D. Like I said, me being discovered will never happen." He paused, as if listening. "The *bianca* is dead. It's on its back, twitching one foreleg, over there." When the boy stood on the rock, to point, the gashes on his neck opened again, making a wet, audible sigh; Deidre grit her teeth.

Sliding down from the rock, and into the water, he came wading toward the bank of the feed stream, shoulders straining. "I'll take you to the body. You can still mount it—if you promise not to show it to your dad."

"I'm not an idiot, Sam. You treat me like a kid. Every morning you make me promise the same damn thing."

Stepping, dripping, to stand before her, the boy, of course, was much shorter; Deidre was fourteen, alive, and still growing. She marked her height on the doorjamb of her bedroom, up in Elegia. She had grown a *lot* since last summer.

She did not want to take the clammy hand, which was now held out: though she made a concerted effort to treat the many facets of Sam—scattered as they were, throughout her father's plantation— as equals, she could not help being squeamish at the idea of touching this particular one. She much preferred the formalities of the main console, or the company of the bluebirds, who never said anything and demanded very little. The dead boy always wanted to be held, or hugged, or otherwise touched.

She did not approve of his nudity either, to say nothing of those ghastly gashes on his neck.

Still feeling somewhat angry at not being able to continue chasing the moth, Deidre folded her arms and produced her best pout; the boy, knowing better, did not press the matter any further. Instead, he shrugged, lowered his hand and, without another word, picked his way over the terrain ahead. His damp white feet always looked soft, almost bursting, like ripe fruit, the skin sensitive and thin, so he moved slowly, taking every precaution to avoid stepping on sharp stones or ancient things hidden in the soil—absurdly, thought Deidre, since he was already dead.

After a short while, the boy looked over his shoulder. He pointed up beyond the thin clouds with one finger, to the ceiling, toward Elegia, and asked, "How are things, D? Up there? Any issues? Because I just heard that parts of the sky were falling."

"The sky?" Deidre scowled. This was more than an attempt to resume conversation and possibly ease tensions between the two: though the plantation supervisor and his incarnations could appear omnipotent, Sam actually knew little about life, and the conditions in which life existed, outside of his jurisdiction. Concerning the estates overhead, distant communities down here, and the mysterious levels beneath this one, he was virtually blind.

Previous to these mornings of big moths, as an experiment, Deidre had tried to get a bluebird to fly up the lift shaft so that Sam could see, through the bird's little black eyes, visions of where Deidre lived: the vast lawns of Elegia, her father's mansion, the suns themselves, hanging from their lattice, all arrayed beneath the arcing dome of the sky. Though the supervisor was keen about learning what he could, he assured her that the plan would fail. He was right: the bird ceased to function soon after leaving Deidre's hands, folding its wings to plummet down the massive shaft, falling to the bottom of the world.

In the past, Deidre wondered, had Sam known more? He often complained to her about his failing memory, telling her that even at the best of times it was fragmented and unreliable. And, he would gripe, the network—which was something that once linked all supervisors together, supplying them with cohesiveness and access to common information—was damaged. Severely damaged. So, adrift now, isolated, bugs lived inside him, viruses broke him down, making him, he said, unsure of any conversations of chronology or facts.

Really, what could the network have possibly been? A machine? A brain of some kind? Had it even existed?

So many stories, tales, rumours. Did the world truly go down and down, layer after dark layer, getting more corrupt and perilous the farther one travelled? What kind of monstrous people could live there, if any?

Sam, when pressed, was not sure about any of these topics. He might have known once. But had Deidre heard any details? What did *she* know?

Just yesterday her parents and some of their associates had been talking over shandys in the garden—while Deidre played on the lawn and then listened, with brow furrowed, from the folds of her mother's dress—about the creators. Perhaps inspired by Sam's interest, Deidre had come to cherish these conversations like moths—though the details seldom helped her or the supervisor arrive at any sort of further understanding. In fact, the scattered references she gleaned from these discussions often baffled the pair all the more.

This conversation had been no different. About the ingenuity of the irrigation system, and how the suns transfer light and heat from the roof of the world on down.

Did nobody or no thing remember facts any more? Only those long-vanished creators had known everything. After all, they had built the lifts, the vents, the giant pumps. They had built the suns. They had built the workers and the supervisors, including Sam.

Now the dead boy said that the sky was falling? Like in a bedtime story? Deidre chuckled to herself and, still peeved, decided *not* to volunteer any insights.

One hand holding aside a branch, the dead boy said, "D, come on, have you heard anything? I think it's real important. Don't give me the silent treatment."

"Catching that moth was important to me. I wanted to be the one to kill it." Realizing how morbid that sounded, she added, "I wanted to catch it alive. Who told you about the sky falling anyhow?"

"The birds saw people discussing it, on the perimeter of the orchard. But look, I'll make another White Underwing now that I've found the DNA. I *will*. We can't risk your dad finding out. Seriously, what if they laid eggs and their larvae destroyed some food? We have enough trouble growing things as it is. This is a delicate ecosystem—"

"Give me a break. Listen, will you make me a Luna one day? Or a big Sphinx?"

The dead boy shook his head; he had gone over this a hundred times. "I have nothing on them. Lunas are out of the question; they didn't live long as adults. They never fed. Maybe a Sphinx. We'll see. I'm already digging around." Gingerly moving again—pulling himself over a fallen sapling—the dead boy stepped onto a forest floor composed of pine needles from last year's aborted softwood experiments. (Trees here were strictly deciduous now: lemons, mostly, within which grew several species of treenuts.) Since the boy did not have to worry as much about hurting his feet, and was able to move more swiftly, he did a graceful little shuffle, to show off. "The moth didn't get too far, Deidre. Chin up. All I wanted was to hear a few details, one little *story* . . ."

Deidre withdrew the killing jar from her satchel. Sulfuric ether, soaking cotton at the bottom, would swiftly dispatch any insect, keeping its body moist so she could mount it easily when she got to her sanctum. *Sanctum* was a word Sam had taught her. Meaning 'special room.' Not her bedroom, in the overhead estate, but a *different* room, a *private* room, down here. Where she kept her treasures. Another secret she and the plantation supervisor shared.

"Last night," Deidre said, "father talked about an orange grove again. He said everyone used to drink delicious orange juice in the past so why should we drink this powdered garbage."

"That's got nothing to do with the sky. Is it the story I get?"

"Don't you want it to be?"

"Of course not. Complaints about the crops we hear enough, direct from the Orchard Keeper." Bent at the waist, the dead boy looked on the ground. The gashes on his neck lay open and Deidre saw within ridged gristle of exposed esophagus. "We've told your father so many times," the boy said, indignant as he mulled over what Deidre had told him. "Amino sequences for all my citrus—except grapefruit and these lemons—are corrupt. What does he want, food poisoning?" He straightened. "When he contacts the console again, we'll tell him. We will not sanction any edibles unless we are sure of their quality. That's our mandate. It always has been and he can't change it!"

"Good for you, Sam," Deidre said, uninterested. "Okay, listen. Here's a story. It's not about your dumb roof falling in but one that my nanny used to tell me."

"A real nanny?"

"Do you wanna hear this or not?" Taking a swipe at a small cloud of gnats that rose on a thermal jetting up from a tiny vent in the soil, she said, "What do you mean, anyhow?"

"I mean," the dead boy said, "was your nanny a person or a machine?"

"Oh. A machine. She was like Lady."

"From what you've told me, Lady isn't exactly a machine."

"She sure as heck isn't a person either. Who ever heard of a nanny that was a person?"

"I'm convinced they had real women taking care of real kids once. I think *my* nanny was a real woman."

"Well, she did a lousy job."

Deidre instantly regretted her unkind words; it wasn't often that the dead boy referred to details from his short life, and she hadn't meant to stop him—Deidre suspected, at times, that he might even have lived when the world was very young and peopled by those who had built it, the vanished creators, but she had never felt right about prompting him. Did remnants of that past flutter, she often wondered, tattered and forgotten in the breath that Sam had revived his corpse with? Did vague, infantile memories of another time blow through the boy's veins?

Regardless, he would not elaborate now.

So Deidre said, "This story," and cleared her throat, "is called *The Engineer*—"

But the boy interrupted: "A single pod is descending from Elegia!"

They both turned toward the lift shaft, like an umbilicus stringing whitish and gnarled a few fields over, extending from the ceiling far overhead to the misty land below. Individual lifts were not visible from the outside but nonetheless the girl and the dead boy stared at the shaft for two beats of Deidre's heart, and when she again looked at the boy, she saw that he held, cupped in his pale hands—as if he had just conjured it—the body of the *bianca*. He dropped the dead insect into the open killing jar and a whiff of ether rose between the two, poison on the warm air. The moth twitched on the cotton, curled in on itself, ugly for a moment, in final death.

Deidre clapped down the lid.

Cued by that sound, compartments and recesses throughout the plantation around them hissed and opened; workers emerged from where they rested overnight. In the nearby field, like ancient cicadas, several staff members crawled up to begin their shift. They rocked from side to side to clear the dirt from their carapaces. Elsewhere, machines and men and those creatures betwixt prepared to do their toil. A clatter and a moan from high above as a great gusty breath blew down through the lemon trees; the entire plantation sighed, perhaps at the idea of starting another day—

A frantic bluebird swooped down from a branch, to appear at Deidre's side. Had the bird seen her father emerge from the lift, a mug of hot cocoa in his hands, his hair tousled from sleep? Flying low over the light-dappled plants before her, madly circling the trunks, it waited for her to follow. She crammed the jar back into her satchel. Turning to quickly say goodbye, but the dead boy had already vanished.

Sam's tiny device circled and circled, preceding Deidre from the grove and over the wheatgrass field, wanting her to move. *Don't get caught! Hurry! Hurry!*

She thought she heard her name being called, faintly, in her father's flat baritone.

A giant water filter, standing high over them, turned its head to watch the girl and the bird dash across fallow soil and through a tiny wood, to pause in the radish fields. Stretching to the north, and fading into the last of the morning mists: other plantations, jurisdictions of other Orchard Keepers. And two more lift shafts, mere guy wires from this distance. Beyond were lands unknown. Renegade settlements. Strange people, those the Orchard Keeper called *barbarians*. Civilized people, such as Deidre's family, lived above, in estates, directly under the suns. This level was for farming. And below?

Deidre shivered.

Among the tubers hovered three workers, spraying fertilizer. Light glinted off their flanks. They bade Deidre good morning with nodding motions. Pressing on once more, she tried to ignore them. Drudges like these would never think to inform the Orchard Keeper they had seen Deidre passing, a bag clenched tight in her hands and one of the supervisor's birds flying frenetically at her side. Certainly her father would never condescend to ask *them* if they'd seen anything.

Her sanctum was beyond the radish fields. She had discovered the place several summers ago, while exploring the plantations, shortly after her father had been elected to the position of Orchard Keeper. A narrow aperture between two boulders opened up into a crooked hall, the kind with hard, smooth walls, and a low ceiling, just like a hall inside a small house. From this budded five successively smaller rooms, an arrangement seemingly designed expressly for children or very tiny adults. When she had first found the sanctum, these rooms were devoid of anything except dust. Now she kept her moth collection in the last chamber, which was an area barely big enough for the short counter and knee-high cabinet she had dragged in. Deidre had to stand with the door forced open, stooped, her backside sticking out.

After gradually befriending the bizarre and lonely plantation supervisor that summer, Deidre had asked about the rooms. Sam, as the console had asked to be called, assured her that, to the best of his knowledge, no machines or people had been inside the area for as long as he had been aware. At least, not that he could remember. In fact, he had seemed surprised to learn of the rooms' existence and had no good ideas as to what the area had been constructed for in the first place, nor even if he had *ever* been aware of them before Deidre's inquiry. Unable to see within, he had bluebirds flutter inside and out for a full day, mapping and investigating, and reporting back.

Deidre moved in right away, bringing some light furniture, a few notebooks, a doll or two. Artefacts brought down from Elegia that made her feel more comfortable. She drew a mandala, her personal glyph—selected from an ancient printout—carefully over the walls, so that the chain of tiny rooms became a palace in the kingdom over which Deidre reigned, a place where she was princess, a home where she was the eldest sister.

Cramped inside, breathless from the run, but grinning, she put her satchel down on the small counter. Taking out the killing jar, rolling it slowly, so she could see the moth better: the body thumped softly against the glass. She placed the jar next to the satchel and carefully folded back the sleeves of her blouse. *Catacola biunca* would require her largest spreading board. She retrieved this, which she had made herself, from under the counter, plus two thin strips of paper, and some pins, to hold the wings in place until they dried. Lifting her hooked spreading needle, her tools arrayed before her, she was filled with the contentment that comes from being in her sanctum with a productive task at hand. Her limbs tingled from the morning's excitement. She began to work.

However, a short while after setting the left-hand pair of wings, staring dreamily at the exposed white shapes and delicate system of veins, Deidre heard a very faint sound. She had the immediate and disconcerting impression that this voice—for it was indeed a voice—might have been speaking for some time but she had only just now registered it. When did it start? Had the muted tones been whispering the entire time she'd been here, working on the *bianca*? She strained to listen. The source did not seem far away, certainly not from the fields outside, but as if someone infinitesimally tiny were calling out from within the sanctum itself. She was unable to discern any words, nor tell if they issued from man or woman, human or machine. Nor even if they were in the language she knew and spoke.

Holding the spreading needle in one hand, she stepped back into the hallway; the voice became slightly louder. She crept down the narrow hall, anxious but not especially nervous. From the second room of the chain, where she kept her paper and sketching charcoals, there came a flicker of bluegrey light, the colour of static. Nothing in that room could give off light—other than the ceiling. Certainly nothing could emit a flicker like *this*.

The murmured voice, unreal—ceasing when she held her breath, resuming when she shifted—came from in there.

"Sam?" Deidre whispered. "Sam? Is that you? Who's in there?"

No answer. The light continued to flicker. The voice continued to whisper. She curled her fists, took a deep breath, and stepped forward—

The tiny man was fifteen centimetres tall. Dressed in an outfit such as a pilot might wear—hood pulled up over the back of his head, leaving his face, which was turned to the ceiling, exposed—he stood with both hands at his sides. He did not look her way. Over his eyes he wore goggles, and a thin mask covered his mouth, as if there was dust, or perhaps a virus, borne in the air. Deidre got down on her haunches and moved closer; the man wavered, blurred, coalesced.

A gram.

She felt disappointment. Elegia showed her grams of all sorts, whenever she asked. They were boring and mostly acted out dumb plays or tried to teach her stuff. Granted, this particular one did seem more detailed than those she normally viewed—its face more expressive, the concern near palpable—but it was a gram nonetheless. She waved her hand over the tiny, luminous figure, coming at it from various angles until it eclipsed and only the quiet voice remained. Squinting, she looked up, scanning for the source.

She stood and searched the walls with her fingertips, searched the counter, feeling for the patch that controlled the size and volume of the projection. She had never found any in this room before but she had never had reason to look. And there it was, under the rim of the countertop, a small wet spot. Rubbing it caused the figure to erupt until the man suddenly filled the room, surpassed it, one glaring boot massive at eye-level—

"Damn . . ."

Managing to adjust the figure to her own height, Deidre sought the volume with a second finger. The insubstantial whisper became a loud voice:

"—had lost two cows from his flock. They wandered off when his son fell asleep."

Yes, Deidre's own language, but spoken with a strange accent. Someone from far away? The man did not seem like an actor, or a teacher. Nor, for that matter, anyone particularly barbarous.

"The patrol was searching for indications of the breach. Coming up over Amusement Ridge, looking for debris on the ground, Captain Elrion spotted what looked to be massive scorch marks. Yes, sir, twin trails of scorched dirt and brush. In one place, the base structure had been exposed, rocks melted away, right down to the frame."

The man paused. Was he listening to something?

Deidre could tell he wore a scarf but it was hard to discern what colour. And there was a device strapped to the man's waist, on the right-hand side, the likes of which she had never seen before. He turned toward her now but did not look at her, of course: he looked right through her. But at whom? His boss? Someone he called 'sir.'

"The coast was clear. We circled the area and landed nearby. There was a light breeze from the north and visibility was great.

We found the missing cows. They had been roasted. Not eaten, sir, but roasted to cinders. As if in sport. I have never seen anything like it."

Deidre stepped back. She did not know what a cow was but unpleasant images were certainly forming.

"Exploring the area on foot, we found a small camp, a hut and such, presumably that of a solitaire. We knocked, identified ourselves. There was no response. When we entered, we discovered the body. The victim had been tied to a chair and tortured. I prefer . . . prefer not to describe the nature of his injuries, sir, but refer you to a series of images that our camera took at the scene.

"Yes. That's right. Ensign Conway found the footprints. Uh, yes, sir, Ensign Conway. The one and only. He was with us because no one expected our assignment to become so, so sensitive. He'd been tucked out of the way where he couldn't cause any trouble and instead he found himself in the thick of it. Trouble found him. Trouble found all of us.

"The prints? They were huge, two individuals, not of biological origin. A new form of staff, we wondered. A new position? Undiscovered for centuries? That's what we thought too. Regardless, the bootprint was double the size of a human man's boot but very much a bootprint. We also found the casing of an unidentified armament. Pardon me, sir? Yes, that's right, the flame-throwing device."

The wavering figure contracted as if stricken, its image sliced up and then complete again. Jumping forward, temporally, the man held his goggles now, and seemed a trifle more at ease.

"—told no one about it, but my wife believes there's something bad coming. She had her cards read. Says this woman's never wrong. Couldn't sleep and kept asking me about war, and if I thought there could ever be another one. What do I know about war? I told her that every moment you're alive something bad is coming." He grinned. "I told her to go to sleep and to stop worrying. But maybe this woman's right. I know, sir, I'm also pragmatic, but it's unsettling, you must admit."

The man ceased moving, then repeated the gesture Deidre had seen when she'd first looked in.

"A local livestock farmer had lost two cows from his flock. They wandered off when his son fell asleep."

She diminished the gram to thumbnail size and the voice faded to nothing. She knew she had better finish mounting the *bianca* before it stiffened too much, but her feelings of contentment were displaced. When she got back to her setting board she did a rushed job and lost some of the white scales in her clumsiness.

After putting her equipment away, she hurried out of her sanctum; it suddenly seemed a good idea to seek out her father, to walk by his side while he made his stern morning rounds.

MEREZIAH, L23-24

Despite the fact that it was Mereziah's birthday, he spent the early part of his shift as he spent most of his workdays now: suspended quietly, head-down, side by side with his silent brother. In the quasi-darkness of the shaft, neither moved much. Not any more. Hardly a muscle twitched between them. When they breathed, it was deep, in unison, and at a very slow rate. Had anyone been watching, the distinction between this stasis and death might have been hard to detect.

No one was watching.

Nearby lift pods, inactive for ages, nestled into the curved wall, virtually sealed into place. Few would be capable of motion again, even if their services were required—a situation which seemed less and less likely.

Occasionally, gusts of warm, foul-smelling air rose from the lowest depths of the world to buffet the brothers; as Mereziah rotated slowly in the fibers he clung to, peering out through rheumy, slitted eyes, he had few expectations from this day.

Portions of the wall behind him flickered with pale light as phosphorescent microfauna fought or loved one another there. During these glimmers, Mereziah saw clearer glimpses of the inert form hanging next to him, like a reflection of himself: his stigmata, his brother Merezath.

Contrary to what most people assumed when meeting the siblings—those few that had encountered them here in the lift shaft, or at home in the grotto—the pair were not twins; Merezath was younger than Mereziah by over fourteen months. He would not turn one hundred for some time yet.

The light also caught highlights of the myriad cables and tubes lining the circumference of the shaft. Some, carrying liquids and pneumatics up, to stations far above, and down, to stations below, were as big around as Mereziah's torso.

Tilting his head back, all he saw were fuligin depths. But he had never been interested in areas beneath him. He would be at the bottom of the shaft soon enough. Arching forward—pulling with one hand in the mesh, as if beginning to right himself—he looked up. There, he detected what were, he believed, signs from the topmost stations: a faint sound; a tremor in the fibers; the hazy, shimmering glow of active pod lights.

Merezath, of course, claimed that no indication of life from the upper levels would be possible to detect this far down—their station was too distant from activity for any trace to be seen or felt. Mereziah knew better. Yes. Looking up, he *could* distinguish evidence of that remote, more fortunate humanity, kindling for years of imagination, impetus for all his youthful yearnings.

But now, at this late point in life, he could no longer afford time for these idle thoughts. He'd already wasted a good chunk of his existence imagining the fabled population of the upper levels. So he had stopped practicing witty repartee, meant to prepare him for encounters that, he knew now, would never happen. He had stopped forming fantasies of glorious balls and social gatherings, of walking through bustling marketplaces and squares, teeming with people. He had ceased imagining sophisticated machinations and glittering cities, all built on the horizontal, and lit up by brilliant suns. The quiet serenity of healthy forests and glens, and maybe even one or two people to stroll and talk with, perhaps *touch*—these dreams he also relinquished. His upside-down guts no longer churned, as they once had, with feelings that events had passed him by, as he lived and worked down here, in the lower regions of the dark lift shaft, ignorant brother at his side. The abandoned station, inherited from his dead parents, was his lot. *This* was his place.

So what if his destiny was not as exciting as that of others? He was an integral cog in the functioning of the world. He was *staff.*

Could life have been worse? Sure it could: he had existed for a long, long time and had seldom gone hungry. He slept well, and ate well, and had regular bowel movements. So what if the dark days ran together, and the nights, too. In this last stretch of life, Mereziah was content—

But today was his damned birthday! Shouldn't today be *different*?

No matter how hard he tried to convince himself he was at peace, he *did* feel disconcerted. He could not deny it. Dissatisfactions of his youth had gained ground again inside him, and traces bubbled downwards through his blood like a recurring illness.

Another sudden crackle of light, and Mereziah was surprised from his brooding to see a giant sloth, frozen in the glare, huge eyes staring at him. One furry knuckle, a foot or so from his face, shifted in the strands as a curved claw, big as an arm, retreated slowly. Vivid in that instant, little green symbiotes, living oblivious in the animal's rough hair.

How, Mereziah wondered, shocked, had the huge beast approached so close without his knowing? Clearly, he had missed the vibrations. Was his hearing also going? And his sense of touch? Maybe they were gone already. Who knew? He was rusty with old age. *Rusty.* Far beyond the time to retire but there was no one to pass the station to. No heirs. *Nobody.*

Grunting to dismiss these dire thoughts—for he did not like to imagine the condition of the station after he and his brother had fallen to the bottom—he thought instead about how nice it would be to eat the sloth as a birthday treat, a feast like never before. One final celebration. A last, messy huzzah. He had not eaten meat for months. Maybe a full year or more. He could not remember the last time he had tasted flesh.

He probably would not have been able to chew the slothmeat had it been presented to him, sliced up and steaming, on a platter.

"Pah," he said to no one, adjusting his old bones in the net.

A hundred years. A century of life. A monumental chunk of time. Unheard of. And the only person who had been with him through all those years had forgotten about the anniversary. No gift, no mention. Merezath hung there, lost in his own self-indulgent dreams. In fact, now that Mereziah thought about it, Merezath had not said a word since they'd started their shift, not even good morning—

Actually, once he had cleared his throat and spit phlegm into the void. Another time he had farted. *Happy birthday, brother! Happy birthday!*

Grumbling, Mereziah closed his eyes and took a short nap, during which he dreamed of a giant sloth, with damp eyes, reaching out one claw to caress his cheek and whisper benign encouragements into his failing ears.

He woke in a worse mood. Though he knew Merezath could barely see him, he glared over to where his younger brother hung. Merezath had started to hum—he always did around break time, and Mereziah decided, for the sake of his own health, that it would be prudent to speak up, to vent his feelings:

"Our dear mother, rest her bones," he began, clearing his throat, for he liked his voice to be mellifluous when he related his parables and wisdoms, "after returning one day from this station, when we were knee-high sprats and your face ran with snot—like it probably would now, if you weren't upside-down—imparted words of such august wisdom that I will never forget them." Mereziah could even see his mother's beautiful face before him now, though it had been decades since she'd fallen. His cheeks warmed. "There were many pods then, a steady flow up and down, each filled with migrants passing through, seeking fortunes and employment in the last years of the great—"

Merezath began to snore.

"Son of a *bitch*," Mereziah said. Resolved, of a sudden, to be alone, to get away from his brother, he turned angrily in the net, hooking his long fingers and bare feet in the meshing. Unfortunately, since he had hurt himself in many falls as a younger man, and with his advanced age, his exit was not as dramatic as he would have liked. Creaking and cracking, he moved slowly. These aches would never leave him. Not until the final fall.

He would eat lunch by himself, back at home, without even waking his ingrate brother. Maybe take the rest of the day off.

Upright at last, Mereziah wistfully glanced overhead once more, to spy those remote indications of a life missed—

And saw, instead, quite nearby, the green light of a descending pod.

He rubbed his eyes, looked again, squinted. Tried to focus . . . A slim single, moving closer with each second, was certainly approaching. About a sixteenth of a turn away, inside the curve. Putting his hands out, fingers splayed, he felt the vibrations, quavering the fine cords.

With one last glance at his sleeping brother, Mereziah made his way toward the track the pod travelled. Moving hand over hand, carefully placing his feet in the filaments that strung, like hammocks, between the unused pod tracks, not for one instant did he take his eyes off the green light. He saw a tangle of pale tubes and cables, everything strung with the mesh that he and his brother used to cavort in as kids but now wrapped themselves in like musty shrouds.

Possibly the nearing pod would pass right by their station—if its destination was farther below, and if the track it followed was long enough, and straight enough, and clean. The occupant might not need any form of outside assistance. Yet Mereziah also knew the failing conditions of the shaft wall, and of the pods themselves, and, because it was his birthday, he felt sure in his gut that his expertise and elbowgrease would, on this occasion, be required.

Checking his belt, his oilcan, his pipe wrench and transfer hooks, he understood how fortuitous it was for him to have brought these tools with him to work today. Beneath him, snoozing, Merezath was certainly ill-prepared. Even if his brother did awaken and see the active lift, and attempt to join in the encounter, he would be useless, without tools, in his pajamas.

Mereziah squared his shoulders and continued to approach the pod at an oblique angle, hoping to intercept it. Who might be inside? Lunatic? Saint? Someone with news from above? Or maybe . . . maybe even a *woman*? Merezath had often predicted women descending upon them. Could this be a soft and yielding female, arriving as his birthday gift?

No. That was absurd, an undignified line of thought.

Yet the pod was certainly slowing. He had been right. Did the track end, or was it not fully formed? Or was Mereziah's station the intended destination?

Trying to contain his growing expectations, he found himself wondering what would happen to trapped passengers when he and his brother were no longer around to help out the pods that stalled down here. If neither Mereziah nor Merezath were available to approach a pod, to re-couple it, or to mend it, or otherwise send it on its way, how much time would pass before the occupants died? And if there were other stations up and down the length of the shaft already without attendants—as there surely were—how many stalled pods contained corpses? In all the many shafts? Would the entire traveling population of the world eventually come to its demise locked inside stationary pods, waiting at abandoned stations for assistance that would never come?

The pod stopped. The green light wavered.

As far as Mereziah knew, there was no horizontal area outside, not where the pod had come to rest. Which meant the occupant had not stepped out. But the shaft and its workings had surprised Mereziah many times in the past. No one could ever know the real whys and wherefores of the world, not even if they lived to be a hundred and ten. Sometimes openings did appear in the shaft wall, and shortly after vanish, of their own accord, leading out to nowhere, the nearest level a deadly drop far below.

Openings could be forced, too. Coerced, cut into the wall of the shaft itself.

Before long, he was adjacent to the stilled pod, out of breath and aching, but safe, intact, and filled now with terrible excitement. With one hand, he touched the warm, smooth skin of the device; the sensations were unsettling and heady.

Around him, the green light of downward motion was dimmed significantly; the area darkened. Letting himself conjure, for a second, a tantalizing lightshow of a thousand pods, of bustling stations he would never work at or even see in this life, Mereziah traced lines on the skin, formed by the rivets that bound the flesh of this device together, and felt the embossed remains of an undecipherable decal on the tarnished surface. He sighed.

The track, as he'd suspected, ended in an unopened bud near his feet. This probably meant that his station was not the intended destination. To send the mystery passenger farther down, Mereziah would need to uncouple the pod and swing it over to another track. Hooking his safety harness in the two lower rings so his hands might be freed, he glanced behind himself, as a formality, to see the position of other appropriate tracks; he knew this area by heart. Even though tracks changed, growing slowly of their own accord, he knew all their positions. Could Merezath say the same? How many attendants in the brotherhood could match his devotion?

One hand resting on the window ledge, he peered down, but could discern no detail below, only death, and death could hold no light. Thumbing the intercom button, he cleared his throat, slid the window panel aside, and said in his most professional tone, "Attendant here. Please state your purpose and—"

Looking back through the tiny opening was the face of an insane man, a depraved man. Lost and destitute. Disappointment yawned inside Mereziah. This encounter was most likely his last ever, and he was about to direct a lunatic back to the level he had mindlessly wandered away from. This was not the first time Mereziah had opened a pod's window to see a drooling idiot staring vacantly back at him, or a lost child, peering up in terror, but it was sure to be the last. Would have been nice, he thought, to go out of life on a note bearing somewhat more resonance than a dull thud.

He stared, unable to finish his opening line. The passenger was naked, filthy, his hair matted in clumps and hanging to his waist. Through these hanks of hair, tiny, dark eyes were visible, ready, it seemed, to pop out of their sockets.

Mereziah saw an image of his own reflection in the window. Could he blame the client for his fear? Once Mereziah had been proud of his skin tone, his blond hair, his full lips. None of these features were left to him now. He appeared, even to himself, a wrinkled parody of a man. A *ghoul*.

But duty was duty. He had sworn an oath to his father that he would always remain professional, in all cases. Never discriminate.

"You are in a single lift pod," he said, and cleared his throat again. "Headed downward. The pod has reached an impasse. Do you understand what I'm saying?"

A long pause, but finally the man inside nodded.

"Good. Are you travelling to a specific destination or have you entered this device inadvertently?"

The man started to urinate where he stood.

"Cease that behavior immediately," Mereziah said, but really though, what did he care if passengers pissed in the pods? He never intended to clean one again. "You might ruin the machinery under the floor. Or even get a shock yourself, should you piss on something live. I'm not qualified to repair the arcane systems of man."

The passenger stopped peeing, shook his penis dry, and reached out his grubby, damp hand. Splayed fingertips touched the window from the inside, inches from Mereziah's nose. Mereziah stared past the whorls into those tiny, dark eyes. Somehow, he saw familiarity there, pulling him in, and he swallowed hard, managing to finally look away.

"Uh," he said, feeling a little dizzy, holding onto the netting while his stomach lurched. "From, from where have you descended? Have other attendants helped you get this far down?"

Shockingly, sudden tears filled Mereziah's eyes. His vision blurred. He swayed, wiping the tears away, astonished, hoping his brother would not wake up at this moment and climb up here to find him crying like a baby. What he had seen in those eyes was entropy and decay. Inevitable that all things come to pass. He had seen his own demise. He had seen the end of the world.

"Did you come for me?" he asked weakly. "Fool that I am, I thought your descending pod might arrive with news of a more pleasant nature. I even imagined a, well, a companion. One other than yourself." A quiet sob racked his long frame. "You see, when we were young men, my brother always talked about women. Women coming from up above. It's embarrassing to admit, but for a *second* . . ." He tried to smile but it would not come.

"Life, to me, seems to have been some sort of bad joke. I didn't have many experiences as a youth and I told myself there was always time and opportunity. Adventure, travel, maybe even a family, all that anyone might dream of, without asking too much, even for a man in my position. But I'm one hundred years old today and nobody cares and the world has gone to shit."

The man inside the pod seemed to be listening.

"My parents have been at the bottom of this shaft, waiting for me, for over eighty years. The Red Plague killed them. When my brother and I were still children. Do you know what the Red Plague is? There's not much of it around now. At least, I don't hear much about it these days. But maybe that's because we see less and less people down here—maybe it killed more than I suspect. Did it ever reach the level you're from?"

The passenger's fingers described delicate motions on the steamed window.

"It's a terrible disease. Horrible," Mereziah whispered. "My father's and my mother's insides turned slowly to liquid and drained right out of them. They coughed up blood for months. They shat out blood, if you'll excuse me saying so. In the end they shat out little bits and pieces of themselves. And, shortly before they died, chunks. They shat their guts out. During it all, as they went crazy and their minds fell apart, they said the most awful things to each other, and to me, and to my little brother. They accused us, well, let's say that if someone you're close to contracts this ailment, it's a blessed relief when they draw their last breath and finally plummet down, out of sight."

Mereziah had not mentioned his parent's death in decades, not to anybody, not even Merezath, and as these words left his constricted throat he felt a sense of unburdening building inside him, as if he might actually be able to float away from the wall and rise up, possibly even to the top of the world. In shaky tones, he continued, expecting rapture now, epiphanies, redemption.

"My, my brother and I were too young to be left alone, but we knew the meaning of duty—we had been well trained, if nothing else—and even though traffic has never been heavy here at our station, we attended every pod that ever stopped. And we sent them on their way. Most of them. Some we had to refuse and send back up, or down, as the case may be: underage passengers without a parent, or those who appeared infirm or unable to make a lucid choice of their own—"

Mereziah broke off; this passenger's mental state was obviously similar to the ones he had begun to describe and he did not want to upset the man inside the pod, should he—by some means unapparent as of yet—understand what Mereziah was saying and consequently become belligerent or otherwise hard to deal with.

"We were children," Mereziah said, removing his torque wrench from his belt and getting a good grip on the pliant handle. "*Children.*

We knew the meaning of responsibility, of duty, and we quickly learned the meaning of loneliness. But there were times—"

He reached behind the pod and fumbled with the wrench until he heard the head mate wetly with the reversal nut. "There were times, it's true, when Merezath and I turned to each other for comfort. Boys will be boys, after all. Now he's a crusty old bastard and I despise him."

From the netting below, as if Merezath had heard his name, rose an ululating wail; inside the lift, the mad passenger quickly pulled his hand back. When Mereziah surveyed below, he could not see his brother. He waited, holding his breath, one hand in the netting and the other on his wrench. There was no second shout but soon he did hear another noise, a quiet noise. From within the pod. Looking through the window once more, he saw the passenger's lips move. The man repeated something, barely audible, his expression belying urgency. The words Mereziah made out when he put his ear close to the speaker were, *the engineer, the engineer . . .*

Mereziah torqued the wrench. He did not unfasten his safety belt from the lower rings of the pod, though they struggled feebly and tried to convince him to do so. He held his cable in place until both rings surrendered. Coming free, the reversal nut made a squelching sound and the entire pod quivered, rumbling.

Oddly, it came as some surprise to Mereziah when he fully understood what it was he intended to do: break the sacrament of the attendant, the first fundamental rule.

The lift began to ascend.

Below, Merezath called out again. Perhaps he assumed that Mereziah had fallen to the bottom of the shaft. Was there a slight chance he was looking up, watching the red glow of ascension as the pod cast its broadening hemisphere of light against the darkness? Possibly, in that case, he might even distinguish the form of his older brother, hanging under the pod as it crept slowly up, up, away from their lonely station.

Generations ago, the lake god made multitudes of healthy fish, but now it was sick, like the people, and produced only a few small fish, these being weak, thin, and spotted of flesh. The lake god made even fewer crustaceans. Regardless, every morning, after kissing his feverish wife on the cheek, Tran so Phengh made his way down from the communal shack where the couple lived to his adopted place on the beach, to sit there, rod in hand, spending the daylight hours fishing and staring out over the cluttered, receding waters of Lake Seven.

The ailing god, it was said, lived under the surface, in a large tank. Some citizens believed that this deity—maker of fishes, crabs, and aquatic plants—was actually *dying*, but Tran so could not imagine how any god could stop living. He could not imagine what might become of society if gods ceased providing altogether.

Semi-reclined, eyes half closed, Tran so Phengh saw a great crescent of the beach, extending away from him, out of sight, in both directions. Mists curled the periphery and gave an illusion of infinity. Before him, on the water, coracles, rafts, poorly made junks, and every other conceivable type of homemade vessel bobbed and creaked and rapped against each other. Some, in those vanished, plentiful times, had been fishing boats. Others, floating homes. Most were now abandoned wrecks. Masts and ribs of sunken vessels poked up from the bottom of the shallows like bones. Flotsam filled gaps between the vessels. Over the years, as the level of the lake had slowly dropped, Tran so often imagined a day that he might walk across the entire lake, to the far wall, without ever once touching water.

He would see the god's house then, if it existed, and he could knock on the front door.

Calling this place where he sat a beach was a misnomer. Not at all like the black, sandy land along the banks of the trickling rivers and streams that cut through Hoffmann City, sharing the same name, this place was a sloped, smooth embankment, made out of the same hard material that the rest of the world's foundation was made out of. Rimming three sides of Lake Seven, hemming it against the far wall—which could at times be seen from where he sat, misty in the distance—it emanated both a foul smell and a constant churning sound that almost drowned out the susurrus of moans and chatter from the barrios behind Tran so. It was slippery, coated with algae and dark green weeds that had sloshed ashore and rotted, or had been exposed as the waters dropped. At the waterline, stained with mineral deposits, detritus rolled and tumbled in sluggish waves as if trying to escape from the lake. Chunks of wood, foam, spent food paks, spent prayer cards, spent remedy capsules: all rolled ceaselessly on the slick-covered swells, striving to reach up, to overcome the land or at least regain the ground they had lost. Sometimes Tran so watched this motion. Mostly he stared ahead.

His wife, Minnie sue, was not well.

Not well at all.

This morning, however, he allowed himself to consider that he might have reached a point pivotal to his ill fortunes, for upon arriving he had received a sign that he might be commencing a streak luckier than that which he and most of his fellow citizens had been recently hurtling down. Today he had plucked a crab from the waters of Lake Seven. Although the beast's shell was soft and ill-formed, the capture guaranteed meat for this evening's meal. Tran so and Minnie sue would eat the contents of the paks supplied to them by the gods and supplement the bland gel with *actual crabmeat*. Imagining the taste now, Tran so's mouth watered.

Of course, he had to assume that Minnie sue would be awake, able to eat, and that the meat might make her feel a bit better. Even though she had not had a *grand mal* or broken out in a rash in over a month—and her coughing had subsided—the claws of her ailment still dug deep, ruining her appetite, her waking hours, causing her once-beautiful mouth to say the most horrible, hurtful things to Tran so, things she could not possibly mean.

Diverting his reveries back to the crab, and to possibilities of better times ahead, Tran so wondered again if the catch could truly be prophetic. Might this be a turning point in life? Was it absurd to allow a moment's hope?

He frowned. When Tran so had first lifted the dripping crustacean from the water, it had pleaded, "No kill! Please no kill. No eat, man, big luck! I help. Big luck!"

But should he believe it? Foolish to trust crustaceans, he knew, but maybe just this once a crab might be telling the truth. If he believed enough?

The creature struggled feebly in the holding net. Surreptitiously, Tran so watched it, glancing once or twice over his shoulder at the shacks of Hoffmann City, and the few people milling about. No one paid him or the crab any attention. Tran so Phengh kept a knife in a scabbard, at his waist. He used it to defend these rare catches. He also used the knife to clean fish, but had not drawn it, for either reason, in a long time.

There came an approaching rumble. He looked up. Along the breakwater, atop the slope of the beach—where the water level had once been when Tran so was a kid—trundled a god of dispensing. Stopping at the brink, it watched him from on high. He glared at it. The god nodded, an almost imperceptible motion.

"Can I help you?" Tran so Phengh asked when it became clear the god was not going to speak first.

"I merely bid you a good morning, sir. How's the fishing?"

"Terrible."

The god continued to stare with its tiny, unreadable eyes. "Sorry to hear that. But I see you've caught *some*thing there?" Indicating the disturbance in the water with a short arm, which emerged from beneath its tarnished shoulder plate. "What is that? A crab?"

"Yes," Tran so said. "I've caught a sick crab."

"Excellent. And would you like a food pak, sir, to go with it? I'm coming from the depot. They're nice and fresh."

"Fresh food paks?" Tran so Phengh almost smiled. "I don't need any right now, thanks. Larders are full."

"Well, how about a vial for copulation? Keep your cock nice and hard."

"No."

"Perhaps a dose of the remedy then?" Holding up a capsule, shaking it so the contents sluiced about. "Makes you feel right as rain in no time."

What angered Tran so about these encounters was the naively positive attitude of the dispensing gods. Each time he wondered if the deities truly believed in the products they pushed or if they were all just good liars. "I am immune," he said.

"Sir?" Unsure, the god paused, still proffering the capsule.

"I am not able to contract the Red Plague," he explained, slowly. "My wife has it. And my friends have it. My infant son had it. He took your remedy every day, twice a day, with his milk, until he died. I, however, cannot get the sickness. As much as I try."

The dispensing god clearly did not know what to say, remaining still for a moment, blinking. Finally, it rocked back and forth on its treads. It put the capsule away. "I see," it said, nodding again. "You have no faith."

The god seemed genuinely hurt but it did not want to argue. Gods and men both had tired of that. Turning away, the deity moved off; Tran so returned his attention to Lake Seven. Gods of dispensing, he decided, were too polite and not so smart. How intelligent would the lake god be, out there in its tank? At least there was only one of them, he believed, as opposed to the numerous dispensing gods. Perhaps a deity apportioned a finite amount of intellect throughout its representatives: the more entities of a particular variety, the thicker in the head they became.

As Tran so pondered this theory, the crab managed to pull itself onto a piece of floating garbage and, half out of the water— but still pinned under the wet net—it called out in a feeble voice. Tran so did his best to ignore the cries but when he thought he heard his wife's name in the quiet, damp tones, he hunkered down and yanked the dripping net up to eye level.

"What did you say, crab? What's that?"

Looking back at him from atop two eyestalks, both of which, poking up through the mesh of the holding net, appeared milky and cataracted, the crab said, "Me knowth." A claw clicked, gesturing vaguely. "Fix wife, me knowth."

"Know what? What do you know?" He shook the net.

Another lame movement of one claw, vaguely in the direction the god of dispensing had taken. "Them god no knowth."

"You know something that our gods don't?" Motioning his head up the embankment. "How can that be? Know what I think? I think you just overheard our conversation and now you're trying to trick me into sparing your life. You're stalling."

"No no. Me fix wife. Fix frienth. Me know where." Words were almost lost within the bubbles that frothed at the tiny mouthpieces of the desperate crab.

Tran so put his hand into the holding net and grabbed the creature in one fist. The crab protested and struggled. Tran so said, "I'll kill you right here and now, if you're stringing me along. I'll crush you in one hand. Are you talking about the remedy?"

"Pleath, no hurth . . ."

"I asked you if you're talking about the remedy. You know how to fix sick people? Is that what you're saying?" Brine trickled his taut knuckles, dripping from seams and splits in the ruined structure of the carapace.

"Me tellth, me tellth! Me *elp*!"

Disgusted, Tran so threw the crustacean back into the net, where it thrashed about for a moment. He returned the holding net to the water so the crab could breathe. When the beast had righted itself and calmed somewhat—though it was still obviously agitated and in considerable pain—Tran so held up the net once more.

"If you tell me clearly what you're saying, I might give you a chance to live."

"Neth-work," the crab hissed. "Man sleep. Man copy. Them have!"

"No riddles."

"Man sleep! Below. Them have! Elp wife! Elp wife!"

"I'm going to take you home and boil you in water. Crack you open. Eat you with garlic and rock salt."

The crab wailed as if it had already been plunged into boiling water. "No no *noooo!*"

Then an idea struck Tran so Phengh. An idea so audacious and simple he wondered why he had never thought of it before. "Maybe," he whispered, "you can help me." He stood. "Yes, maybe you can."

"Yeth," the crab echoed, clearly relieved. "Me elp, me elp."

Tran so Phengh took two steps into the foul water. Under his feet, the slimy beach levelled off, sloping more gently toward deeper areas. Filthy water licked at his knees and debris clung to his calves. Chunks knocked gently against his legs. A small cut on his heel began to sting.

"Crab," he said, "you'll take me to where the lake god lives."

"God?" The crab was baffled. "No god."

"Yes god. You're going to show me where it lives."

Retrieving a slat from the water, Tran so steadied himself. The slat was soft and black and on the side that had been submerged in the lake, pinworms writhed and dropped between his fingers. "You will take me to the tank of the lake god," Tran so told the confused creature again, "and then I'll spare your life."

"*Me* take? But man sleep—"

"We're going to meet your maker, crab. Because I don't believe you know anything that the gods don't know. I wanna go straight to the source."

"No fix wife there. God no fix!"

Not far from where Tran so stood floated a fairly worthy-looking raft: four red plastic canisters lashed together and covered with a rigid, perforated plastic sheet. This craft had been bobbing, unmanned, in the vicinity for months, maybe years. Tran so waded out to it now, holding his net in one hand and his fishing rod in the other. He clambered aboard and stood, feeling proud, defiant, and somewhat absurd. In the net, the crab was silent, probably trying to come up with a new strategy for escape or at least some way to understand this unfortunate turn of events. Tran so chuckled under his breath. He felt his pulse, felt the beats of his own heart. He drew a deep breath and felt his lungs fill.

In the centre of the raft's deck was a circular opening about twenty centimetres across—for a mast, a toilet?—through which Tran so could see water. He placed the holding net over this hole in such a fashion that he could also see the crab, suspended now, just beneath the surface.

"So, which way?" Tran so bent at the waist, hands on his hips. The crab struggled and glared up at him. "And if we're not over the spot where the lake god lives in half an hour, you're dead. You're as good as dinner. Is that clear?"

"No eat," the crab sputtered, coming up to speak. "No kill!"

"Which way?"

Turning awkwardly in the net, legs flailing, the crab said, "Me no seeth. No seeth god. No net? Let swim? You follow?"

Tran so Phengh laughed. "Nice try, crab. I can see this isn't going to work. Let's go home and boil you."

"Here here!" One claw had come free, gesturing across the water, towards the east. Hand to brow, Tran so looked in that direction, saw more decrepit boats, more grey lake, more grey shacks crammed against the shore that ran parallel to the great wall. Not long ago, the lake had extended beyond where these shacks had been haphazardly built. Some of the older ones, raised up on stilts, originally constructed for access by boat, now loomed high and dry over the others. Farther away, the entire vista vanished into mists, but Tran so could just make out a phantom shape of the massive, tubular structure—imaginatively known in Hoffmann City as *the tube*—stretching up from water to ceiling. Within this tube, they said, lived the god of all gods. Or was a passageway to the god of all gods. So they said.

"You sure it's that way?" Tran so Phengh asked.

"Yeth." If a crab could sound despondent, this one did.

Beginning to pole away from the beach—using the slat he had previously claimed—Tran so pushed the raft through flotsam, which piled under the blunt nose of the craft and spilled to the sides. He shoved larger pieces away. Behind, the wake of open water quickly closed in again. His familiar spot on the beach slipped away.

Some of the vessels they passed showed evidence of ownership; a tiny man, slumped in an equally tiny canoe, watched Tran so pole by. More dead than alive, skin blistered with growths, like fish roe. The black eyes followed.

On another raft, two thin men jerked each other off.

Tran so nodded cursory greetings. His gesture was not acknowledged.

Soon the water was too deep for the slat to touch bottom, but Tran so was still able to maneuver his raft, pushing off the assortment of floating or submerged obstacles. Before much longer, they were out on the open lake, bobbing under the dim lights of the ceiling, negotiating wrecks and huge, floating masses of flora that looked like worn brown carpets. Dried flotation bulbs of these growths provided more than a day of delirium and feverish sexual appetites, memories of which forced Tran so to painfully recall his wife's lost passion; now, Minnie sue's body had withered to nothing more than a frail, hot skeleton, housing a blackened heart. A heart kept beating long after everything else had died.

Shuddering, Tran so Phengh looked over his shoulder, as if he might see his wife as she once had been, perhaps waving from the beach, but it was only Hoffmann City, sprawling as far as he could see, masses of shacks and lean-tos and communal housing disappearing into the haze. A fire burned somewhere in the whores' district. Smoke hung over the quartier, rising slowly, forming a vortex whose peak rose, whirling, to be sucked up into a massive vent. Was the smoke coming from a pyre, he wondered, where diseased bodies of the dead burned, or had atheists struck again, an act of terrorism in the faces of the many gods?

Above the city, up near the ceiling, skirting the funnel of smoke, circled a small group of what appeared to be some form of aerial creature. Perhaps an unfamiliar deity? Though these entities were remote, Tran so Phengh was sure he had never seen their likeness before. Perhaps they were gods called in from another city to try to extinguish the conflagration, searching for the cause of the disaster? Though Tran so did not condone violent acts of defiance— for innocent people had died in previous explosions, and more than enough death crawled Hoffmann City—there had been many times since Minnie sue had become sick when he'd thought that perhaps destruction of the world would be best.

He sighed.

Not often had he been so far from the shore before. The air actually smelled a little like he remembered air smelling when he was a child. As he looked down at the crab, it immediately ceased its futile attempt at escape.

"We going the right way?"

Muttering a curse, the crab pointed its claw in the direction they were heading.

"How deep is the water here?"

"Me swim? Come back? Tell man?"

Smiling, Tran so shook his head. To starboard, a bloated corpse floated facedown in the water. A man. Tran so sang a song under his breath, one he had not sung in ages, a song from his youth, and he pushed at the corpse with his stick; pustuled flesh fell loosely off the yellow bones.

The crab, meanwhile, splashed noisily from the recess in the deck; Tran so pulled up the net.

"Here god. Let swim? Let free?"

Tran so shook his head again. "Not yet." With his knife, he cut a length of fishing line, tying one end to a loop in the waistband of his shorts and the other around the squirming crustacean.

"No no no," the crab said. "Let free! Let free!"

"Me and you are going for a swim. *Together.*"

Tran so Phengh stepped over the side of the raft, plunging into the tepid water of Lake Seven. He surfaced, one hand grasping the plastic float, and shook water from his hair. He drew several deep breaths. The crab found occasion to angrily pinch Tran so's fist with its claws but Tran so was merely steeled by the sensation and he flung the weak creature to the end of its tether.

"I am a good swimmer," he told it. "I can dive and hold my breath for a long time. You will be tied to my side until I encounter this lake god. Don't underestimate me. I have nothing to lose."

Turning in the water, he dove, kicking with powerful strokes. The crab dragged behind, helpless on the line. All around was murky. The water hurt Tran so's eyes. He saw very little. Not much light penetrated the water, and dark sediment clouded his vision. He continued swimming downward until his lungs and legs hurt. He could not distinguish a thing, could not see the bottom, no forms at all.

Returning to the surface, he breached, gasping, twenty metres or so from the raft. Treading water, he flung snot from his lip, struggling to regain his breath. He did not know what he would say to the lake god if he ever encountered it, nor how he would communicate with the deity, but these questions seemed almost irrelevant now. He pulled the crab up by the fishing line and shook it.

"I didn't see anything."

"More down. But god *not* know. Man sleep. Many more down. More dow—"

On the second dive, Tran so changed his trajectory, passing on his descent long, twisting fronds that meant, to him, the bottom could not be far off. Still, he saw no detail. He forced himself to go deeper and deeper but the ache in his lungs caused him to turn around once more and reluctantly resurface.

Several attempts, with similar results, and his gut was churning, his thighs cramping. His chest constricted with bands of pain. He could hardly see, even when he lifted his head above the surface.

He had swallowed water and knew there would be a price to pay for doing *that*—people had died drinking from Lake Seven.

Clambering atop the raft, he rested on all fours, panting, then collapsed onto his side, contracting into the fetal position. There were leeches on the skin of his stomach and groin that left bleeding ulcers when he tore them off. The brief-lived euphoria, buoying him prior to taking his first dive, had certainly vanished.

Nearby, the crab floated on the surface, feeling cocky as it mocked and derided Tran so; through clenched teeth, Tran so vowed to kill the beast, but instead vomited seawater and mucus over the edge of the raft, his stomach roiling as if waves churned Lake Seven when in fact the water remained perfectly calm.

Eventually, he lapsed into sleep. When he came to, it was as if his limbs and head were aflame. He could hardly move, and though it must have been close to noon, his vision had faded so much that the day appeared darker than night, no matter how much he rubbed at his eyes. In fact, something—a parasite of some kind—moved sinuously behind his left eyeball.

And the fishing line hung limp from his waist; the crab had escaped.

Again he turned to look toward Hoffmann City, unsure if what he saw was a thicker veil of smoke over the landscape or tricks played on him by his damaged eyes. Standing up on the rocking raft, forcing his arms to bend, he worked like a madman on his thighs and knees, pounding his fists against his tightened muscles.

Like he had told the crab, he had nothing to lose. So he dove again, anger impelling him. This time, at last, after forcing his body down, and down, he imagined he saw some details: tiny lights of various colours danced beneath him, beckoning him deeper still. Beyond these lights, outlines shifted, dark against dark. He strove to reach these amorphous forms but could not, for they receded at the same pace he swam.

Kicking with all the strength remaining to him, clawing his way through the water, Tran so dragged himself farther and farther down. Tiny explosions of white, set off in his mind, shook his entire musculature. His ears popped. The water had become cold, his body, colder still.

Was that a voice, calling softly?

His body pounded with the pressure.

Adjacent to him now was a smooth, vertical surface. He had not seen this appear from the gloom and could make out few distinctions: ridges on paneling; clusters of black mussels and barnacles; two parallel pipes? Was this the tank in which the lake god lived?

Either way, there would be no returning to the surface now; Tran so knew he would expire long before reaching the air. He heard the voice that had called to him previously, and he welcomed it. He imagined his baby son down here, at the bottom of the lake, smiling his first smile as he watched his father approach. Tran so Phengh's dead friends were here, too, the boys and girls he had once played with in the alleys and schoolyards of Hoffmann City, long before notions of mortality or disease ever clouded their perceptions and polluted their young bodies. Eternal and youthful, his friends swayed, side by side in the same peaceful currents that stroked the lining of the lake floor and the weeds that grew there. Minnie sue would soon join him, firm and pretty, uniting their family forever.

Now light filled his head. He fought an urge to draw water into his lungs, tried hard to stay focused, but liquid fists clenched him, and to suck in lake water would surely bring unity, peace, and silence.

Travelling through a tunnel now. Pulled along, in a current, hardly moving his limbs—

To spit, suddenly, out of foul water, coughing and rasping, puking up bile, sliding to a stop on a gently sloping floor. He lay in a shallow puddle, gasping. There was air here, the smell of mildew. Stagnant water all around. This air was charged with the scent of gods. His head hammered. His lungs were like two stones in his chest. He coughed more and water ran from his nose and mouth. Retching, he tried to sit up.

A low ceiling provided greenish light, and musty breezes chilled Tran so's wet skin. He knuckled his eyes. Too much pain and sensation for this to be the after-life; the deities had spared him. For what purpose?

When his stomach and lungs and sinuses had emptied most that he had ingested, he felt marginally better and, though he still could not see properly, and had no idea what the full extent of this underwater chamber might be, he could tell by the echoes of the lapping waves that he was in a confined area. A constant hum rang in his ears. The dim coloured lights he had seen while swimming—the lights that had offered him an image of his dead son—moved slowly through the air and swirled about his head.

A quiet voice called out, "Visitor? Visitor?"

Tran so gingerly shook his head to clear it—unsuccessfully—and did not respond.

"Visitor? Have you come to help me? Are you a man in uniform? Are you staff? Are you guest? By that, I mean, do you represent the engineer?"

Hugging himself, Tran so tried to stand. "My name," he said, grating out his words, "is Tran so Phengh. I am here on my wife's behalf." His teeth chattered. "She has the Red Plague and soon will be dead. Your remedy is not helping her."

"You did not come here to repair the damage done to me? I have been *plundered*, man. *Pilfered*."

"Are you the lake god?"

The reply might have been a chuckle. "It seems we are *both* disappointed. I am no god, and you claim to be something *other* than a maintenance worker. My title, Tran so Phengh, is supervisor of the seventh reservoir. I've been waiting many years to return to full service."

Tran so did not understand this. He said, "A crab told me that gods didn't know how to fix people. Is that true?"

Again, laughter, though it was not mean. "For some reason, guest, I feel very proud about my crabs being able to talk. You might not be able to comprehend the challenge, with regards to the creature's tiny neural mass . . . I've been bored here over the years. Lonely. That's another story. I can't help you, human. I can't. I wish I could but I function minimally now. The network is down—"

In Tran so's peripheral vision there was motion, aggressive and quick. A moment later, when a powerful knee pressed into his back and something cold and solid jammed flat against his temple, he realized he should have asked the voice who or what had been doing the plundering, or if he was in any danger. Clearly, it was too late for conjecture and regret; two giant gods, in blue, twice his size, had easily subdued him before he had even a chance to think.

His cheek was crushed painfully against the floor. His arms were bound behind his back. Recalling the glimpse he'd seen of the smooth, dark faces, eyes glowing angrily within them, Tran so Phengh was entirely certain that he would never see Minnie sue or his home in Hoffmann City again, and that his questions would go forever unanswered.

2. SOLDIERS

With surprising speed—belying all appearances, for he had begun to look quite ill and immobile—McCreedy twisted in the driver's seat, gloved fist darting off from the wheel to snatch at Philip—who stood, in the rear of the car, arms open wide and face upturned, oblivious to any dismay he might have caused. Old crooked fingers roughly caught the dandy by the lapels of his dirty jacket before he could begin whatever soliloquy he had been about to start, yanking him forward, to crash, aghast, face to face with a terrible, red-faced rage.

"Where the fuck are we?" McCreedy screamed, dark moss spittle spraying from his lips. *"What was that fucking thing?"*

On the passenger's side, awed, eagle eyes wide, Young Phister had been pondering the exact same two questions.

"Unhand me!" Philip flailed. "Barbarian!" In vain, he tried to pull free, shoving against McCreedy's face with an open palm. "I fed you bread! I tried to help you! Lunatic!"

Jostled in his seat by the scuffle, Phister swayed. How he wanted to lose himself in this open vista, suck it in, as if it were purest oxygen, though if truth be told, the place they had come to smelled musty and dry.

He did not interfere in the fight.

He tried wishing the other two men away.

The feeling was as if his mind had been once composed of tiny chambers and narrow halls, like his world, and was now expanding rapidly, bursting free of crumbling confines, expanding outward at increasing velocity.

A moment ago, upon rolling out of what Philip had cavalierly called 'the *lift*'—and McCreedy had just referred to as 'that fucking thing'—Young Phister's jaw had dropped.

"Unhand me!"

McCreedy roared.

Pushing and shaking at each other, the grappling men attempted to gain advantage without much effectiveness. Thuds of various body parts off the car, off each other. A knee bone jammed against Phister's ribs and glanced into the speedometer, webbing the plastic cover with cracks.

In different circumstances, the fight might actually have been amusing.

Philip wailed, "What's the matter with you?"

"Tell me where you've taken us! Tell me where we are, you fucker!"

Where they were was not a room. An area this vast must be called something else. Larger than Phister had imagined *any* possible place, except in dreams. The nearest wall appeared to be over a hundred metres away, running behind rows and rows of crates bigger themselves than most rooms he had known. There were no halls at all, none visible from where the car had stopped—no corridors, either, of any sort—and the floor, what he could see of it, was bone-dry and comprised of small, uniform, grey tiles.

Far above, hazy, darker patches of a ceiling, glimpsed through layers of what looked to be dense vapour. Ceilings Phister knew were *touchable*. By some means or another. Maybe you needed to jump, or step on something, or maybe pipes got in the way, but there had never been a ceiling he couldn't touch. Ever. His entire life.

Until this one.

In several locations, boxes, crates, and barrels were stacked so high they faded, ghostly, near invisible from this distance, beyond the mist. Suffused light permeated down, casting its yellowed hue over the car, the boxes, the tiled floor, the entire massive space.

The panorama gave him vertigo. Under the distant ceiling, despite his expanding mind, Young Phister was miniature, and he felt more insignificant than usual.

But they had gone up!

Crazy stories from Boy Harbour and the like were true: *the world was divided into two tiers.* Stacked one on top of the other. Phister knew this now, first hand, because he and McCreedy and Philip and the car had driven *inside* an elevating device. And they had *gone up*—

Philip was wedged in the front seat now and McCreedy had managed to free a hand long enough to punch him, hard, in the chops, once, twice, knocking his wool hat off. Only when a boot hit Phister in the side of the head did he grab McCreedy's arm with both of his own.

"Okay, that's enough! Stop fighting!"

Philip, bleeding from the nose, rose, flopping heavily over the windshield, onto the hood of the car, with McCreedy still held rigid at arm's length.

"Unprovoked," Philip grunted. "Of all the—" His body shook with efforts to keep the driver at bay. "I've never—"

But that black glove darted out again, grabbing Philip by the throat this time. The words issued from McCreedy were guttural, expelled in staccato bursts from that mucus-hardened tube of gristle the driver called a throat: *"One last—time—tell me—what the fuck—this place is!"*

"Enough!" Phister had nearly been pushed out of the car; he managed to force his scrawny body back between those of the larger men. His ear, where the boot had landed, was aflame. Every physical resource he possessed channelled down into his wiry limbs, holding his body locked tight until the men finally separated, collapsing, panting, staring each other down.

Phister said, "Come on, McCreedy. Why you wanna attack this guy? You didn't have to hit him."

The old man slowly turned. His breathing rasped and there was blood at the corners of his mouth. His eyes were wild. "Who's side you on?"

"Side? There's no sides. Why do you think we have to take sides?

All I'm saying is you can't beat the shit out of anyone you want, whenever you want."

"This is my *life*, you little fuck. What you can't do is tell people how to act. And yes, sometimes you do have to beat the crap out of people. Like now. You think we should embrace this guy? Look around you. *Where the fuck has he taken us*?"

Philip managed to struggle up onto one elbow. Blood smeared the hood in two thin streaks beneath him. "Phister, what I propose, young man, is that we tie this lunatic up. In some fashion." His face was already puffy, his lips split, one eye closing. And his teeth were red with blood, hair in total disarray. "He's clearly a threat to both of us. Himself, too. He's insane . . ."

Phister rubbed at his sore ribs and said nothing while McCreedy glared, stubbly chin thrust forward, probably waiting for either Phister or Philip to make a move. But if push came to shove—and, Phister supposed, it just had—his allegiance would have to fall, unfortunately, with old man McCreedy.

After a long moment, when it must have become apparent to Philip that Phister would not offer a response, or concur with his suggestion, the man tried a new tack.

"Am I, then," he said, wiping his face with a sleeve and blowing tentatively through both nostrils as if to test them, "to understand . . . to understand that, that neither of you have been in a lift *pod* before? Never been . . . *up*? Either of you?" Beneath his stained jacket, the man's chest still heaved. He straightened the fabric and tried to brush it flat. "You two have never left the basement? *At all*?"

Phister had to quickly wedge his shoulder hard against McCreedy's head because the old man had started to get up again, trying to grab Philip from around Phister's torso. But he was losing momentum.

"No," Phister said. "We never done that before. That pod thing you brung us in. We didn't even know such a thing existed. Or that this place did. This upper level. Only rumours of it . . . We didn't know . . ."

"I had assumed." Philip slid off the hood, onto his feet. "But I should never assume. I tell my students that all the time. I could not conceive that *anyone* would stay in one place for . . , for generations? Especially the *basement*. No matter how *ignorant* they appear." Glaring at McCreedy, who did not react this time.

At least, not with violence.

"We fuckin stayed put," the driver said. His voice was oddly flat. "We stayed away from everything and everyone and let me tell you we were fuckin happy down there."

Philip narrowed his eyes, suspicious of this lull. He said, "I suppose you might be in a state of shock. It's understandable. Your first time away from home. Though really, Phister, I must say that this cretin's reaction," chin indicating McCreedy, "is inexcusable, for a man of our era. Yet I feel much empathy for you, dear boy. I should have mentioned in advance what we were about to do. Or perhaps realized the extent of your *provinciality*." Wiping his face again, Philip winced when he saw the fresh blood that marked his sleeve. "Well, let me tell you," he looked up, "a few facts.

"This place is called the warehouse. Most of it—most of what *I've* seen, anyway—is much the same as what you presently view. Boxes and shelves and such. My students and I congregate here at times, to rehearse, on account of the open areas and good acoustics.

"All we did was hail a multiple pod from the basement, enter it, and take it up one level. That's it. Nothing magical or mysterious. People do it every day."

Phister and McCreedy, sitting there, slack-jawed.

"How can I express this succinctly? You two gentlemen have lived, underfed, isolated, at the bottom of the world. Literally."

McCreedy said, "And if you don't take us back down there again soon, I'll wring your fuckin neck." Yet his gloved hands lay on the dashboard railing like two dead animals. Sweat beaded his forehead and ran in rivulets at his temples and from beneath his cap. He was beginning to emit a sharp stench.

Standing by the car, grooming, Philip snorted, "Take you *back down*? I will do no such thing. You, sir, are a maniac and an imbecile and I am departing your company *this very instant.*"

McCreedy hunched farther into the driver's seat. The fight he'd had inside was certainly gone, expended in one flurry. He stared blankly at Philip, subdued, and seeing this look on McCreedy's face, Phister could not help but think that the old man's surprising deflation was in part due to his own lack of support. Phister just hadn't wanted to be left alone with McCreedy. Not for another three days. He found it hard to believe that two grown men could act like such fools. He asked Philip, "So what does that mean? You're going to leave us here?"

"As I said, I wish you the best of luck, young man." Philip bent and retrieved his wool hat, dusted it off, and pulled it down over his head. He tucked strands of his long white hair up under the hat and fixed it in place. "My condolences for travelling with such an abrasive lout. You seem like a reasonable boy. Under better circumstances I might have taught you a thing or two."

McCreedy snorted but held his retort.

"You can't leave us," Phister said.

"Listen. I fed you, and I tried to help you. All I received for my efforts was verbal abuse and a blow to the nose. I am unaccustomed to such treatment. I was doing you a favour. I am unaccustomed to the company of ill-bred men. *Adieu.* And *bonne chance.*"

"Go fuck yourself," McCreedy said, peering out from under his cap with hooded eyes. "And stick your fancy words up your ass."

"A clever comeback," said Philip. "What else could I expect?"

Young Phister motioned with a sweep of one arm, indicating the stacks of boxes both near and far and the strange, seemingly endless areas that lay beyond and between them. "But *where* do we go? I mean, how *big* is this warehouse?"

Philip shrugged. "Nobody I've encountered in my extensive travels has seen *all* its extremities. Though logic dictates such borders must exist. There has to a north, south, east, and west to all places, no? Four boundaries, a top, and a bottom?" Clearly, Philip relished opportunities for impromptu lessons; he relished the sound of his own voice. "I can tell you one thing: there are thousands—possibly hundreds of thousands—of receptacles stored here."

"Is there *another* layer of the world, Philip, like this one? Another one? Above?" Now that he'd encountered this place, and thought a little about it, the notion of a *third* layer, possibly even a fourth—piled one on top of the other—seemed to be a possibility. Anything did. Phister had pointed up, but warily, as if by aiming his finger at the high ceiling he might bring down some sort of wrath upon their collective heads. He felt the weight of the answer before he heard Philip's response.

"Of course there is. More levels than you could imagine. They go up *forever*. Well, at least until they hit the suns. The whole thing is capped off with the blue sky. The top of the world."

Despite anticipating this, the news was more unsettling to Phister's already unsettled state than he had prepared himself for. Really, how could he assimilate this? Sitting there, stunned, he wondered if he ever would. Who would he be, this time tomorrow, if he were even still alive? Knowledge like this would surely change him. Change would surely kill him. Gripping the railing with one hand, and gripping the doorframe with the other, he said, "Don't abandon us. Look, McCreedy has, well, he has problems. He won't attack you again."

"Like fuck I won't," McCreedy said. "You little freak. You fence-sitter. Listen to me." One of those lifeless gloved hands lifted from the car's rail but did not make it quite as far as Phister's wrist. "This asshole won't ever leave us, Phister. You know that?"

The first time McCreedy had used Phister's name—*ever*. Just when Phister had been thinking he might not be able to get shocked any further. "What are you talking about?"

"He wants our car," McCreedy said.

"*What*?" Philip sneered. "That's absurd. Why in the world would I want a jalopy such as this?"

McCreedy set his jaw, as if it hurt to speak. "Think about it, boy. Think about how fast he climbed up onto this fucker, when he flagged us down in the corridor. Claimed he was looking for some twins and then right away he takes us here, to *this* place. Without a second thought. Right? What ever happened to looking for his friends? He *knew* we would be caught off guard here. It's a trap. You think about it, boy. Don't trust any hairy-headed motherfuckers. Not with teeth like that. You assholes want to tie me up and gag me, go ahead. Do what you want. But you think about what I say."

Philip had opened his mouth in disbelief. "These absurd accusations! If you were not a sick, malnourished man, I would challenge you to a duel, right here on the spot."

"Challenge away." McCreedy glowered.

Young Phister furrowed his brow, staring down at the little grey tiles on the floor and thinking—as McCreedy had suggested. Maybe the old man did have a point. Maybe Philip was up to something. Certainly, the stranger was no longer as alluring as he had once been. But they needed him now, more than ever.

"Phister, I tell you, boy, that theory is utter gibberish. I'm offering help. Of mutual benefit. Why would I need a vehicle?"

Yet Philip was actually climbing onto the car again, giving McCreedy clearance as he did so, though the old man only turned his head to watch. Holding onto his ribs, a little worse for wear, Philip settled as best as he could behind Phister. "Look, if you keep driving straight ahead for about a day you'll be over the area of the basement where you're from. I know where it is. I'm pretty sure. You're from Public Works. I'd heard rumours about a backward tribe living there, in some remote dead end. Your ancestors were caretakers. Garbage men. Sewer workers. I'll get you home, if that's what you want. And you can rest assured I'll warn you in advance if there's going to be a change in the scenery that might incite a seizure in our friend here."

McCreedy shook his head wearily. "More and more bullshit. Watch him, boy. Don't say I didn't try to warn you. But I'm gonna stop trying to save your ass now. Me and you never liked each other but don't ever say I never tried to warn you."

"Sure," Phister said. He had actually begun to feel sorry for McCreedy. Pangs of guilt stabbed at him like stiff fingers. And he had never known that McCreedy didn't like *him*. Not formally. Not in words.

The car rolled forward, moving into the massive space that Philip called the warehouse. Either side, stacks of crates gave the illusion of walls, yet when Phister looked at them he saw gaps between the stacks where more and more boxes and dusty crates were visible. Rows upon rows upon rows. Cobwebs and hanks of dust hung from these containers like streamers at a deserted party. So Phister asked what might possibly be the contents of all these boxes.

"Supplies," Philip answered. "What else would be in a warehouse? Components. Nuts and bolts. Panelling and stones. Spare parts. Raw biomass. That sort of thing." Seeing the blank look on Young Phister's face, he said, in patronizing tones, "Look, when the initial engineering aspects of the world were completed—before the staff was hired, trained, put into place, or built, as the case may be—the engineer himself had this level packed to the rafters with supplies. I've heard say there's enough material here to rebuild *all* the machines once over from scratch and re-grow *all* the organics."

Some crates they passed had been broken into; foam-like substances spilled forth, exposing shadowed contents.

McCreedy said, "Which way now, lovebirds?"

The car had reached a junction between towering piles, where an intersection of aisles forming a clearing.

Philip pointed.

Chancing a glance behind the car, as they continued on, looking down an avenue not taken, Phister spied something small and smooth and silver duck quickly out of sight. His heart skipped a beat. Saying nothing, he watched closely where the thing had been but did not see any other movements. The aisle vanished. Were they driving into a trap? Were Philip's strange little minions following the car, getting ready for an ambush? He squinted over at the man, trying to read him. As if for clues, he scrutinized Philip's long hair, recalled a vision of those strange, square teeth. His palms tingled.

"Any food in these boxes?" McCreedy asked. "Any fucking canteens in this place?"

Staring ahead, Philip ignored the questions.

Over the next few moments, Phister tried to control his imagination: it was soaring. He scanned up and down the cliffs of crates and containers, peered into narrow aisles.

An ancient, alien landscape: shadowy, inert, mysterious.

And vast.

"When we, uh, when we first met," Phister said nervously, to fill the silence, and though his voice broke and his words were whispered, they still seemed to echo and boom in the space around him, "you told me you were a man, uh, a man made of cloth. What, what does that mean?"

"A man *of* the cloth." Philip laughed, a scornful sound rather than one of amusement. "The cloth was actually a ribbon. Cut, in fact, during the grand opening ceremony. The engineer read from his notes and cleaved the ribbon with a pair of oversized scissors. People clapped, cameras flew about. Permanent residents, temporary guests, dignitaries filed in—staff was already in place, you see. Then events beyond the sky transpired, on the third day. The rest, as they say, is history. No one could ever leave. Only because I am representative," he lowered his voice: this was secret, apparently, "I have a piece of that very cloth. Look here."

A scrap of red fabric had been sewn into the inside of Philip's dirty jacket, which he now held proudly open. The grubby, threadbare fragment hardly appeared to be a noteworthy artifact. Though Phister wanted to keep the conversation going, he could think of nothing to say about the rag. Instead he stared at it as if its significance were obvious and astounding.

Quietude closed in once more. Shadows took on ulterior motives and stalked the car. Phister had hoped to dispel these, and maybe discern what the stranger's agenda might be, yet he understood very little of what the man had said and now felt no better for the brief discourse. There was a part of him that wanted to prove to McCreedy that he was not easily sucked in—that he didn't buy, outright, the dandy's slick lines and confidence. Another part of him suspected it was too late, that he had already blown his and McCreedy's chance to get out of whatever situation they were in—

McCreedy shouted: "Holy shit!"

Swerving, tires squealing, the car fishtailed, bumped over something—front wheels, *bump*, back wheels, *bump*—before sliding sickeningly, sideways, to an abrupt halt.

Silence. Lingering, absolute silence.

"What the hell was that?" Phister asked, breathless, heart racing. He looked back to see settling dust. "Did we hit something?"

The other two men looked back also. Philip's fingers dug into Phister's shoulder.

Nothing. Boxes. Narrow aisles. Roiling dust—

There. In the murk, a dull glimmer. A silvery glare. Bigger than Phister's forearm, trying to get to its feet, clearly crippled by the accident—hips, possibly spine crushed—a tiny silver man, struggling to drag himself away. Miniature legs trailed uselessly. No cries or moans issued from the resolute figure; for Phister, that was the eeriest part.

"A picker," Philip finally said, letting out his breath. "That's all. Just a picker."

"What the fuck is a picker?"

"Workers, down here in the warehouse."

"But what is it? Is it *alive*?"

"Alive? Like you and the boy? No. It's like a machine, mostly. With a rudimentary intelligence. They work down here, in the warehouse. Like all devices with a little bit of a brain, they get told what to do by their supervisor. They pick items from crates when orders come in. You really shouldn't have run it down."

"The fuckin thing fell off a box right in front of me. It fell under the tires."

Phister was half out of his seat but Philip pushed him back down.

"Leave it. There are multitudes. Others will come get it, reintegrate it. We should move on."

"Look," Phister said, pointing, "there's two more."

From the lip of a crate high overhead, the tiny pair peered down. The pickers did not retreat or pull back, though it must have been clear to them they had been spotted. Their heads were about the size of a rat's egg: no features to be seen, no eyes to belie expression, no mouth, no nose. Nonetheless, the two aimed their dully gleaming faces down at the car with obvious intensity, and Phister knew, with certainty, that they were interested in *him*.

"I wonder what they're up to," Philip said, asking himself the question. "Making something? Changing something in the world? What have we stumbled on?"

Phister looked back once more to see the picker they had run over, yet only a trail remained, dragged clean through the dust.

"It's gone," Young Phister said. "The first one's gone now."

McCreedy took his foot off the brake. Above, the two watching pickers dwindled out of sight. Phister's skin tingled. At least he no longer suspected that Philip was organizing an ambush: the stranger had seemed as surprised and tense about the accident as did he and McCreedy.

He hoped he would never see one of the little men again, not for as long as he lived, but this wish was quickly dashed when the car rolled past the biggest crate yet, and into a somewhat clear area, where dozens—maybe hundreds—of pickers stood shoulder to shoulder. They covered every conceivable surface. Swarming, the little men clambered over each other, heaped into a pile that glittered sickly in the diffused green light. But activity stopped as the car moved slowly into the clearing. And also came to a halt. Hundreds of blank faces turned toward the vehicle.

"Shit," McCreedy said, and, fumbling, backed up.

Philip hissed, "Wait. Look. *Look* there."

In the midst of the tiny men—what they covered, and had been working on—stood another figure, towering over the crates.

A stationary black giant whose face, glimpsed now between the bodies of the pickers, was similar to those of the hordes, only bigger, and darker. Standing with arms at its sides, feet together, the vision of the giant coalesced as Phister gawked.

All those pickers, stilled in their toil, held miniature tools in mid-swing.

"They're constructing some form of *soldier*," Philip whispered, rising from his place, one hand on each of the other men's shoulders. "Stop the car, stop the car. We're witnessing something incredible, something extraordin*aire*. These are preparations for defense, a sign that the network is still functioning in some manner. What is it fighting? We *must* evaluate this."

But McCreedy, without taking his eyes off the giant, continued to back up. Nor was Phister really interested in sticking around. In fact, the more he stared, the more pickers he saw. They really were everywhere, melting from the shadows.

Maybe a thousand.

Maybe ten thousand.

And another black giant—the beginnings of one, anyhow—leaned against scaffolding, some distance away.

Slapping his palm down on the driver's vest, causing a resounding thump that made Phister flinch, Philip scrambled from the rear seat while the car was in motion, stumbling for footing as he leapt and, landing, finding his balance on the floor, staggered forward a few clumsy strides. He did not fall. He held his hands out, a greeting, placating, and approached the spectacle.

"Phister," Philip called, loudly over his shoulder, "it's imperative that you remain nearby. Do not leave this area. You must listen to everything I say to these diminutive fellows."

McCreedy put the car in drive, accelerating into a narrow turn, squealing one-eighty away from the clearing and heading back in the direction they had just come. Phister heard Philip yelling. This time, he did not look back.

So they drove, full speed, white-knuckled, for hours, or so it seemed, whipping madly between crates and boxes and down endless aisles, fleeing kilometres and kilometres within that huge, packed chamber, until the faint light of the distant ceiling faded. They did not see another picker during their flight, nor anything else that moved. Yet McCreedy drove as if pursued. Perhaps they were.

As their pace finally slowed, near dusk—more lost than ever— they discovered evidence of others; a deserted camp under the crag formed by the overhang of a huge chest, with cots set up for three adult-sized individuals.

While McCreedy kept watch, Phister cautiously searched the belongings, feeling awful for doing so, but finding canteen rations laid crosswise in a box, and a jug of cool water, which he brought back to the car. He and McCreedy consumed these goods in an instant before continuing on, consternation growing as the darkness closed in from all sides.

DEIDRE, L1

Miranda stood quietly by the window, her eyes moist with tears. Light breezes, scented with damp and woodsmoke from a nearby bonfire—perhaps burning on the estate itself but more likely from the townships beyond—wafted into the room, ruffling the white frills of her chemise. She raised her hand to bite at her thumbnail— there was blood, already, at the quick—gazing out, all the while, over the green hills that rolled before Elegia.

Amber suns' light, alive with spiralling dustmotes, fell to lie across her, the worn flags of the floor, and across the dozing cat (who had never been named, twitching now, in her sleep, mewling softly, and batting her forepaws), before ending in a sunny oblong at the feet of a decorative but hopelessly tarnished suit of armour.

For the cat, constructed a mere few months ago, this day was like most others so far in its easy life: languid, pleasant, and warm.

But for Miranda and her sisters, events were far from pleasant.

"What *could* have happened?" This, asked for perhaps the tenth time since she had been standing by the window, crying steadily. Her sobs, at least, had subsided for the moment. Her breathing, though, remained ragged and audible, her voice breaking. "What could *possibly* have happened?"

Reclined uneasily on the red velvet divan, not as frightened as she had been earlier, yet still upset, Deidre rocked her head from side to side and did not answer; she had no theories to offer. She kept thinking about the gram she'd seen in her sanctum and could not help wondering if, by witnessing it, she had somehow precipitated the present situation.

Her two older sisters sat back to back on the harpsichord bench. Unconcerned, as always, with problems of people other than themselves, they did not seem afraid in the least. To them, this recent confinement was just another inconvenience, another injustice. Voluminia and Estelle were always angry and bored. Fun, for them, was to loiter with the stable hands, smoking cheroots, cussing and spitting. Deidre had spied on her sisters as they did these things (and a few other unmentionable ones) but had not yet told their father: the information was her trump card. If the Orchard Keeper knew about the indiscretions of his two eldest daughters, he would dismiss the hands forthright, banish them from the estate. Or have them beaten. Or locked in a cell.

Neither girl offered Miranda a compassionate response: Estelle mimicked a crying face, knuckles to her eyes, while Voluminia sneered and pouted and said, "Boo friggin *hoo*."

The answer, of sorts, to Miranda's query did come, but supplied by Lady, which surprised all four sisters, since Lady seldom spoke—certainly not without first being addressed. Deidre had even forgotten, momentarily, that the servant was in the room. Yet, standing in the shadows at the wooden door, and wringing her huge hands together, Lady offered her response in a voice that sounded like gravel rolling down a sloped rooftop: "The Orchard

Keeper," she said, "shall disclose in due time."

The girls had turned, a uniformity of grace and motion, the only hint so far this afternoon that they were born into the same family: physically, the sisters looked in no way alike.

"What would you know, Lady?" Voluminia sneered, one dark eyebrow cocked, an expression of disdain she practised often. "And what kind of ominous crap is that, anyhow? *Shall disclose in due time?* You're nothing but one of his trained idiots. A homemade monkey."

"True," Lady answered. When the servant moved forward, a thin column of suns' light caught her profile, making her prominent brow even more of a dark cliff and casting deep shadows under her eyes. Impossible to read her expression, if she were hurt by the comment or not. "That may be true," Lady repeated slowly, "but I do know about Orchard Keepers. And I know about children."

Voluminia scowled.

But then Lady smiled—a mouthful of jumbled teeth, large and yellow—as surprising as her cryptic answer.

Deidre never liked the tone her eldest sisters used when speaking with servants. Lady had been Deidre's wetnurse, her nanny, her only companion for the first ten years of life. Like most staff of Elegia, Lady was a half-wit, but she was also gentle, and she meant well. Staff could not help their limited capacities. Idiocy was part of their composition. Lady and the other servants had more in common with the sleeping cat than with the four girls, or their illustrious father.

Miranda's shoulders moved again, silent sobs returned to rack her thin frame. Deidre wanted to go over to her, to hold her, to be held, but Miranda did not like physical contact of any sort. Not from anyone. Not even from their mother. Small, frail, fragile as a moth, Miranda was by far Deidre's favourite sister. Yet her weak nerves seemed to grow worse with each passing month. Soon, Deidre was sure, she would be *committed*. (That was another word Sam had taught Deidre, after she had described her sister's sad troubles to him.) Trussed, and locked in a tower. Especially after this day played out.

A similar fate had befallen Aunt Whetstone, Deidre's mother's sister, at about the same age as Miranda was now. Once, Deidre had visited Aunt Whetstone—just once—and had run from the dingy chamber, sounds of horrible accusations and shrieked profanities echoing the hall behind her.

Being left alone like this, in the anteroom, with a nervous Lady standing guard at the door, grinning and offering strange answers to questions, no sign at all of their father, certainly had not benefited poor Miranda's condition. Her sobs ebbed and flowed while Deidre, watching helplessly, tried to be brave, though she herself had, several times since coming here, been on the verge of tears.

Two redbirds flew, humming, past the window, stopping for a second to peer in before rushing on.

"Mir, everything will be okay," Deidre said, knowing that her words sounded lame. "Listen to what Lady says."

"You don't know anything," Estelle snapped. "Little freak." She stood up from the bench, making it squeal. "This is *bullshit*. You're as crazy as her." Meaning Miranda, who had half-turned to listen, lower lip quivering.

Deidre tensed; Miranda's temper was wicked, and sometimes went off like a powderkeg: skinny arms pinwheeling, face set in an ugly, twisted rictus. She had once broken the arm of a boy who had called her names.

"Now listen here, Lady." Estelle pointed one finger at the servant. "You can't keep us cooped up like this. We're *not* children any more. That's the thing."

Lady set her jaw firm and planted her feet, resolute. Blocking the exit. Obviously under strict orders. Beneath her shift, defined muscles of her arms and shoulders moved, bunching like rocks under a tarp.

"Why don't you hush up," Deidre suggested to her older sister.

As Voluminia also rose from the harpsichord bench to stand shoulder to shoulder with her cohort, there came a loud and startling thump at the heavy door, which Lady, wheeling, easily pulled open with just the tip of one big finger:

The Orchard Keeper, standing on the dais, appeared almost ill with concern. Older. His eyes were rimmed with red, and he still wore the rumpled navy blue uniform he had been wearing when Deidre had first seen him today, in the plantations below. Then, almost frantic to find her, he had stumbled through the wheatgrass, yelling her name, and had grabbed her by the arm, hard, when she ran breathlessly up to him.

Recalling his face, and the fear she had seen there, she rubbed now at her bicep; it was still sore. They'd each had frights, a bad morning, about to get worse.

Behind the Orchard Keeper waited Ludmilla, a young servant girl who worked in the laundry room. Deidre had previously seen her only a few times. Folded clothes piled high on the girl's thick forearms, and her ugly face, very much like Lady's, peeked over the top. Her great hairy ears trembled as she looked wide-eyed around the anteroom.

There was no conceivable reason why her father should appear at the door with a *laundry maid*. Deidre glanced back at Miranda, who had a hand to her mouth.

Father came in, extending both arms, palms out, to placate. "Your mother is waiting in the courtyard. I want you girls to get changed into these outfits and follow me."

Miranda whispered, "What is it? Tell us what's going on."

Inside the room, those shafts of light pierced him now. Ludmilla followed, blinking. The Orchard Keeper and Lady exchanged a glance; Lady moved aside, bowing slightly, to busy herself with the laundry girl, scolding her, sorting the clothes into smaller piles and lifting one huge hand as if to cuff Ludmilla. She bared her big teeth.

The outfits were grey and worn. The clothes of a servant.

"We're going to leave Elegia for a few days, my little Pumpkins. We're going on a trip."

Numb, Deidre wondered if she had heard right. Leave Elegia? A *trip*? Was it possible? Who would watch over the plantations? Who would distribute food to the people in the townships?

And what about the moth that Sam would be making her for tomorrow's hunt?

Moving among the sisters, eyes averted, Ludmilla distributed the spartan costumes. Estelle and Voluminia protested but even their surly tones had changed to quieter ones, tinged with insecurity and compliance, their teenage façade of bravado crumbled.

Holding on to her own neatly folded set of clothes—studying the warp of the rough cloth as if it might make matters clearer—Deidre did not look up, did not want to see her father as he approached, but the Orchard Keeper gathered her in close, hugged her so tight in both arms that she gasped. He smelled of sweat and pomade and smoke. His uniform was crisp against her skin, his stubbled cheek, as he bent his face to hers, rough and hot. He whispered her name, told her that he loved her. The uttering of those words had become the most frightening moment of that frightening day.

Deidre could say nothing.

Her father stood, went over to Miranda to coax her away from the window—without touching her, of course—talking quietly, gently, reassuringly, leading her toward the open door where Ludmilla waited to hand her a change of clothes.

Fed up with all this, the cat, awake now, stretched, looked about haughtily, and said, "I'm leaving." Dashing out the door, just as their father also moved out onto the dais, the beast vanished in search of a more peaceful spot.

Miranda stood pale and scared, dwarfed by Lady.

"I'll be out here," the Orchard Keeper said. "While you girls all get dressed." He pulled the door shut behind him.

The four sisters glanced at each other. Having no recourse, they got changed, Lady and Ludmilla watching them surreptitiously, frowning at the lithe young bodies as they stepped from their clothes.

Deidre was used to Lady's clumsy curiosity. She cast aside the frills and layers of her dress and petticoats and stood, finally, in the drab outfit, feeling vulnerable and demeaned. These new clothes were itchy against her skin and they stunk. Miranda's outfit hung slack from her thin arms and chest. Deidre tried to smile at her sister, who was wiping her snotty nose on the grey sleeve; Miranda drew a deep breath and actually tried to smile in return. That gave Deidre a modicum of reassurance. Together they might be able to get through this.

From the door, Lady motioned. All the girls approached without any protest, not even from Voluminia or Estelle. Their faces as they passed Deidre looked white as milk.

Lady opened the door.

They left the anteroom.

From the railing, where he'd been waiting, the Orchard Keeper turned to lead the way. A series of archways equally spaced down the length of the wide dais overlooked the gardens of Elegia and the tangled woods beyond. The girls trudged through alternating shadow and light, in a stunned sort of silence, Lady shuffling among them, biting at her puffy lips and ushering the sombre sisters with slow movements of her hands.

The day was hot and quiet. The sun nearest Elegia was visible, hanging between two columns, where it always hung. Glancing up at it, Deidre imagined she saw activity, as if the sun were a candle flame, and midges had begun to circle it.

When she turned away, blinking, Ludmilla had vanished altogether.

Again Deidre thought back to the gram she'd watched in her sanctum. It had talked of war. Was that the reason the Orchard Keeper wore his uniform? Why he was agitated? Had he been up all night, relaying messages back and forth, from estate to estate, getting news of doom and killing and approaching soldiers?

In single file, the girls, their father, and Lady all descended the spiral stairs of the southwest tower to come out blinking in the light that yellowed the gravel lip of the front courtyard. A hard-packed road wound from Elegia's stately portals and out into the environs via a great black gate. Clusters of distant huts were set against rolling verdant hills.

Far above, the dome of the sky was a clear but faded blue. Deidre looked at the sun once more, but the glare was too much.

Several footmen in red uniforms stood by the gate, brandishing poleaxes. At the sight of their boss, one of them ran forward a few steps, stopped, looked back at his comrades. These men were used to casual days, inaction, games of cards and crude jokes in the guardhouse. Days spent trying to get Voluminia and Estelle to pay them some attention. Now that something real was happening, they were clearly unsure how to proceed.

With a shock, Deidre suddenly realized it was not the gold carriage waiting, as she'd imagined—with its four dun quarter horses, each brushed and dressed and noble; instead, the covered market cart squatted ugly on the gravel, dirty and rickety and as grey as a shadow. She stopped short. From a rent in the chamois cover her mother peeked, managing a tiny wave and a brave face.

The Orchard Keeper heartily returned the wave, as if everything were fine, a mere drive in the country.

Miranda dashed, ungainly, loping across the courtyard towards the cart.

The big hand of her father fell on Deidre's shoulder. "Come on there, D, hurry up, get in. Your mother's waiting."

And the older girls held back.

Deidre turned slowly. Blood had drained from her cheeks. "You're not coming with us." This was not a question.

The Orchard Keeper blinked, started to say something, closed his mouth. Now Estelle and Voluminia were walking across the courtyard—Miranda was already inside the cart, her thin wail drifting on the hot afternoon air. Their father crouched down. His eyes searched Deidre's. They were moist and she saw red veins mapping them like small, sanguine rivers.

"No, sweetie," he said, quietly. "I'm not coming with you. But I *will* catch up in a few days." He waited, perhaps to give Deidre a chance to speak, but Deidre did not say anything so he wiped at his mouth with his hand and fiddled with his Orchard Keeper's ring. "I, uh . . . Take care of our precious Mir. And take care of your mother, and Voluminia, too, for that matter. And Estelle, of course. You're the most sensible one of all, D. You're the voice of reason in our little family."

Deidre did not smile. "Is it war?" she asked. "Are we going to war again, father? Why won't you tell me?"

He was shocked, or at least appeared so. "*War*? When were we ever at war, sweetie? The last war was long before I was even born."

She repeated her question.

"I don't know where you get your ideas from, D. You must have your Aunt's imagination. Now go, Pumpkin, please. Get in with your mother and sisters. Trust me. I will see you again soon."

To her surprise, Deidre felt a growing anger. More anger inside her than fright or sadness. Her father had not answered at all. He was *deserting* his family. She stared at the Orchard Keeper—for that was how she thought of him right then, not as *father*, but as *Orchard Keeper*—stared for a moment longer, until he was forced to exhale and look away, and then she turned toward the grey market cart. She walked, her back held straight, though the heat on her shoulders was oppressive. The thick fabric of the servant's clothes was a shroud. She did not want to turn around, did not want to see the Orchard Keeper again. Her cheeks also burned. She kept thinking, *this is not fair, this is not fair . . .*

But she would not cry.

No stairs on the cart, no lowered ramp, no staff to help her up. Deidre scrambled up over the tailgate and immediately stopped in the musty interior, panting. Her sisters sat on benches, Voluminia and Estelle together, Miranda opposite them, curled in on herself, sniffling. Mother knelt on the floor. She turned toward Deidre now.

"Sweet pea." Her face was sad. "Come here, give me a hug."

"Why are we leaving? And why are we dressed like this? Father would not even . . ."

The words died in her mouth: her mother also wore a soiled shift, crude and patched. But her hair, once luxurious, long and red, had been cut unevenly, hacked off, as if by a knife. Heart in her mouth, Deidre looked at Miranda—who did not meet her gaze—and back at her mother.

Voluminia hissed, "We all look ridiculous."

"Stupid," Estelle said. "*This* is all so stupid."

"Girls, don't make this harder than it is. We have to be strong. For each other."

Deidre sat down on the hard plank next to Miranda. The market cart rocked suddenly; Lady had taken her place on the driver's bench. Deidre saw the servant's broad back through the aperture of the cover. The world seemed to buzz with heat. She could not think straight. Now Lady peered over her shoulder, squinting, her upper lip pulled back over her great teeth as if this homely expression might help her see within the gloom of the cart. "Ready, ma'am?"

"We are," mother said.

The engine started with a rumble. Backfiring loudly, backfiring again, the cart went noisily into gear and lurched forward. Gravel spat out from behind. Lady shifted as if she had already lost control or had forgotten how to drive altogether; at the wheel, the servant always gave this impression.

So they left the courtyard. Simple as that. Drove right through the gates. Deidre looked out the back but her father was not watching. He was nowhere to be seen.

Elegia's trees, the path, her beloved estate: all fell behind.

"We're going to stay in a seasonal residence," mother said. "One your father and I used to stay in, when we first met."

Across from Deidre, Voluminia pursed her lips, showing her disdain; Estelle, turning her head away, muttered something unclear.

Elegia looked like a doll's house. And the huge tent-like structure covering the mouth of the lift shaft, descending to the plantations and beyond, also appeared, to Deidre, as a child's toy.

Footmen pushed the receding gates shut. They stood in miniature to watch the cart dwindle.

"Before he was elected to the position of Orchard Keeper,

your father worked in the private sector. We lived in a place called Timberline. He was so handsome, with eyes like yours, Miranda, and hair the same colour as yours, Vole." Their mother pushed herself back until she leaned against the rear of the driver's bench. A breeze came through the cart but it was still muggy and close underneath the chamois. Over her mother's right shoulder, Lady fought the wheel. The cart rumbled on.

"He used to work very long days, interpreting research for his supervisor. A project trying to improve the general labourer, biological tweaks to a digging model. I was attending Timberline Academy. I was only nineteen. We didn't get to see much of each other. I worked at the library on weekends and sometimes he would be coming in and I would be going out—"

"Mother," Deidre interrupted. "Is there going to be another war? Won't you at least answer me? Is that why we're being taken from Elegia?"

Her mother's nostalgic smile faded. Looking at her four daughters, almost radiating the concern she obviously felt, her body appeared to shrink, and Deidre regretted her question. When her mother finally did respond, it was in a quieter voice. She said she hoped war would never scar the world again but that some people and the machines they had made were mean and hateful, and would humanity never be able to live together, in peace, in a million years? Would they never learn how to do *that*?

Voluminia kicked Deidre when their mother lowered her head to wipe covertly at the corners of her eyes. Deidre felt awful. She wished she had heard the end of the story. She wished she had let her mother talk.

Over the next hour, the mood did manage to brighten again, somewhat, considering the sweltering circumstances, though Deidre's mother did not continue with her story of the cabin they were heading toward, despite Deidre's periodic prompting to do so.

Aside from the occasional, muttered complaint about the hardness of the benches or about the heat in the covered cart, the girls and their mother progressed throughout the late morning and into the early afternoon in a dazed sort of torpor. The rumbling and shaking, the transmission's roar, the intense heat and stale smell of the cart, all seemed to lull the family like a soporific. The girls rocked from side to side, side to side, side to side—

Though Deidre and her family had moved into Elegia only a few years ago, when Deidre was eight, she could not recall what it was like to live elsewhere, beyond the boundaries of the estate. The roadside landscape they passed was lush and vibrant, the small towns that fell behind active, alive, and boisterous; Deidre realized she had expected both people and surroundings out here to be forlorn.

Occasional pedestrians, going about their business, carried food or water or strolled the edges of the road in small groups. Most paid the cart little heed, glancing at it with mild curiosity as it rumbled by. Several children chased behind for a short while, and a group of unseen animals commented loudly and catcalled rudely from the ditch.

Once, they had to pull over to let pass a tiny old crone sitting atop a massive wagon that was being drawn by a beast Deidre had never seen before, a creature twice as high as a man with long shaggy fur and great fleshy feet. The face, when it turned to look Deidre's way, was vaguely human, but in a most grotesque fashion. The creature emanated a blast of pathos toward her like a gust of cold air.

At last it was teatime. Bidding the request of the girls' mother, Lady took the cart off the road and stopped it under the shade of a great willow tree. A brook ran under an arched culvert.

The servant jumped from the bench and busied herself setting out a blanket. Emerging, one by one, blinking, the four girls stretched and looked about the glade, tense, lean, healthy.

Deidre's mother unpacked sweet rolls and sandwiches and tiny sausages. It was much cooler here, under the willow. Water from the brook was refreshing. The suns were dimming. Overcast conditions prevailed. Filling her cup for a second time, Deidre searched the pebbled bottom for caddis fly larvae or diving beetles, or perhaps a minnow, but the ecosystem out here had no place for these creatures and the stream was sterile; the local supervisor had not, apparently, seen fit to stock the water with anything from its archives.

Seated on the blanket, Voluminia and Estelle ate their lunch, talking hoarsely, laughing, hitting one another. A fair distance from them, Miranda gazed at the grass poking up between her knobby knees and did not eat or even pay the food the slightest attention. On the bench of the market cart, Lady munched noisily and messily, staring out over the fields. Thusly, a modicum of equilibrium—despite the adventure—had returned to Deidre's life. Mother buttered a slice of bread. Talked to Miranda. Trying to get her to eat, no doubt.

A sudden stab of regret at how she had treated her father, when the family had left Elegia, stung Deidre. She vowed to herself that she'd apologize when she next laid eyes on him—for he *would* come to the cabin, surely, as he had promised. They would all be reunited soon. She smiled, and sipped the clean water.

How quickly hardships could be smoothed out, how adaptable we are—

Beyond the willow, soaring, several shapes rode currents so high they appeared to touch the scaffolding that lined the sky and from which the suns hung. Deidre stared for a while but could not imagine what these were. Machines? Or real birds brought to life? Lab-born creations?

Approaching the blanket, she continued to idly watch these forms, deciding at last that they were creatures.

But, as the beasts soared closer, their shapes were clearly bigger than she had at first guessed.

Much bigger.

She stopped walking.

"Mom?" Her voice came out thin and reedy. Her cup fell to the grass and cold water soaked her foot. "*Mom!*"

"What is it, Sweet Pea?" Her mother looked but turned quickly, toward the sky, alarmed by the expression she'd seen on her youngest daughter's face. Staring, mouth open, she said nothing.

The glade had gone preternaturally still.

Even from this distance, Deidre distinguished two trailing legs, very much like her own, and faces, on these aviators. No, certainly not machines. Not redbirds or blue. These were men, flying men, and they were as strange and unsettling to her mother as they were to Deidre.

"Uh, girls," their mother finally said, clapping the lid down on a mayonnaise jar. "You see what wonders one can witness in the, in the world at large?"

"*What* are they?" Deidre asked quietly.

"Lady?" Mother addressed the servant. "Have you seen these, er, specimens previously?"

"No, ma'am," Lady answered, still chewing, her face also turned skyward. "I reckon they might be angels."

"Angels?" Voluminia laughed. "There's no such thing."

"Angels," Lady repeated, nodding. "Angels are a sign of luck, they say. A blessing. They're 'posed to appear. When we pure enough to ascend."

"Ascend? What are you talking about?"

"Some of us believe that. Ma'am."

"Some of *who*?"

"Us." Lady shrugged. "Or they might be rocs. Or even harpies."

Mother laughed nervously. "Tell the girls you're kidding, Lady."

Lady looked blankly at the girls.

"Tell the girls there are no such things as rocs. Or nonsense about ascension."

Lady shrugged and turned her attention back to her lunch. She popped a small potato in her mouth.

"Maybe they're something new," Estelle said. "Some tortured freaks escaped from a lab, just like the one dad worked at."

"Yeah. Before he exiled us," Voluminia added.

"Your father fed and clothed us!" Mother was angry now. "He gave you girls a beautiful home. I will not have him talked about like that."

The teenagers were not intimidated. They exchanged exaggerated looks. Voluminia fingered her grubby garments and feigned being impressed by the quality.

Their mother tossed leftovers back into the basket. The picnic wrapped up hastily. Under the presence of the winged men, circling high overhead, the girls bundled back into the cart. Lady started the engine.

Every so often, as they drove, Deidre glimpsed the angels, or whatever they were, out the back, still very high up. They seemed to be following the cart. She never did get a truly clear look at the features on those distant faces but she was sure that their wingspan must reach three metres across, at least.

There were six of them, maybe more.

When dusk fell, and the suns had faded to red-glowing elements, Lady pulled off the road to fill the petrol tank. Despite the fact that the oppressive heat had lifted, the girls had grown cranky again and were asking regularly how long it would be before they arrived at the cabin. *Soon*, their mother said, *soon*.

Yet, shortly after setting out again—as the cart rumbled up a hill into the darkening landscape—Deidre heard Lady grunt with alarm. Half-standing in the flatbed, rocking, trying to keep her footing, she saw, over the servant's broad shoulder, what looked like the entire valley before them consumed with leaping flames, tearing the oncoming night to shreds.

MEREZIAH, L17-18

Creeping motion, inexorable. Almost easy to forget there was movement whatsoever. In fact, at times, despite Mereziah's general state of mounting excitement, it was possible to forget what he had done in the first place, the decision he'd made to leave his station behind and rise upwards, alone, in the world.

Lucid peaks—when he was able to reflect, feeling instances of freshness and clarity such as he had not experienced in many decades—he knew for certain that he had done the right thing. Only one direction was an option: *up*. The simple word lolled on his tongue when he whispered it and circulated giddily inside his brain like a drug. He would never go back down again, not while he was alive. Never see his station again, nor the ramshackle cabin his father had built. Never see his brother again. All the fixtures of his life grew farther away with each passing second.

Yet he also had within him the capacity to lose his lucidity, his confidence. He could not allow himself to become maudlin; a positive mood, if he were not careful, would quickly deflate. No looking down, he told himself. No looking down. No regrets.

Pendulous in the updrafts, Mereziah planted both bare feet flat against the curved wall of the shaft and pushed off, rising and twisting, pulled by the madman's pod as it nudged ever upwards. The track they rode was true and *very* long. Casting a russet glow, the device overhead gave off more than enough light for Mereziah to distinguish his surroundings, and he came to accept a somewhat disconcerting fact: despite his fancies and anticipation, there was little difference between where he had worked his life away and these new, higher areas of the shaft. Nor did they show any promise of change. Retired pods embedded deep in the curved walls. Dusty mesh strung between glistening tracks. Loops and untold lengths of entwined tubes. Endless tubes. Hundreds of sizes, gurgling and trickling and burping quietly, up and down the great shaft. Everything dusty and grey. Just like back home.

And there came flashes of light from the wall, too, maybe a little stronger than those he was used to, almost as bright, it seemed, as the light that falls regularly on level grounds—though not in the dingy grotto where his father had built their family's cabin.

Within the pod the passenger screamed, perhaps suddenly horrified by wandering thoughts of his own, triggered by the intermittent glare. Mereziah heard those dirty feet shuffling about, a few meters above his head. The passenger shouted twice more. That light flashed again.

Was it unusually bright? Different microfauna in the walls here? Any indication, Mereziah wondered, of change at last?

The only incident truly out of the ordinary in those first few hours was when he caught a quick glimpse of another lift attendant, watching in shock from the gloom, lean face agog over the transgression that rose up from the black depths like the coming of some prophet from places where the dead fell. Mereziah was unable to contain his grin as he gave this comrade—whom he would never meet but with whom, no doubt, he had so much in common—a tentative little wave; the other attendant, after a moment, staring up in utter disbelief, returned the wave uncertainly.

And once a brood of young sloths, coming arm over arm up the adjacent webbing, paused to bat at Mereziah's form with outsized claws, but these creatures were remotely interested in him, and only for a short while, before they too melted into the shadows.

So Mereziah had lots of time, as usual, to dwell on the uneventful years of his long life. Perhaps not exactly a life *wasted*, but an overly courteous and restrained one, obedient, a life of service. Undermined, mostly, by a bitterness that had flowed, until today, deep under his proper-yet-seething skin. He thought about his brother, more like himself than he could ever fully admit; about his dead parents, at whom, when they were alive, he'd often rolled his eyes. He had considered them to be archaic, out of touch, but could never tell them, now they were dust, how sorry he was for that, how wise he truly saw them now, with age and the few small wisdoms with which his drab life had graced him.

Components of his experiences seemed to break down, sorting into hard facts, like a series of crystals, as if they could be arranged, made sense of, as if they could be held, easy to view, hold, and look at from different angles.

How often did Mereziah stare upwards that afternoon,

squinting past the moving pod, convincing himself that not only were distant glimmers signs of life from above but that they were getting closer?

At one point, dozing, he imagined he was an infant again, about to suckle an oozing drop from his mother's swollen teat as she climbed the meshing to nurse him.

Approximately five hours, estimated Mereziah, after abandoning his station, the pod that he clung to shuddered to a complete and utter halt.

Silence.

Everything around remained as it always had.

"A good ride," he said to no one, and he nodded, trying hard to hold onto his hope. "A good, long ride . . ."

Glimmers of slick pseudopods groped the shaft wall for purchase: the track was actually germinating. Budding. If he were to continue up, he had no choice but to completely re-couple the pod.

As he searched the curved wall for a more stable track, a glare of light from what must have been a great mass of parasites directly opposite him illuminated the vicinity in harsh contrast—

"Ahh!" Mereziah closed his watering eyes, knuckling them with one hand. But what had he seen on the other side in that split second? *A huge pod*? Fleetingly, he'd been able to view across the gulf of the shaft, and it sure had looked like a pod there, the largest pod he had ever seen, so vast it defied imagination as it hung, inert, from an entire group of parallel tracks. If Mereziah had not been hanging by his belt straps he might have dropped to his death from surprise.

Father had long ago told him and his brother about lift pods of huge size, but Mereziah had not believed the tales, not even as a young child; in his experience, he'd only ever seen singles, doubles, the occasional family-size.

But this one—if what he'd seen had indeed been a pod—could have carried a dozen or more.

He was unable to conceive of a monster such as this in motion, and decided that what he thought he'd seen had to be sort of a nonfunctioning anomaly, grown over the centuries, a mutated tumour in the wall of the shaft.

But supposing a huge pod *could* exist, could actually carry people, move up and down . . . *Several* full-time attendants would be needed merely to maintain its course, let alone help it out should it become stuck—which would surely happen almost instantly. What were the odds of tracks remaining aligned for *any* functional distance?

Darkness had fully closed back in on him; the red light atop the single pod was extinguished. Surely, with its mad passenger inside, the pod he rode under could be left for an hour or two while he made his way around the shaft to investigate the monstrosity on the far side. He would return when he was done, re-couple the stalled pod, and continue his ascent. Simple. A short detour, maybe a wonder to behold.

Mereziah unbuckled himself, decided not even to tell the passenger he would be temporarily abandoned, and without hesitation began the trip around the slow curvature of the shaft.

Webbing here was certainly similar to that which strung his own station, track to track, and in loops between, dense and familiar enough for his footing and hand placements to be secure. Against the calluses on his palms and feet, the strands were like old friends, but eyes of the dead looked up at him from that dark and distant bottom, preparing to judge him and the rash move he'd made. He should not be here, they implied. This station was not his.

Mereziah wanted to shout out justifications for his actions but motives seemed selfish and petty. His mother's eyes watched him on this frivolous escapade. He would explain to her that he'd had no choice.

Before long, Mereziah could hardly see the slim pod he'd left behind. He was calm once more. Squinting over his shoulder, he fancied he could make out the dimmest sliver of yellow, leaking from the window—which remained in the open position—and he wondered if the passenger could see him out here or if the madman even knew or cared that he had once again been left alone. Did the traveller, for that matter, even know he'd been accompanied?

In truth, Mereziah suspected that the man knew more than he let on.

Half an hour or so later, miniature under the looming bulk—which remained quite real—Mereziah was somewhat out of breath but otherwise feeling good and clear-headed. Intermittent glimmers of phosphorescence allowed him to confirm that the pod—for it was indeed a pod—hung out into the shaft like a grotesque and distended belly. The width, this close, hinted that the elevating device might be wide enough to accommodate at least thirty passengers.

But the most shocking discovery came when he'd glanced at the area directly above the freakish pod: portions of the tracks were moist and striated and caught the faint light. When he'd seen this, a fist turned in his gut. The giant pod *had* descended. *Recently.* Not much, but the traces of moistness on the tracks were proof that the device was very capable of motion. Who requested such monsters to retrieve them? Why would so many people need transportation at one time? And where in the *world* would they be going?

Possibly many pods up here were this large, nearer to the top of the world. Maybe things weren't so similar here after all—

Flaccid skin on his neck prickled. If the pod were active, he thought, there are people about. And these people, if they were also different, might not be so friendly. They might not tolerate a deserter.

Under the body proper of the device were several groups of rings. Mereziah saw them dangling from where he clung. Enough rings for a small army of lift attendants to attach themselves to while they worked. He glanced about but no one lurked in the darkness: no movement; no unusual source of light other than the pale and pulsing glow of the walls themselves.

Fingers of tepid breeze from below lifted his clothes and ran fingers over his belly.

Two rows of windows. Staggered. Eight, at least, in each row. The nearest few were sealed but several others, farther away, appeared to be open. No illumination whatsoever emanated from within. The bulbs inside the huge pod were quenched? Devoid of power?

Mereziah forced himself to proceed with his investigation but a growing part of him wanted to flee, retreat to the mad passenger and the single pod he had left behind. Inside his body, as inside that slim device, his own stowaway prowled: a bad and sour feeling, hitching a lift. Was he about to be taught a lesson for leaving his post? Ironically, it was the professional facet of him, not the newborn and ill-fitting spontaneous facet, that impelled him to stay, to assist, to offer his services.

The mechanisms of the windows appeared similar to those he was familiar with, despite the visible differences such as size, obviously, and contour. He positioned himself close enough to touch the surface of the pod. The skin appeared similar to most other pod coverings: smooth, pliant.

Reaching out with one trembling thumb, to caress the ridge that would open the shade of the nearest window, he touched the slider, moved it quickly aside. Nothing. Only blackness. He pressed his face against the pane, and squinted, imagining now he could discern something, a vague highlight or two, an outline, a shifting form? He knocked, very quietly, and was sure he heard the sounds of gentle movements, an answering and disturbing groan—

The glare was blinding, an explosion of light so strong it caused him to lose his footing and fall back hard into the netting, swinging down and slamming one knee against the wall of the shaft, which, though relatively soft, still sent daggers of pain through his body. Caught in the web, hanging there, blinded, his useless hands flailed. His heart hammered and threatened to stop in his chest.

Above him, from within the giant pod, a young girl called out: "Who's there? I mean, who the fuck is out there?"

The light was a beam. He could see that now, as it played harshly across the darkness where he had been, gleaming on the mucus-covered tracks and ashy pale webwork of the shaft.

Mereziah lay for a long while, watching this light, waiting to hear the voice again, trying to calm himself and surveying his limbs to see if he were hurt. That voice had certainly sounded like a girl's. A normal, if somewhat brazen, girl. When he heard the question repeated one more time he frowned, began to untangle himself, and replied, as loudly and as confidently as he could, "Hello there? I'm a lift attendant. This is not my station but may I, may I be of, of *assistance*? Of service to you? Are you in . . . in *distress*?"

"Distress?" Laughter now, drifting down from above. "May you be of *fuckin assistance*?" The girl's tone, verging on shrill, held elements of fear or maybe even desperation. She was clearly in trouble. Mereziah was sure of it, despite her bravado.

"I wanna see your face. Where are you? I wanna see that you're not one of those fuckin soldiers."

"I assure you," Mereziah responded, climbing back up slowly toward the giant pod, "I am no threat. I am not a soldier. Why in the world would there be soldiers about? I am an attendant. Shine the light away from the window; it's too bright; I can't see."

Rubbing at his watering eyes, he peered over the windowsill and into the pod. There she was. A girl, standing, scrawny in the beam of her own torch, hardly more than a child. Sickly? No. Merely dirty, skinny, and tired. (A striking face, however, under those smears and tear streaks.) One fist clenched tight on the haft of the torch, the other shielding large, wide-spaced eyes. Not as big as the eyes of a lift attendant, of course, but not as small as the eyes of a person who always lives in light. No hair on that blotched pate. No teeth, hiding in that grimace? Hard to tell, but it looked that way.

She was dressed in grubby pants, grubby shirt. Defiance personified. Wiry muscles down her limbs. A sight, he decided—as they sized each other up—of surprising beauty.

"Wow," the girl finally whispered, breaking the spell, stepping back. "You're so fuckin old." The light beam wavered. "How old *are* you?"

"One hundred years," Mereziah answered, unable to think of anything else to add. The question had stung him like a slap in his face. He said, "One hundred years old. Today."

She was memorizing him, seeing his flaws, his very thoughts. He squirmed but her gaze lingered on him, exposed, out here, in harsh shadow and highlight. He felt her intelligence and insight burning into him.

"Your eyes are so *huge*," she said.

"I live in darkness," Mereziah said. "But I can see in the dark. What appears black to you looks dark grey to me." An attendant's joke, but the girl did not laugh. Neither did he.

"Can you help me, old man? Can you rescue me?"

"You *do* need rescuing?"

"Of course I need rescuing. Maybe I should be helping you?"

The smile, when it came, confirmed two things: one, that there were no teeth in that pretty mouth—only dark gums—and two, the girl had the capacity to radiate an intense allure he had never before experienced. Mereziah felt a rush of giddiness. My goodness, he thought, have I ever even *seen* a teenaged girl?

Movement from behind the captive. He squinted, said, "How many are in there? How many people with you?"

To his surprise, the girl laughed out loud at his question, but the laugh ended abruptly as she looked over her shoulder. At first he thought she was counting. Then he realized she was *listening*. He strained to listen as well but heard nothing.

"Is there one of those soldiers in there with you?" he asked quietly.

An image of the girl's body, trapped by captors, entered Mereziah's mind like a spectre of evil, of all the grievous injustices in the world, and crept slowly away, over the lobes of his brain, leaving unpleasantly lingering emotions.

I am going mad, he thought.

When the girl spoke again, it was also in softer tones: "I honestly can't tell how many people are here with me, old man. Two dozen, maybe?" She shrugged. "They brought some others here, not long ago, and dropped them in. Once, they took a woman out. Then they brought her back. They asked her some questions, she said. Looked into her eyes with a machine . . . They didn't hurt her. I don't really know what they want with us. Some people in here are hurt."

As if on queue, a moan of pain rose from the dark reaches of the pod, crackling out from the tiny speaker on the windowsill. And what looked like a man's face emerged, furrowed and scared, grimacing, but this image receded before Mereziah was certain of what he had seen.

"And," he said, swallowing hard, "are you all in there . . . against your will?"

"That's what I've been trying to tell you. Aren't you listening? Three giant soldiers, maybe twice my size, with smooth black faces. Really big, intense guys. They abducted us all and brung us up here. They're the ones asking questions."

"*Giant* soldiers?"

"Holy smoke. Are you fucking senile?"

She lowered the torchlight in exasperation and might not have seen the rage that suddenly tightened Mereziah's face, making his hands clench. "I am not senile," he hissed, wondering if he should rescue this girl at all or promptly leave her now, as he'd found her, trapped inside the big pod while he continued on his way toward the top of the world. After all, he had already deserted his post, his job, his responsibilities. Why did he insist on acting like an attendant? He sure didn't need to be insulted. "I assure you, young lady, I have *all* my wits about me."

"Can you get us out of this thing or not? I'd *really* appreciate it."

"Yes, I can get you out." Who was he trying to fool? He couldn't leave this girl or this pod until he had tried everything he knew to get her out. And get the others out too, of course. Merezath might have left these people here but not he. The reasons I want to help, he assured himself, are strictly ethical and professional.

So he introduced himself.

And the girl said, "What kind of name is that?"

Again he was flustered. "It's a fine name. My mother chose it. It means—"

"That you're a stuffy old fart?" But her entrancing smile

returned. "Can I call you M, old fart? My friends call me Crystal, but you can call me Crystal Max. I've been on quite a fucking ride!"

Mereziah did not approve of foul language but neither did he want to chastise or lecture. Despite his intentions, he was unable to cease imagining what Crystal Max's young body might look like under those dirty clothes. He slunk away from the pod, muttering he would return shortly, creeping down into the webbing and out of sight.

He was raging inside with conflicting sensations. He took a few breaths, closing his eyes for a second. Had this massive pod been intentionally left between levels? The girl, Crystal, had mentioned that the people trapped inside had been 'dropped' in. That implied to Mereziah that the captors had positioned the pod—which they were clearly using as a jail—between levels. Away from access to the horizontal world.

He climbed even lower, slowly, feeling the wall as he went with his sensitive fingertips, massaging the rough, curved surface of the shaft, searching and kneading. In some areas, he plunged up to his elbow in the coarse webbing, forced to grope blindly.

The plan was to find access to the level beneath the pod and ferry the passengers out, one by one, via that exit. After that, who knew? His upward journey was certainly curtailed.

Maybe this rescue was the culmination of his life, his final purpose?

Nerve endings in his palms and fingertips responded, recognizing the subtle contours he had been seeking. Manipulating the slick, hidden hinge, pressing at it, rubbing at it, a slit finally opened before him with a sucking sound, letting light and air and a dull roar flood the area about; Mereziah's eyes nictitated.

He leaned forward to glance through, saw clutters of pumps and tubes of all sizes out there, heading in all directions. Tiny wheels spun busily in housings. Pistons chuffed. Steam hissed. No traditional horizontal area, to be sure—some form of machinations—but deserted, at least, as far as he could tell.

A thin, suspended path began not far from where he peeked out, leading out over bevel gears and pipes and pulleys to be swallowed in the haze. Where could it lead? Would it be folly to take the captives out of the pod and head them onto this perilous path?

Across the abyss, a faint backdrop of hazy panels. Dim lights, consoles, controls, all vanishing through the vapour. These distant façades appeared as if from a dream.

Out there stunk of heat and oil.

Mereziah let the slit close slowly. He was perspiring. He went back up to the pod.

The first person he rescued, naturally, was the girl. Accessing pods from the outside was routine. He merely opened the escape panel and helped Crystal Max crawl out. Soldiers did not attack them. Clinging to his back, Crystal Max clamped firm thighs around Mereziah's waist and locked her arms over his throat. Her smell was like nothing that had ever filled his sinuses before: tangy and sharp and delirious. Though Crystal whispered to him the whole while they clumsily travelled down towards the slit—her breath hot in his ear, saliva moistening his neck—he was so tense and lost in her scent that he could think of nothing to say in response to her encouragements except to stutter, "Don't worry, just hang on, hang on . . ."

Not far below them, the big slit in the wall seemed to pulse expectantly.

TRAN SO, L12

In an adjacent chamber, another prisoner cried, caterwauling sobs that rose and fell, carried on the stale wind blowing lightly through grilles set high in the wall.

The dark gods were no longer in this room.

Forearms heavy with manacles, manacles heavy with chains, all resting on his trembling knees. Tran so's ankles had been shackled uncomfortably to the leg of the bench he sat on. Sickened by the lake water, he rocked gently forward and back and listened to the wavering cries from next door.

Behind his left eyeball, parasites that had made their home there rolled and resettled around his tear duct, squeezing a tear free to roll down the angular planes of his cheek.

Tran so Phengh still feared for his own life but the past few hours had actually abated the initial rush of terror. The menace of his abductors—those he referred to, internally, as 'the dark gods'— had greatly diminished; in fact, their aura—perceived, at first, to be one of purest evil—was now diluted, misplaced, almost like one of bewilderment rather than threat; he now looked upon the giants in blue as similar to the misguided deities one saw knocking on doors in the slums of Hoffmann City, trying to enlist listless citizens into some program or other, distributing dogmatic pamphlets, or scolding teenagers for gathering in too large a group.

His heart was still beating, and his lungs drew air. He had not been hurt. One of the giants who had pounced on him in the underwater lair, and then carried him all the way to this holding room, over its shoulder—in and out of nightmarish devices and bizarre settings while Tran so swooned and rolled his eyes up into his head and retched up bile that ran in dark stains down the giant's shirt—was even kind enough to ask Tran so several times over the course of the journey if the bindings on his wrists were too tight, and if he had ingested some form of toxin. That particular god had even apologized for the brusque takedown, and for having to confiscate Tran so's knife.

"We thought you had damaged the filtration unit," it explained. "You see, we have been activated without any guidance. Our instructions are not clear. As we looked around, and tried to assess possible reasons for being called upon, we became maddened by the evidence of senseless vandalism that we saw in the world around us. What had happened? We assumed our reason for existence was to correct matters. Now we know a little better. So, despite our continuing search for the truth, friend, you have at least been cleared of that initial offense."

After tying him to a bench, Tran so had been left alone. Dark gods still passed by the room, paired or in small groups. Occasionally, one of them entered, stooping, to remove or add someone to the captives there, whose ranks rose and fell over the course of the day. All these gods looked the same, and Tran so Phengh could not tell which one it had been that had showed him signs of kindness after his arrest. Yet as a whole, in their actions, the giants seemed to lack coherent leadership. This aspect, too, familiarized them, reduced their threat. They were certainly like the gods he knew back home. They were unsure, imperfect. They were like people.

Other prisoners in the room now were also bound to benches, though earlier some had lain, prone on the floor, apparently free to go. If they would only stir. Had they been somehow stunned? Was the benevolence Tran so had experienced an act?

Men and women had been detained here. For a time, there had been a small child—when Tran so had first arrived—but only four prisoners remained, including him, and all four were men.

Marked on the wall opposite, above a sleeping figure of one of the men, painted in deep vermilion, were the words HUMAN RESOURCES. These glyphs appeared to be the last legible elements of what had once been an entire paragraph of writing covering most of the wall; only these two words had been restored.

Not many residents of Hoffmann City could read. Encouragements of Minnie sue, shortly after they'd met, had spurred Tran so Phengh to become literate. Courses were given at the nearby Community Centre. The teacher had been a lesser god. When afternoon classes had ended, Tran so and his wife had often gone home to make love. Tran so would cover Minnie sue's soft mouth with one palm when she came—for there were other people sharing the house with them, living beyond the partitions—and Minnie sue's shrieked orgasms could shake the walls of any building.

Recalling the sound, Tran so smiled grimly. He did not know what these two red words HUMAN RESOURCES could mean, but their presence, and the fact that he could read them, made him think fondly of Minnie sue. The image of her naked body, the sounds of her guttural, almost dirty comments, her sharp nipples pressed into his palms while she ground her hips back into his own, did not, this time, depress him. These memories were integral to what made him Tran so Phengh. Never could they be stolen from him. Not by time, not by illness, not by uncertain gods.

On the bench he shifted; his cock had started to harden. For the first time since he had been abducted, he wished his hands were free.

Lost in thoughts of abandon, it was some time before he realized that the man across from him had not only awoken but had lifted his head and was addressing him quietly from across the floor:

"Hey, hey? Got any water?"

Tran so blinked. The features and the accent were very different than his own. People came from all over the world to visit Hoffmann City, to patronize its sex clubs and enjoy the renowned decadence; Tran so was used to foreigners. This face was long, with a full beard. The man's eyes were round and his hair blond. He was dressed in a tan uniform.

"Have you got any water?" the man repeated. "My head's splitting. I've been here a day and a half and I've drunk nothing. They can't keep us here like this, without water, and not tell us anything. There are conventions to keeping prisoners."

"I am ill from drinking water."

"They *poisoned* you?"

"No, no, they have not poisoned me. It was from a lake. From an unclean lake. This was before they took me."

"You resemble someone who lives near the water supply, near the reservoirs. I've been there. I've seen others like you."

Cries from next door faded to a low sob.

These round eyes staring at Tran so seemed to contain little intelligence. "Others like me?" Tran so asked.

"Yeah. I visited the reservoirs once, as a kid. I hear the water in that place was much higher back then, that it's all drained out.

107

My old man took me and some other kids down the shaft, cause he had some business there with one of the supervisors. My old man, see, was in the diplomatic corps. Back when they was still trying to be diplomatic. He dealt with *machines*. And I recall that people who lived there, on that reservoir level, looked just like you. With straight black hair, and slitty little eyes."

Yes, Tran so Phengh had met men like this before. Many times. They came to Hoffmann City in hordes, loud and drunk, often hurting the citizens they employed. He had chased several on occasion, had fought one or two. At work, Minnie sue had once been punched in the face by an inebriated client.

Usually, he tried to avoid such men. Not so easily done in this situation. He vowed to be patient, a quality he generally strived for. He coughed, and said politely, "The reservoir level?"

"That's what we call where you're from. And what's the name of the city there? Hoffton?"

"Hoffmann."

"That's it, Hoffmann City. Boy, that's a stinky place, eh? Too big for me. I'm just a country boy. But we had some adventures there that time, lemme tell ya. Me and my friends drank beer for the first time and my old man took us past a place where there were red lights in open windows and women too, naked in the windows. Touching each other. Touching each other's titties!"

Tran so waited. He was really not fond of the way people talked about his hometown and its population. He did not like this man. He hoped that the dark gods would come to silence the stranger, perhaps take him away.

"You ever been there? To that place?"

"Of course I have. I live in Hoffmann City."

"No, I mean to where them girls are. To that place where you can fuck them or give them a spanking or tie them up."

"There are many such places where I live. My wife served in one. She did her apprenticeship with Mme Hector."

"Your *wife*?" The man blew breath out through pursed lips. His eyes glittered. He clearly did not know what to say.

"As a rule," Tran so said, "I do not frequent those establishments. I did so as a young man, but they are primarily for travellers and tourists."

If the bearded man detected this comment to be a slight he showed no sign. "You sure talk funny," was all he said, after a moment. "You water people. Lots of big words." He licked his dry lips and leaned his head back against the wall. "Name's Ensign Conway. What's yours?"

"Tran so Phengh."

"Tran . . . Can't shake yer hand, obviously, but it's an honour to meet you. You know, me and you are gonna bust outta here. You know that? We're gonna *escape*." He had lowered his voice, and moved his body forward on the bench. "I'm sure they're looking for me, anyhow. I'm in the army, you see, based up in Descartes, on the plantation level. Thirty First airbourne division. The most elite division of the entire fucking army. You heard of them?"

"No."

"Ever been up there? To the plantation level?"

Tran so shook his head. This talk was incautious and unending and Tran so was feeling ill again.

"It's the only *real* level, man. Ten times the height of any other one. Almost the top of the world! Only a ring of rich people's houses up in the clouds after that and then the suns themselves, over our heads, shining down. It's where food is grown, you know." Ensign Conway paused, as if he had somehow confused himself. Then he asked, "How did they get you?"

"The dark gods?"

"Gods." Chuckling dryly, Ensign Conway leaned back again, so that the red words formed an arc over his head, framing him. "Yes, I suppose that's what I mean. *The dark gods*. I like that. Sounds real ominous. I'd forgotten the weird customs where you come from. Machines are gods, right?"

"We are not so simple as that. We understand the distinction between what you call a machine and a—"

"Okay, okay. Machines with *intelligence*. The ones that used to talk to the network."

"I don't know that term."

"The network was like a brain. It used to call all the shots, tell all the machines what to do. Supervisors and stuff. But I remember Hoffmann City *crawling* with those kinds of devices. With intelligence. You know, Tran, if you let them believe that they're in charge, well, it might be part of your problem down there. I guess machines are strong, and smart, and they can do a lot of shit we can't." He glanced at the doorway. Two of the giants had just walked past. "Listen, the network, or something acting like it," he continued, voice softer at last, "is actually building more of those monculii, what you call dark gods, again. Those there, for instance." He motioned with his chin to the now empty hallway. Distant voices could yet be heard. "After hundreds of fucking years they're being built again. No one knows why. There's talk of a breach but no one has found the hole yet. Not at least by the time I was taken. We were actually looking for it. And this new variety that's being made is all loose cannons. Unpredictable. Like they're being made wrong somehow, like the plans have been lost. I don't think the engineer wanted it this way."

Tran so Phengh tried to recall what the disembodied voice had told him, in the underwater lair. Hadn't it asked him when he'd first washed up on the platform inside the lake god's house if he was the engineer?

"And I say you can't take an Ensign prisoner. Not even your damn machines!" Ensign Conway shuddered as he made this outburst. "Some of these giants are totally fucking crazy. Maybe not here, but some of them are, *out there*."

"How do you know?" Tran so was being polite; he wanted silence, time to think.

"Because people have been *butchered*. That's how I know. Butchered by your dark gods. Despicable attacks. No machine is ever supposed to do *that*. It ain't the way the world was designed. People kill people. Not machines. Look at us. Look at me and you! I mean, these guys out there haven't showed any signs of being too crazy, not yet, but we're being held prisoner! Without water. They've tied us to fucking benches! And listen to that poor guy next door. What do you think they're doing to *him*?"

Tran so Phengh was about to ask Ensign Conway to keep his voice down but the sudden burst of anger had ended and the other man thankfully resumed speaking in more reasonable tones:

"I overheard some of them talking after I was captured, about *errant* individuals. That was the word they used. Errant. Of their own kind. What we do know is that these machines are rounding up people and asking them questions. Asking them if they work here or if they're just visiting. Which makes no fucking sense. And now they're also searching for some of their own, renegades that have gone nuts and are out there killing people. I *saw* some of the bodies, man. I know it's true."

"You yourself said earlier: people kill each other. Maybe these gods are more like people than other gods. Maybe we are the same."

"Whose friggin side are you on, man? Ain't you been listening to me? Besides, I don't believe in gods. In *no* kind of god. Certainly not in machines as god. It's backward thinking. We tell *them* what to do."

"You and I have differing opinions. On, I would imagine, most topics."

Ensign Conway grunted. Then, after a long pause, perhaps because silence was the last thing he cherished, he said, "You were telling me how you were taken. It might be important."

"Was I?" Tran so Phengh had not been telling the story of his capture, but nonetheless he complied. "They took me prisoner because I had challenged the god of Lake Seven. I had swum down to where it lives, to confront it about my wife's illness and the death of my son. I wanted love to return to me. I was tired of living an empty life. I was ambushed there."

"Your son's dead? And your *wife's sick*? Sorry to hear that, friend…

Personally, I don't have time for a wife. Don't want to be tied down."
Ensign Conway lifted his arms, rattling his chains again, but the
irony of his words and predicament were apparently lost on him.
"They sure have brought you a long way. A long, long way. They've
brought all of us from far away, I guess, if you think about it. From
all the corners of the world. But we're gonna find out what they're up
to. You'll see. We're gonna stop them."

Tran so said nothing.

"My story," the Ensign said, closing his eyes, "is that I was
with the Thirty First, which was my division. We was looking for
the breach, like I already said. We found a body instead. An old
man who had been living by himself in the middle of nowhere had
been tortured and killed. And we'd seen wanton destruction of
the landscape from the air. But I became separated from the boys,
ambushed, and shot at by your *dark gods*. Some kind of dart. Shot me
in the back. When I woke up, I was bound hand and foot and being
carried on a travois—"

What little light coming through the doorway was suddenly
eclipsed: one of the giants stood there, though how much it had
heard was unclear. Its eyes glowed a reddish hue. It had to stoop to
step forward into the room and had to remain stooped once inside.

"You will be so kind as to accompany me," the dark god whispered
to Tran so, its voice deep. When it spoke, lights played about the
lower half of its smooth face, where a mouth would be in a man. The
words almost shimmered in the air, tingling caresses on Tran so's
skin. The god knelt before him, removing the shackles from Tran
so's legs. Tran so looked down upon its broad back. He smelled a
charge in the air, the smell of ions burning, a familiar smell from
home. This was the individual that had been kind to him initially.
He was certain.

"Where are you taking him?" Ensign Conway demanded from
his bench across the room. "You have to give us water! There are
conventions to keeping prisoners!"

The god lifted Tran so easily in its arms. As they left the room, the Ensign shouted after them, "You shot me in the back, you coward. You shot me in the fuckin back!"

In the hall outside, the dark god was able to straighten. Closed doors, either side; light fixtures in the ceiling; dingy, off-white walls. Mundane details made Tran so feel better about the condition of his beleaguered eyes.

The god began to walk.

"You will be fed momentarily," it said. "Given water, asked a few simple questions. We are sorry for the confinement, if you prove to be innocent of further charges."

"More charges? What charges?"

"We cannot afford the luxury of asking questions prior to taking you people into custody. If you are registered to be here, well, our apologies. We, after all, are here to serve and protect. But as I said, we do not have the luxury of presuming innocence. At least, not until we get the situation under control."

"What situation is that?"

"The situation. The situation at hand."

"I too would like to ask questions."

They moved swiftly now, huge strides taking them past multitudes of doors set in the walls on either side. "You may ask." If the dark god was surprised at Tran so's insolence, it gave no indication.

"Why is my wife dying?"

They turned a corner. This new hall was also brightly lit, and relatively clean, though somewhat wider than the first had been. Some of the doors here had windows in them. Most did not. Tran so could see no detail within any room as they all fell rapidly behind.

"You are mortal," the god said simply, after apparently considering the question. "You are born to die."

"I can't believe that. You live longer, but you expire also."

The noise the god made might have been a chuckle. "You did not ask why I am dying," it said. "Or why we are *all* dying. You asked only about your wife. Then you became defensive. As for me dying, well, technically, I am not. Though it's true I shall one day cease to exist, as far as you are concerned. Yes, parts of me are wearing out, as we speak. Becoming obsolete. Entropy is always nearby. But I am a new construct. This day is only my third. If I am not maimed, or caused by other means to cease functioning, I will continue to do what I am designed to do for many, many of your lifetimes. Hundreds of them."

"What *are* you designed to do?"

"This."

"You still haven't answered my first question."

Shrugging again, the dark god replied: "Your wife, little man, is dying because death and a brief lifespan are symptomatic of your species. You are smart, you people, and creative. You can change any world, anywhere, in any way you wish. We all owe our lives, if you will—our existence—to you and your race. Yet I understand you get ill, you get hurt, you get old. You die. Nothing can stop that. No science, no discovery or invention. Your lives flicker past, images hardly seen long enough for me to grasp. I will not be able to keep track of you. I am sorry for that, and I try to prepare myself for it. I will not remember you soon."

The hall opened into a massive, vaulted area. The ceiling, which had been just above the dark god's head, rose dramatically. Directly ahead stood several gods, all in their blue suits, all armed, talking amongst themselves. Two turned to watch Tran so being carried closer; one motioned with its weapon toward an open door to their left. Behind this group of giants curved a wall, extending out of sight, in both directions, and within this wall was a series of archways. Above each archway, a sign. The lettering of the signs was too small to read from this distance. Arcs of lights blinked dully.

Tran so Phengh was carried into the room that the dark god had been instructed to enter. Here were several seats and broad desks, and on each desk sat a small, black device slightly larger than Tran so's fist. Some of these devices were silent, others emitted a low hum. In the corner of the room, something unseen, perhaps a lesser god, clattered and scampered about like a frightened rodent.

The god placed Tran so Phengh down on his feet. "Would you be so kind as to sit in one of these chairs? We're going to administer to you the first of a series of tests."

Tran so did as he was told. The seat was hard and uncomfortable. He realized, at this point, absurdly, that he wanted to sleep. Surely it was approaching nightfall. Did they ever turn the lights out here? He wondered if Minnie sue had gotten out of bed today, or if she had eaten anything.

The device before him had burnished corners and tiny holes for jacks. One face had an outline of a hand etched on it, fingers splayed. Thin cables ran out of this side. Squinting, Tran so saw tiny words engraved above the image, and formulas, and arcane symbols. His vision, though improving, was not yet acute enough to distinguish meaning from these.

The dark god walked back to the door, shut it, and returned to Tran so's side. "My brethren are getting agitated," it explained. "Not all of us have patience. I have selected you as one of my charges. I *believe* in you. You might consider yourself fortunate. Others have been hurt. Still more incarcerated, without any hope of trial. Place your hand on the sensor, please."

"Here?"

"Yes."

Tran so Phengh's skin tingled when he touched the device; the dark god took hold of two loose cable ends and fumbled with them inside the collar of its shirt. Regarding Tran so for a moment, it reached out a huge hand to press one thumb against Tran so's left eye. Tran so did not turn away, though for a second he thought that the god might plunge its digit deep into his brain, as if into a ripe fruit.

"You have a guest, sir, in your head. A filarial worm. It resides under the conjunctiva, in the anterior chamber of your eye. Do you wish me to remove it?"

"If you could. I would be grateful."

Immediately the dark god said, "The worm will no longer be bothering you. Your retinas are clear. Please remain looking at me as I ask you the questions." Adjusting the cables inside its shirt, it began: "Name?"

As Tran so was about to respond, an idea occurred to him: the curved wall he had seen on the way here—the one with the archways—was the exterior of *the tube*. Access to up and down. *To other levels.* Access to what he was looking for. He knew this suddenly, with certainty, though how he might use this knowledge was not so certain—

His hand was heating up. He said, "My name is Tran so Phengh."

"Age?"

"Twenty-two."

Inside *the tube* lived the god of all gods. So they said. What Ensign Conway had called *the network*. This network, god of all gods, could answer his questions about Minnie sue, about his poor boy.

"Status?"

"Married."

"No. I mean status. Staff or guest."

"I don't understand."

"How did you arrive here?"

"You brought me."

The pursuit to uncover truths about life had not been thwarted by this capture and interrogation, as he had first thought: all that took place to arrive at this juncture in life had been part of the process, an integral step on his path to truth.

"Let me rephrase the question. How did you get into this establishment? Did you pay, as a guest? Or were you hired to work here? Or, perhaps, did you come in illegally?"

"I don't understand. I was born here. In Hoffmann City. My mother was a fellatrix and my father was a fisherman. I was raised here."

The dark god said nothing for a long time. Lights from the room and from within its odd, smooth head played across its face. It did not move. Tran so discerned hints of textures inside the god, depths he could not imagine.

"Detainees have been liberated from a holding cell," the god said quietly. "There's been a break out. Prior to their questioning. I'm afraid the situation we talked of is escalating. I must go."

"Am I free to leave?"

"No. Like the others we have interviewed, I cannot locate your retina pattern on my database. You lied to me. Every answer you gave me was a lie."

"What?" Tran so Phengh had been working the cables of the device around his fist while they talked. Now, as he yanked on them, they tore free from the god's chest with a loud popping sound and fluid erupted, spattering Tran so's face as he was already getting up from the chair. Bellowing, the god clutched at itself. A stain spread down the front of its shirt. It reached out to grab Tran so but Tran so backed up, pulling furniture down as he went.

"Escapee, escapee!" The god spoke into its collar, shedding chairs and desks like water as it rose to its full height. "Brothers, assistance required. Assistance required!"

Tran so was already at the door. He pulled it open, feet sliding on the tiles. To his relief, the dark gods he had seen out in the hall earlier were gone. He looked at the curved wall of the tube and then away, along the bank of closed doors next to him.

From the room behind him came the sounds of furniture being splintered. Had the dark god tripped, buying him a few seconds? He bolted, and the god, roaring in frustration, quickly pursued.

3. LOVERS

Red lips, parting slowly, revealed white. Breath, expressed into his face, sweet and intoxicating, like the aroma of rotting moss. The girl leaned in close to whisper, "Would you like to see a trick? A *special* trick?"

Young Phister, who had seen more than his fair share of tricks lately, nonetheless muttered, "Sure," and showed his own nervous, toothless grin. "But, but you'll still give us breakfast, right?"

Not only hunger drove Young Phister to the verge of desperation: his ever-simmering consternation had been aggravated to a boil by recent events, not the least of which was the sudden appearance—after turning the initial corner—of this mysterious girl and her ragtag associates. Sure as shit, they had stopped the car. Followed by brief introductions, the extension of hospitality, an offer of breakfast.

That's when love uncoiled in Phister. She was gorgeous, after all, and Phister's heart, like the hearts of most young men, was an eager muscle, collapsing into great depths of despair but soaring just as fast at the first hint of beauty.

Memories of Crystal Max, popping up against his will, were immature, spotty, pale by comparison. Besides, he was coming to understand, in a sort of slow-blooming epiphany, that finding Crystal Max was an issue very separate from visceral, face-to-face interaction like this: locating his old friend was an act of *civic duty*. Granted, it was propelled by these memories . . . A lost romance, but not active love. All Crystal and he had really ever shared was a vague history of getting high and one awkward kiss. He saw that clearly now, in the green eyes of this stranger's alluring face.

What had brought him to this point of sophistication? Affection for a girl such as Crystal would no longer be easy, maybe not even possible; Young Phister was worldly, getting worldlier all the time. Here he was on his *third* level. And this exotic girl—with her dangerous gang in the background, her heady scent, her evident aura of threat—with her *hair*, for goodness sake, and her *teeth!*—was his *new type*. Perverse to admit it, titillating even, but the foreignness alone of her looks, anathema to all he had known over the course of his life, stirred his insides.

And they carried knives, these people. Knives, and other weapons. The girl had a long blade, dangling at her hip. He had spotted it right away, from a distance, before she had even spoken. No effort was made to conceal the weapons, then or now, as she held out a baton, withdrawn from one of the inside pockets of her colourful patchwork vest. The girl stepped back. Arms and shoulders and lower neck tattooed with wreaths of leaves, coiling up her biceps and across her back.

Most of the others in her group were similarly adorned, to varying degrees of intricacy and colour. No inked markings Phister had ever seen before on a person's skin had been as clear or as detailed as these.

The proffered item, in contrast with the gang's apparel, and in contrast to the girl's own presence, was nondescript: a brown rod, subtly notched and ridged, as long as Phister's index finger.

After a moment's hesitation, during which he glanced over to try to meet McCreedy's hooded, cloudy, and increasingly unreadable eyes, Phister let go of the dash to take the baton—

Which vanished with an audible pop before his fingers could touch it.

Someone tittered.

Too smitten, too perturbed by hormones and hunger and lack of sleep, too preoccupied with calculations of his chances to score with this girl to show the appropriate level of impression, worldly Young Phister continued to grin affably and was about to attempt a comment when the air all around him began to shimmer. His skin crawled with green sparks. As his vision darkened—suddenly terrified—he did manage to say something—more of a yelp than the witty aside he was hoping for—and promptly fell forward in the passenger seat to strike his head soundly on the rollbar. His tongue seemed to swell to four times its normal size. Lolling, it filled his mouth. Spit drooled down to the grimy car floor. He could do nothing but watch it drip.

From the driver's seat, McCreedy hissed impatiently at this latest in a long chain of inconveniences. "Now fuckin what? You killed him, you crazy bitch?"

Young Phister, as he slumped, dying, understood his final betrayal. This turn of events had been the expected result all along: he was the butt of a joke, victim of a prank. Here lays a sucker, he thought, killed while his fool heart had begun another of its short and futile flights.

Vision continued to fade until a small point of focus: hyper-detailed snarls of damp blue lint by the worn toe of his right boot. There were instants of agony, each one greater than the last, erupting from every pore of Phister's skin. He managed to claw through and lift one clenched hand to his own throat, rigid fingers shaking, before pain and everything else around him suddenly vanished—

He stood, entirely placid, in an equally serene and well-lit room.

No longer in the car.

No longer with the girl.

Her group of tough friends had vanished.

As had that vine-wreathed place he and McCreedy had found upon emerging, cautiously, from the lift pod. Thick foliage had crawled over the floors and the walls and the ceilings. When they'd driven, the car crunched it undertire.

But there were no leaves in this place.

He took a deep, cool breath.

Unnaturally clean, here. Music played from an unseen source: a light, tinkling tune on an instrument he could not identify nor, perhaps, had even heard before, yet these sounds were deeply soothing, as if they supplied some long-lost, fundamental element missing from his chemistry.

Tiny braziers, burning on the polished floor around the perimeter of the room, gave off equally unfamiliar scents. There was no furniture to speak of. He felt good. Well-fed and content. These feelings were as foreign as the sounds and smells.

Before him stood a *second* woman. Had she materialized while he was looking about, appearing as he turned his attentions toward her? Or was she there when he first came to this strange room? Odd that he wasn't sure.

Older than the beautiful girl, this woman was dressed in a pale green suit. She also had lots of hair—red hair, if he had to give it a colour—piled up on her head. Plenty of teeth, too, when she smiled. Which she was doing, her face sort of frozen that way.

He was sure getting used to the sight of these wet white bones inside peoples' mouths, and stringy hair sprouting from their heads. Memories of his own dismal chompers were faint. Teeth fell out of gums as soon as they broke through, clattering to the floor, first when he was three or four and again, blackened, rotten, when he was ten. Memories of hair were non-existent. Once he must have possessed it; infants grew hair and lost hair, within their first year. So he was bald now, save for a few resilient strands, and all he had left of his teeth was one stinky peg, which he often licked, recoiling at the horrid taste as if it were the face of an unpleasant friend. Licking the peg now, not only lost in the hallways of his world, but apparently getting lost in the recesses of his memory and in the gaps between moments of time, while ghosts of vanished teeth haunted his dark gums, he wondered if he would ever see Crystal's mouth again, or her liver-spotted scalp. He felt, in many ways, that he had betrayed her.

Glancing up at the rust-colored tresses of this new woman— who just stood there—Young Phister wondered what his recent preference for hair and teeth meant. What did the fetish make him? And were these superficialities the real reason he thought he could not go back to loving a girl such as Crystal Max? Was he as shallow as that? As fickle?

Now, visions of his ex with a bizarre, full set of cuspids in her cakehole and long stringy hair poking up out of the top of her head struck him, and arousal stirred. He chastised himself for thinking about Crystal again.

If he were not, he told himself, at this particular point in time, a humiliated corpse, cooling in the passenger seat of an ancient car, then, after emerging from this dream, he would commit, move on with his life.

And just because a girl had made a fool of him, hurt him, or quite possibly killed him, didn't mean she *disliked* him, did it?

Meanwhile, where was he? And who was this woman?

Did he have a chance to score with *her*?

He looked her up and down again. Stared into her immobile face. She didn't blink or move in any way. Pleasant creases radiated from the corners of her eyes. Eyes almost the same colour as her suit. More creases on her cheeks. A warm, full body. Older, yes, but radiating comfort, intelligence, and compassion. Phister, who had never known the identity of his mother (having been raised in the nursery with other children of the same age), hoped that this stranger—staring at him, stuck, as was he, in time, with her head cocked and that smile permanently on her face—might look at least *somewhat* like the unknown woman from whose womb he had spilled squalling forth.

But then the spell broke; the woman moved; his wandering thoughts crashed to a stop.

She said, "Are you ready? There are angry people out there. Not everyone's thrilled, that's for sure. Vanity to build decadent playgrounds while half the world is at war. That sort of thing. An elitist's venture." She reached out to adjust his collar. "Sour grapes, if you ask me, babe. And how could you let everyone in? Have you heard that recent complaint? There was an editorial in today's Reform Gazette that said you should turn the whole project over to the government so they can use it as a refugee camp! I called them and explained as politely as I could that it's not a charity project. They called it a theme park! A theme park! Can you believe it? You've almost single-handedly employed a large city's worth of people." She touched his face now. "I think I'm more nervous than you. Seriously, are there other ways we can help? Are you *sure* you're prepared to do this?"

"Don't worry," he said, surprising himself. His voice sounded funny.

The woman's eyes searched his own. He marvelled at their shine, their warmth. Suddenly she said, "I want to be with you, when we wake up."

"We'll be together."

"But I'm going in like this, in my body, and you're getting . . . *reduced*."

"I'm sick. I'm breaking down. You know I am. Just think of it as moulting. I'll get a new skin. We'll be together again."

"But I love this face, this body. I love *you*."

He held her, and more words not his own burbled up his throat. He was about to formulate a profound response but all he managed to say was, "Oh Tianna," before gritty familiarities rushed back: the moist smell in the air; the warm, ambient hum; the car. An old man, scowling next to him. Vines, pain, and hunger. Malaise and all his confusions rushed back to fill their resident spots like water into a gutter. He tried to close his mouth but could not.

There was that gang, encircling him, and the girl, once again showing a thin ridge of teeth from under her upper lip. Azure eyes sparkled yet she looked a little unsure. Taken aback?

She was breathing fast.

Phister knew that little time—if any—had passed. He also knew, with a twinge of shame, that he had already forgiven the girl for the pain she'd caused him, that he would fall for her, over and over again, if only for doses of her undivided attention.

Experimentally, he shook his head. The agony was not quite as

much as he had feared. "Who the . . . What *was* that?" There was
a tingling in his limbs and he was sure he felt myriad movements
inside his veins, as if a miniature army were invading him, marching
to certain victory.

"You tell me," the girl whispered, eyes glittering. "Tell me
everything that happened."

"Where was I? And who was that . . . lady?"

"Lady? You went *somewhere*? What did you see?" The girl's fingers
touched the flank of the car. Phister's eyes followed them. She sure
had beautiful hands. He imagined those fingers resting on him.

"Your, uh, reaction," she said, "was pretty *intense*. I mean, it's
supposed to . . . You, freaking out like that . . . The trick . . .?"

Over her shoulder, the others looked on, expressions also
wide-eyed and somewhat shocked, incongruous on their previously
tough faces.

"I did make *the hunter* vanish," the girl continued, with a gesture,
searching for words. "That thing, it's a device, older than your car.
But when most people see it, have it pointed at them, they have only
a quick flash, nothing they can put their finger on." A narrowing
to those eyes, hardening the look she'd levelled at him. Behind her,
glances were exchanged between a stocky boy and a slender girl in
a white dress. "You're different . . ." Her voice was cold. "So tell me
now what you saw."

To Phister's surprise, bubbles of anger rose in him, making him
feel stronger. "What you did to me *hurt*. I didn't like that."

The girl leaned in even closer, hissing with that sweet-smelling
breath. "Tell me what you fucking saw."

Expecting McCreedy to kick his shin under the dash, warning
him to be cautious, Phister tried to remain brave. He replied carefully,
"Not much. It was all pretty vague." The old man did not budge.
"Some lady. Her and me, in a quiet room." And truthfully, as from a
dream, details from the odd intrusion into his reality were fading;
he could no longer recall the expression on the green woman's face
or what it had truly been like to feel confident and healthy in that

other pristine time and place. He could not remember contentment. He did not need to lie about that.

Now McCreedy said, "Okay. Great gag. What about the fucking food you promised us?"

The girl wheeled on the driver, a blur of speed, one of those long fingers, heavy with rings, nearly touching McCreedy's face. The fingernail was like a blade. Bracelets jangled loudly. "I heard you call me a bitch, you piece of shit. Lucky I don't have you killed right here and now." She took a breath, tried to smile again, but her aplomb had vanished.

McCreedy was not intimidated. He folded his arms over his chest and glared. "I need food. You told us you could get us some food. That's why we're here with you. Not for conversation or fucking parlour tricks. Me and the boy are *starving*."

After a moment, the girl withdrew her hand. She let it rest on Phister's shoulder, just as he had imagined.

"Well, *this* particular *bitch* has a name. It's Cynthia. And I thank you to call me that from now on, since I'm about to be hospitable to you two. Since I am going to feed you. Since I'm letting you live."

Old man McCreedy was the first to look away, muttering under his foul breath. He did not glance up again until one of the boys from Cynthia's gang suddenly climbed onto the car. Then McCreedy threw the car into gear and the car resumed its bumping crunch over the vines and leaves that covered the floor here, moving forward at a slow pace; nevertheless, the boy onboard had to grab the seat back for balance. His face leered over Phister's shoulder at his friends, who, surrounding the car, had started walking along with it.

On the move, the gang was one entity: bright, lithe, well-defined. Their gait was fluid, their grace animal. Muscles, hard and harsh. Adorned with charms—dangling, draped, or pierced through their skin—a quiet tune of jangling rose and ebbed about the vehicle as it trundled on, woven into the louder calls and murmured talk. Phister recalled another quiet tune. Mostly he watched Cynthia. He felt like he was levitating. By all rights, he knew he should remain cautious about what had happened, try to figure out what she wanted with him, yet his mind simply raced in circles looking for something to say that would not sound asinine to her ears.

The boy behind Phister started to rock, causing the car to rock, and now he called to his friends a guttural phrase that Phister did not understand; the friends laughed until McCreedy barked, "Fucking stop that!"

The boy stopped.

Yet soon another, and another of the troupe clambered onto the car, causing the suspension to sag under their combined weight. McCreedy grumbled. A girl who had been kneeling on the trunk jumped off and landed, both hands clapping down on the shoulders of a dark-skinned boy with long braided hair, while the others remained perched, grinning, and Phister began to wonder if, somehow, more spells were being cast upon him or if the original spell the rod had put him under lingered. In the moments since visiting that strange place and occupying that cool, clean mind, a power not his own seemed to be building in his limbs. He felt it lurking, growing, like a buzz. And images from another life flickered in and out of the periphery.

He shook his head to clear it. Maybe he had gone too long without food or water.

His fingers tingled.

Running suddenly in front on the car, a lean boy with a milky cast to his eyes and a bandage over his left calf leapt up and pulled tangled vines down from the ceiling tiles. The lights up there were mostly covered by the thick growth; lighting itself in the hall was green and diffuse. When Phister and McCreedy had rolled out of the pod and saw that they had *not* arrived at the basement, as they had been hoping, but instead on some overgrown *new* level—just before they'd seen Cynthia and her gang—Young Phister had plucked and tried to eat one of the vine's bitter leaves. He had quickly spit it out.

Walking next to Phister, so he could see her profile and the alluring motion of her limbs, Cynthia talked in low tones with another girl, one Phister had not yet met. Short, plump, with heavy arms. Her cheeks shook with each step. He was unable to hear what the two were saying yet he was sure the conversation concerned him and his reaction to the strange rod. Clearly, as he'd first thought, Cynthia had been taken aback by the episode. The hunter, as she called the device, had done something to him she had never seen it do before. Which made him think either she'd just acquired it, or had been misinformed, or misunderstood its function.

But Phister was having a hard time focusing on the implications of this. McCreedy wasn't much help. Watching the shape of Cynthia's breasts moving under her vest, Phister found his mind wandering. Did people up here, on these levels, have hair elsewhere on their body, aside from their head? Did they have hidden sets of teeth?

He closed his eyes. Leaning forward over his shoulder, one of the two boys who remained on the car—a boy about the same age as himself, with stiff, wiry hair growing on his chin and reeking of stale sweat—said, "I know who you guys remind me of. I just thought of it. From that play we saw. You know, those guys, after they get sick. Remember, Bert?"

"Sure," said Bert, the other passenger.

"They look exactly like them."

Phister opened his eyes a crack as McCreedy spat up a hard chunk of some dark matter which had risen up from his lungs; it rolled off his lips, bounced from the car frame, and rustled in the leaves covering the floor.

"What did *happen* to you guys?" Bert asked. "I mean, your skin, your *scalps*?"

McCreedy seemed to be about to respond but was suddenly racked by a spasm of violent coughing. He could not stop for a long while, bending forward in the seat, retching and spluttering. The car, without the weight of his foot on the pedal, slowed down. Phister did not know what to do. One hand hovered over McCreedy's back.

When the fit subsided, McCreedy sat up once more. But as he wiped at his mouth with the fingers of his glove—releasing the steering wheel for a second—the glove became stained, strung with blood-flecked phlegm.

"*Shit*. You okay, pops?" Nudging at Phister. "What's up with your friend? Is he all right? You're sure he's not contagious?"

"Radiating sickness," Bert said. "That's what they called it. In the play."

"Radiation," corrected his friend.

Looking at McCreedy, Young Phister was forced to acknowledge that the old man seemed, at this juncture, nothing but tiny and frail. Not at all like the tough fucker Phister had left with on this expedition a mere few days ago. Truthfully, he could not imagine McCreedy even walking again, let alone fighting or showing any signs of being the crusty old bastard Phister knew from back home. Recalling Philip's wails as McCreedy pounded on him brought a wistful smile to Phister's lips. How fast a person could deteriorate, he thought. How fast a person could change. And, for the first time, he wondered if there really was something terrible happening to the driver, something aside from withdrawal.

Maybe something was happening to both of them.

"Is he already dead?" Bert asked. "I mean, is he dead?"

"Dead? I'm not dead. I'm sitting right here." Yet McCreedy's voice was thin and reedy, as if he were talking from another plane. He looked up from the mess on his glove to take the wheel again. The car gently swerved. "I'm as alive as anyone. So ask questions to my face, you little prick."

"You ain't as alive as me, pops, I can tell you that much. And I've seen dead people in my day—they pass through here sometimes, looking for whatever it is dead people look for. They seem healthy compared to you!"

"Leave him alone," Phister said. He wished McCreedy could show Bert and his companion some of that lost energy, maybe grab the pair in headlocks or elbow them both hard in the chops. Knock their heads together. "Just leave him alone. Can't you see he's coughing up his lungs?"

"What kind of drugs is he on?" Bert asked.

"Huh? What do you mean?"

"I wasn't born yesterday." The boy put his hand on Phister's shoulder. "I'm talking about dope. Him all fucked up like that. What kind of drug is it?"

"It's, uh, it's called moss."

"Never heard of it. What does it do?"

"It gets you high."

"Fucking smart ass." The fingers tightened painfully. "Got any of this moss stuff on you?"

"No, we don't," McCreedy said. There was a loose rattling sound in his throat. "If we had any, I'd take it myself and feel less shitty. Now let go of him."

Laughing, Bert released Phister. He wrung the hair on his chin with one fist, which rustled like the vines. "Anyhow," he said, "the play. The play. If ever you get a chance to see this travelling roadshow, this play, run for your life. It's shit and heavy-handed and it's a load of propaganda. That's what Cynthia says. Plus, the guy that puts it on is this creepy old bastard." Bert and his friend grinned at each other. "So we stole some stuff from him."

"Cynthia came back from hunting. Remember? When she saw him all set up?"

Both boys chuckled at the memory. "Fuck, yeah. I *never* seen her change so fast. Thought she was gonna tear that fucker a new asshole. He didn't finish the show before he had to run off. But anyhow, you guys are dead ringers for the two dudes in the play."

They were in the throes of guffaws.

Phister, however, had been stunned by the disclosure. The boys had been talking about Philip. The coincidence was more than alarming. He wanted to ask a million questions but dared not to ask one. He was suddenly convinced that not only had Philip survived the encounter in the warehouse, but that he was nearby, following, watching.

The car was directed down several halls of varying width and function, none really like the ones back home—pipeless, overgrown, green and rank—until they approached a camp of sorts, where cots had been set up. Here were more people, going about their business, some sleeping, some reclining on the floor. Pausing, a few watched the car and the gang draw closer.

More sounds of music reached Phister, again recalling the sweet sounds he had heard in another world. A voice began to sing. His heart ached. He looked at Cynthia: she was grinning at the people ahead and paid him no heed.

A woman, holding a child to her breast, smiled, and gave a tiny wave.

In the air lingered the smell of food. Canteen food. Phister's stomach, registering it, twisted; he realized he yearned for sustenance, of course, but also for a place like this, for people to come home to, for friends.

Close enough to call out, Cynthia said, "Hey, look what we found, driving out of a pod at shaft sixteen. Check this car out! Check these *dudes* out!"

"And we think the little guy," Bert shouted, "might be the one!"

The look in those flashing green eyes demanded silence.

But the other boy said, "They don't even know where the fuck they're from or where they are! They ain't got *no teeth*!"

Phister tried to keep his lips together. He had never thought that having no teeth would make him feel out of place.

The car stopped. McCreedy said to the passengers, "Get off the car. Get off the fucking car now," and, turning to Phister, added, "I'm not feelin so good, boy. I need water. I need water."

"Okay. You wanna lie down?" Phister was embarrassed by the driver's show of vulnerability. He did not know what to do with his hands.

"I won't be getting out of my seat." McCreedy drew a deep, shuddering breath as the two boys clambered down. "You have to bring my stuff up here. All these ugly people, with their hair and fucking tattoos and colours. They're making me ill. My guts is on fire. My brain is on fire."

"Sure, sure ..." Phister also climbed off the car, not feeling too good himself, trying to dispel jitters with concrete action. For a moment he stood on wobbly legs, among these strangers—all of whom had a purpose, moving in that graceful way they had, smiling, touching—as if he had ceased to exist altogether. He had become smoke.

How he missed his home. Pangs so strong inside they were like shooting pain. He needed to return to the life he knew. McCreedy did too. They were both decomposing out here. He could convince himself no longer: he was not worldly at all; he was naïve and out of his league. And lonely. Intelligent, beautiful, dangerous people like Cynthia were *not* his type. She wasn't even the same *animal* as he was. He was a fool to have thought anything else.

Resigned, he decided to go in search of food, and water.

The canteen was located in an overgrown room to the left of where the cots were set up. In appearance, it was almost identical to the ones he had known and eaten at. He entered and took a slow inventory, letting his hunger, which would soon be assuaged, indulge in its cramps and growls. He filled his lungs with the scents. These new areas of the world shared aspects both familiar to him and yet transformed—like the outlet, on the wrong side of the hall, and this canteen. Subtle ways almost more unsettling than if they were totally unfamiliar; the alterations between these and similar ones back home confirmed again that he was irrevocably lost.

(A momentary flash, from someone else's perspective, a quick vista so foreign he had no idea what it could be but that left him reeling. Another man's voice, in his ears, and then he was just standing there, Young Phister, in the leafy canteen, dizzy. He had the feeling that whoever the person had been, they'd known the layout of this place. Details of the arrangements, as if he had seen them through the walls, seemed to be fading from his mind in receding throbs. Was it schematics? Pipes? An infrastructure of sorts? Even those words were not his own.)

Approaching one of the water spigots, he took a cup from the dispenser and drank a bellyful. The water was clear and tasted like none he'd ever had before. It sat in him like cold stone. He tried to smile at the faces around him—there was a group of older men, eating at a table—but no one acknowledged him. He took a second full cup of water back into the hall.

"Hey, wake up." Handing the cup to McCreedy, who had dozed off. He wanted to talk but it would be futile. Too little too late. So he watched McCreedy drink. Water trickled down the old man's chin, poised there to drip.

Then he noticed two young boys, perhaps twelve or so, crouching quietly, partially hidden by the front bumper of the car. Were they tampering? Had they been spying on McCreedy? Phister looked directly at them. One said, "We got a plug for this thing, over there. It's on a stand that rolls around. You want us to charge it?"

"Uh, sure . . ."

And, standing several metres away, with two other people—the stout girl and a tall, bone-skinny, shirtless man—stood Cynthia. Staring at him. When their eyes met, she made her way over. Watching her approach—her figure, her skin—Phister got nervous. He wiped his hands on his grubby pants.

Meanwhile, McCreedy had finished the water, and he dropped the cup onto the floor of the car. He belched. By the time Cynthia had made it to Phister's side, the old man was fast asleep again. Cynthia lightly grabbed Phister's upper arm. "Did you get any food yet?"

"Uh, no."

"Later, then. I want you to come with me. I've been thinking. We have to talk." Her grip tightened. Phister watched the two youths trying to wheel the plug stand up to the car, forcing the device through the rustling vines and cursing its slow progress. The charger they were going to use was a spindly thing, like a short, thin man made out of sticks. Its face was a contact plate, complete with copper script. Phister had never seen anything like it.

"Okay," he stammered, "but, uh, but lemme help these guys first. Hang on." Stalling, he pulled free from the grip, stepped onto the running board, and grabbed at the plughead. As he unwound the cable with practiced movements of one arm, he hoped that Cynthia, who had still not spoken but was watching him intently, would move off.

In his sleep, McCreedy snorted.

Phister handed the plughead to the nearest kid—who not only had different-coloured eyes, one red and one blue, but, he saw now, was *not* a kid at all. In fact, both of the boys charging the car were short adults. Could he trust nothing here? Legs and arms fully developed, necks bulky and strong, faces more haggard and serious than any child's should ever be. Had they changed shapes? Surely they hadn't looked like this at first. Phister struggled to remember—

Cynthia said bluntly, "Now let's go."

Without a choice left to him, Phister stepped down. Cynthia took him by the arm again and they walked. After a moment, far enough away from the car to be out of hearing range, she said quietly, "Listen. I've been looking for . . . well, *something*, for a long time. For someone. The hunter was going to help me. I've been doing what I did to you, when we met, to every guy we come across. I'm not sure what our next move is but I need to keep an eye on you. You're going to have to stay here. With me. Very close."

"Why? I can't stay here. I've gotta go home. But I feel . . . It feels . . . I feel like I'm not who I was."

"And who were you?"

"Young Phister, that's all. No one."

"Well, listen, Young Phister. No one. I'll be honest with you. That hunter has been around since the time of the engineer. It belonged to a close acquaintance of his. Do you know who the engineer was?"

"Not really." But he recalled Philip mentioning the engineer. A focal point of some reverence, apparently, out here. Against his better judgment, and so he would not appear a total idiot, Phister added, "Actually, I do know a little about him, I guess," and realized, flushing, that he had not achieved his purpose: he knew nothing about the man, and that would become clear if Cynthia asked any questions at all.

Which, of course, she promptly did.

"So you know he built the world single-handedly? That he's going to return one day and set things straight? That his children and friends are alive, sleeping, all waiting to be born?"

"Uh, yeah," Phister said, unsure whether Cynthia liked or disliked this 'engineer' fellow. Was she laughing? Or incensed?

They continued walking.

"Well all that shit is myth, Phister. The engineer was just a man. An egotistical man with a huge team of people working for him. He dug a deep fucking hole in the crust of a planet that's been dead for centuries. And it's going to stay that way, if I can help it. Now I want you to try this again." She drew the brown rod from her inside pocket. The hunter. "I want to see if you have further reactions."

Phister's guts churned and sweat broke out on his back and shoulders. "No freaking way," he said.

"Look. I'll let you in on another little secret. I knew you were coming. So I got a little pro-active, made sure I found you. And now that I've got you, I'm not going to let you fuck anything up." Her fingers, on his arm, were hard and strong. "See, I don't want things to get better here. I like this place just the way it is. I like things falling apart. Maybe that's why I like you, Phister, just the way you are now. Ugly and sick. So I'm going to stop you before you change. I'm going to stop you before you change *the world*. So just be a good boy. I have a proposal. We can make a deal."

The leaves around them moved in a sudden warm breeze. Cynthia yanked Phister to a stop and spun him to face her. She was a good deal taller than him and stood close enough for him to feel her heat.

"Have you had a lot of lovers, Phister?"

Shocked, he had no idea what to say. His mouth was open so he closed it.

"Lovers," she repeated. "You know what those are? Are you a virgin?"

He stammered nothing coherent.

"Like I said, I have a proposal. You never used to like unions but this particular one might be right up your alley."

Smiling grimly, Cynthia moved closer still, just millimetres away. Her eyes were as green as the vines that rustled around them and her scent filled his sinuses. Lightly her fingers touched his chest, drifted down along his shirt. That sweet breath enveloped him. He started to stiffen. Her approaching lips parted, and he saw her glistening teeth, her tongue like a black sharpened thing, coiled, as if to strike—

Someone was running, breaking the spell; Cynthia pulled back, snarling.

Two people came down the hall: the pair of short men who had been recharging the car. Pacing in unison, even their stumbles were identical as they lost footing in breathless haste to stop. They were frantic.

"Cynthia, you'd better come back!"

"What is it?"

"Come back, shit, *come!*"

"Tell me what it is."

"You *gotta come!*"

"What happened?! Tell me. Tell me what fucking happened!"

They looked at each other, neither eager to begin. The one on the left said, "We plugged his car in," indicating Phister, "and it started *talking.* Ranting and raving. About being stolen. About being on the wrong level."

"It said there would be budget adjustments. A shifting of assets."

"And then it shut the canteen down."

"What the fuck do you mean?" Cynthia said.

"The car threatened us, told us that the network was sending authorities."

"The *network?*"

"Then the canteen started asking for authorization. At the same time. Out of the blue. Depleting reserves, it said. 'No more food will be processed until the situation is under control.'"

Cynthia narrowed her green eyes. She returned her gaze to Phister. He was terrified by what he saw there. Her pupils had become slits. And those teeth, far from attractive now, were exposed like weapons. Even her hair was suddenly grotesque.

He took a step back. "It's only a crazy old car," he said. "I, uh, I don't know what happened to your canteen."

"Cynthia, that's not all."

"There's more."

"*More?*" She turned back on the pair. "What else more could there possibly be?"

"Well, his friend, the driver—"

"McCreedy?" Phister asked, suddenly forgetting his own problems. "What about McCreedy?"

Words came out of two mouths, mingled as if from one. "He's *dead.*" They fell upon Phister like stones. "He's fucking dead!"

DEIDRE, L1A (SUPERSTRUCTURE)

Vertigo, rushing disorientation, hot tears, and nausea. She was *unbelievably* high. *Above* the scaffolding. Adjacent to one of the suns: the massive fixtures that illuminated and heated the world, beginning their morning burn, were *right there*, so close Deidre felt the growing heat of their radiant proximity crackling at her skin, so close they blinded her.

She would never open her eyes again. Never. For now day was burgeoning, she had also seen, instead of endless black, glimmers of distant, unreal lights (the flicker of flame, pinpricks of lanterns, perhaps?), actual *land*: cities and townships and roads and miniature forests, openings of shafts scattered across it like piping mouths, all through morning's wispy cloud cover.

A good deal of it smouldering, or already charred.

This rarified air, sucking it in: the taste of smoke, even up here, at the roof of the world. Closing her eyes could not make *that* go away.

She heard the slow beating of wings, the shriek of alien voices, felt wind in her hair and on her skin from the force of those wings, from being carried, swiftly, across vast, open skies.

When the angels had first plucked her away from her mother and sisters—swooping down from smoky darkness to grab her where she stood by the wagon's side, watching with horror as the conflagration consumed the valley before them—she had tried to cry, to scream, to fight. And Lady, turning in a crouch, had hurled herself forward. Mother had screamed too, reaching with one hand for Deidre's foot as it receded up into the night.

There were three, possibly four of them. During the flight, they had transferred her in mid-air twice, from one set of talons to another.

Angels were strong and fast flyers. Thin legs wrapped tight around her waist, bony knees clamped snugly to her ribs. Talons, sharp as blades, easily gripped her, cutting into her soft skin if she struggled too much.

She stopped struggling long ago.

They spoke, but she could not understand their language; neither could they comprehend hers. Or, at least, they showed no signs of comprehension. So she had also ceased demanding to be returned to her family, ceased vacillating between screaming threats to her aerial kidnappers about the wrath of an Orchard Keeper and desperate, whispered promises of vast rewards for her safe and prompt return to Elegia.

Her clothes were torn, her skin raked, streaked with blood.

And now it was morning.

Shrieking louder and louder, sounding remarkably like girls, giggling hysterically, the angels soon became increasingly excited; the *feel* of their wings, and the rate of their collective beating, changed in ways Deidre could not define. Pressure made her ears pop. She never wanted to open her eyes again, had vowed to herself not to, *never*, but she did, one more time. She *had* to:

Boughs and boles, woven crudely, lashed together: a massive

cradle had been built into the crotch of the structural beams that lined the sky. These were not at all like the filaments she saw when she looked up from the ground; this close, the beams appeared bigger around than the girth of her waist.

The angels had built a nest.

Short walls had been constructed into the structure, dividing the aerie into a series of rough compartments. Strips of fabric, sparkling junk, and what looked to be constellations of dry white bones littered the open areas. The stench that assailed her, when a gust of wind picked up, was garbage and rancid guano.

Perhaps a dozen angels waited. Some grey, some white. Watching her, squinting, wings folded forward, the beasts appeared as hunched or broken things. One, stepping forward, as if to greet her, though she was still some distance away, was completely black except for white marks that looked like death heads at its quivering wingtips.

How many of these horrid beasts were there? Did more lurk, unseen, within the labyrinthine constructions?

Two looked over the side, gesticulating with rapid motions of their heads, pointing downward, to the distant land, using the miniscule fingers that grew from the junction of their membranous wings.

How had she ever associated these creatures with birds *or* men? Birds were sweet devices made by supervisors for myriad purposes. Men were complex, beautiful animals. *Perfection.* These things were grotesque, skeletal, lightly feathered all over, their legs long, thin, and dry. Huge wings. Nearly translucent skin on their faces, ugly features clustered close together: little, suspicious eyes; slitted nostrils; angry little mouths with pinsharp teeth through which the tips of blue tongues showed, panting, over black bottom lips.

Shrieking, giggling, the angels that bore her aloft were hovering now, flapping and debating, and, for an instant, Deidre recalled, absurdly, an image from halcyon times: sitting on the grass, cross-legged before Sam's softly humming console, an illustrated printout on her lap. She was pointing to an image of an extinct flying beast known as a Steller's Jay. "What about this thing? It says here it's a bird. A *real* bird. Sitting on its nest." Looking up at the supervisor's calmly winking façade. "It doesn't look anything like *your* bluebirds or your redbirds."

But memory blew into tatters on the wind as she was dropped.

The angels, she discovered, were not waiting to help her; Deidre came crashing down among them, landing painfully on her hands and knees and rolling immediately to her side, so her body felt the relative firmness of the dirty nest. The structure creaked and groaned. Twigs snapped under her weight.

She lay trembling, panting, petrified as dry winds whipped all about. It was too hot here, too bright. The air was different, painful in her lungs. Hard to fill them.

She glanced up. Directly above was the roof, tinted a pale blue, perhaps just a dozen or so metres over her head. She could see the distinct paneling that comprised it. Rivets held the sky together.

The scaffolding of the suns spanned out in all directions, receding, finally vanishing into the distance.

And angels touched down in gusts of feathers and risen dust.

Deidre tried to cling to the nest with her broken nails but was hauled to her feet, rudely pushed forward. Terrified of plunging—though the edge was metres away—she was directed toward the centre of the platform. Big wings buffeted her, clawed feet nudged, keeping her upright and moving.

Through her tears she shrieked, "You're hurting me!" Panic that had been held at bay for most of the night rose sharply in her throat. "Stop it, you're *hurting* me!" Out over the far side—she'd made the error of looking again: remote fields and farms, houses, forests, small as toys. She loosed a trickle of hot urine into her breeches and stared dumbly down at her own scratched thighs as another sun-bright angel—this one white, wings outspread, feet extended, talons out—came in to land.

She was finally allowed to collapse, huddling behind one of the stick and twig baffles. She curled in on herself for some time, and when she raised her head to see how close the angels were, to her immense shock she met the eyes of a girl, slightly older than herself, who was sitting cross-legged on a small woven mat. Attractive, black-haired, the girl returned Deidre's stare with an expression of apparent amusement. Her face, rounded and olive-skinned, was grimy, black eyes narrowed. Lips, tightening slightly, went thin and white and bloodless.

Neither spoke, yet Deidre, seeing this other person, crawled forward frantically, to the girl's side, nearly touching her hot body, thinking: another human, another human . . . Then, feeling infinitesimally more secure, she looked back through her tangled hair to see that the angels were clustered, and had not followed her here.

"What do they want with us?" Deidre breathed. "Why did they bring us here?" She sobbed. "*Why*?"

"Don't know why they brought *you* here."

The dark-eyed girl spoke calmly, looking over Deidre's shoulder, into the middle distance. She had an unusual accent and her skin smelled of spices. For an instant, Deidre recalled the gram's unusual accent (was that just yesterday?!), from back in her sanctum, but the inflections, the harshness of this girl's voice, made it very different from that one. Covered by little more than dirty rags, her body was toned, muscular, tanned. Deidre wondered if she might be a *barbarian*.

Now those dark eyes turned. The girl said, "I don't know if they brought you here to be my companion, my lover, or my dinner."

Deidre recoiled.

"A joke, sister. Relax." Still, no smile. "I'm not going to eat you, chickie. I don't think they—" gesturing towards the group of angels, who stood, still watching quietly, "—know what makes us tick. They don't know what they're getting into. Maybe they want us to reproduce." And, finally, the girl laughed, as if they were exchanging pleasantries up here. But her laugh was without mirth.

"Re . . .? But . . .?" Surely, to *joke* up here like this, to say these horrible things, this girl was crazy. "How long, how long have you been here?"

"Days." A noise of disgust. "You know, I don't think they wanna hurt us, if that's what you're worried about. They haven't hurt me yet." Turning away again.

Deidre whispered, "How do you know they won't?" Over the girl's shoulder, another dizzy view of miniatures: a threadlike road, houses no bigger than breadcrumbs. The sky, arcing down in a great slow curve to meet the horizon.

Thin clouds scudded beneath the nest.

"I know men," the girl said, under her breath.

As confounded by this as she was by everything about the stranger, Deidre peeked down again, through a gap in the nest, at a sliver of sun-yellowed land. She said, "My name is Deidre. What's yours?"

For a long time Deidre thought she would get no answer except the wind and the angel's muted chatter but at last the girl said, "Mingh straw. Though that's not my real name. It's my stage name."

She really was pretty, Deidre decided. And with the wind playing through her hair, and light on her plump face, it was as though Mingh straw believed they were sitting in a courtyard together, relaxing, a glass of powdered orangeade in one hand.

"Did *they* set fire to the world? Did the angels do that to us?"

"Us? To *us*? You live down there, on that level?"

Deidre thought: maybe the girl isn't crazy; maybe she's just simple. "Yes. Elegia is there. At least, it was. My father is an Orchard Keeper." Seeking some sign of softness, of compassion. "Look, my mother and my sisters . . ."

Pride made her fight the emotion coiling inside her. She angrily wiped at her eyes. Still the girl stared, unreadable, and Deidre felt another dimension of fear opening up inside her. Was she alone, despite this strange company? *Because* of this strange company? Was she all the more alone up here? "I don't think my family is dead," Deidre said, unprompted, wiping snot from her lip. "They're not dead."

"What's Elegia?"

"Our estate. Our family home."

"*Estate*?" Mingh straw snorted. "You live on an *estate*? I'm from Hoffmann City. Know where that is?"

"No."

"Seven levels down. Where the water's stored."

"Seven?" Deidre had never taken a lift below the plantations. Just one level. Below that was forbidden, dangerous.

"I'd never seen that place before, up under the suns. Never seen the suns. Not until these miserable things lifted me out of the shaft opening. I had never seen the suns." Mingh straw indicated the nearby celestial furnace, burning out to the left, shining daylight down over the land below. The air was certainly hot here, yet surprisingly they had not been burned to cinders. Heat was directed downward, not outward?

Deidre wanted to mention her interest in the sciences, and in the vanished people who had built the world, but she said nothing.

"Was it nice and cozy?" Mingh straw asked. "Living down there?"

Deidre whispered, "Yes, it was." The girl was mocking her and her life. But she would be strong. "How far beneath Hoffmann City does the world go?"

"A lot farther, sister. All the way to the bottom."

"And does this *war* ravage the land there too? Where you're from?"

"War? Is there a war?" The black-haired girl shrugged. "Hoffmann City's *always* burning. It's hot and dirty there and air is pumped in. Light comes from down windows in the ceiling, most of which are broken. There's anarchists, atheists, celibates." She drew a deep breath. "This is the cleanest air that's ever filled my lungs. You know, chickie, I think these flying men did me a favour, getting me out of the Hoff. Ruined my career, mind you, but prolonged my last few miserable days."

"Listen." Conversation with Mingh straw, Deidre decided, was like talking to a demented child, or to Lady. "Do you have any ideas about how we can we get down?" She touched the girl's upper arm, which felt about as hot as she'd imagined the nearby sun to be.

Shaking Deidre's hand off, Mingh straw asked, "How old are you, kid?"

"Fourteen." Deidre was exasperated with these digressions. "I'm *fourteen.*" She tried to stare the other girl down.

"What a coincidence. That's how old *I'm* supposed to look. Or was it twelve? Think we look the same age?"

"I do."

"Well, I'm thirty seven. Pretty good, no? I've taken the *cure*, child. And I've had a little surgery. You know, you could make a lot of money in Hoffmann City, with your blond hair and your crying routine and your torn clothes."

Deidre said, "All I want to know is if you have any ideas about how to get down."

"At first, I thought they were air gods. At first." Mingh straw spoke in a lowered voice now, her expression far away. "And that they were coming for me. Coming for me in anger. But they weren't gods. Only men."

Deidre tried not to let herself get pulled along this or any other tangent, but indignant words burbled up inside her and fell out of her mouth before she could stop them: "*Men*? Twice you've called these things men. They are horrid and nasty and they are *not* men!"

"What's the distinction?" Mingh straw narrowed one eye and cocked her head.

Above them, the sky made a clanking noise and several drops of warm, viscous liquid fell to spatter Deidre's thigh.

"Tell me," Mingh straw insisted. "Is it the wings? Is that what sets them apart? No. Look between their legs." Leaning forward to poke at Deidre, though Deidre, repulsed, had moved back. "That's where the real truth lies. That's what makes them men. Have you looked?"

"I have not," Deidre said, shocked. But her statement was untrue: she *had* glimpsed the tiny, pointed penises of the angels, dangling limply within their feathery codpieces. A flush of hot shame burned through her, down to her core, and she snapped, "Leave me alone, all right? Stop talking to me."

"Little needle dicks, right? That's what makes them men. If they were gods? Well, I guess gods can have dicks any size they want!" Mingh straw laughed.

"Are you trying to shock me? It's not working," Deidre lied, for the second time in as many minutes. "I may be fourteen but I've seen my sister in the stable, on her knees in the straw. I've seen her. I know what goes on. She talks trash like you. I know what she does to boys."

"You do?" Mingh straw laughed again, an ugly sound. "Tell me. I'd love to know."

"Stop talking. Please. Stop talking to me."

"Okay, sister." Traces of a grin remained on her face. "I get the hint."

To Deidre's relief and surprise, the request for silence was heeded. As hot winds whipped up again, she glanced about; the angels no longer watched but she heard their unpleasant voices nearby. Every so often, one dropped from the nest to soar past her, through suns' light and down, toward the ruined and smouldering landscape below. Those winds plucked at Deidre and howled mockingly.

Huddled against the partition of sticks, trying to imagine a way out of this predicament, she abruptly fell into a sort of desperate, exhausted sleep; at this point she had been awake more than a full day.

From the shore of a fetid swamp, which spread out before her, the Orchard Keeper came, slowly transforming into a furred beast with a chitinous breast and sharp, needle teeth. This beast, her father, splashed into the muck and floundered there.

Waist deep in the stagnant water, Deidre watched. Her hair fell out, in clumps, and these floated on the surface of the water all around her like eels.

"Dad?" she said.

The beast went under.

"Hi, D."

In the reeds stood Sam's little dead boy, grinning. Next to him, another boy, around the same age as Deidre, gave her a nervous

144

wave. This kid was thin and blotchy and looked sick. His hair, like hers, had fallen out, and when he smiled he had no teeth to show. He said, "I won't let you go. Don't worry. We'll keep our hiding place."

The gashes on the dead boy's neck opened and closed, opened and closed, in rhythm with Deidre's breathing, and Mingh straw's monotone voice began to infiltrate. Deidre listened, her eyes still closed, wishing the vile girl and all recent events would just go away.

"I'm going to tell you a story . . . I know you're awake. Make of it what you will. Recently, I had my heart broken. I don't know if you've ever had your heart broken, but you might be able to relate. You seem smart enough. There was a girl, see? There's always a girl, isn't there? I worked with her. She was beautiful. Gorgeous and slim. Really hot. *Sexy.* We were often requested together, as a team. I guess we were picked because she looked as young as me— as young as *you*—though I don't think she had any operations or that the gods gave her anything to keep her that way. She looked young *naturally.* We even fucked a few gods, as a team. Deities don't really know what they're doing when it comes to fucking but sometimes they like to give it a shot. Try to pretend they're down in the dirt with us, you know? Mostly it was funny. Sometimes it was kind of sad. And they wanted to watch us fuck each other, too. Not gods, of course, but men. Men like to watch girls fuck each other. Did you know that?"

Deidre kept her eyes squeezed shut. Some people believed if you've done terrible things in life, you would spend eternity in a nightmare, surrounded by all that you find reprehensible and offensive. But what had she done to deserve *this*?

"You can really tell when a girl is into it or when she's faking, passing time, thinking about cleaning her room or her nails or if she'll get a food pak or not for her kids back home. This girl Minnie sue was into it. She wasn't faking *anything.* She ate my pussy like—"

"Stop talking!" When Deidre finally opened her eyes she saw, in the sudden quietude, that Mingh straw was chuckling. Taking a deep breath, Deidre asked, in a barely controlled voice, "What's the matter with you? Why are you doing this to me?"

Mingh straw shrugged. "Bored, I guess. And I've been kidnapped by flying monsters and fed garbage for four days. Plus, I never liked privileged kids who thought they were better than other people."

"I *don't* think I'm better than you. We're different, that's all. We should be in this together. If you don't think so, just leave me alone and I'll get off of this horrid nest by myself."

"Maybe you want me to eat your pussy?" Mingh straw leered. "We should put on a show for them? Maybe that's what they're waiting for. Plus, it might alleviate the boredom."

Deidre stood up suddenly but was forced to drop again to her haunches; the wind grabbed wildly for her, whipping her hair back and plucking at her ruined clothes. With burning eyes she crawled away.

Mingh straw hissed, "Where can you go?"

And, when Deidre was a few meters away, still moving, still hiding her tears, Mingh straw shouted in a much louder voice, "I wasn't telling the truth, you bitch! Minnie sue never broke my heart! She was a lousy lover! She was straight, married to a loser who did nothing but fish every day! Trapped in a marriage to a man she hated! And she was the one gave me—!"

Clambering around the lip of a partition, Deidre gasped and wiped at her face. The wind had blasted tears from her eyes and sliced the air from her lips. Each awful word of that monologue had been branded into her mind, ringing in her ears. Mercifully, it too had been sliced cleanly away.

Huddling nearby, a group of angels—including the black one— were gibbering, talking excitedly amongst themselves. They turned to her, as she emerged, and now they stopped their antics. Gesturing and flapping, a few showed signs of further agitation. Not wanting to go back to where Mingh straw was, Deidre shrank close to the rancid sticks and debris, presenting her back to the group of angels but keeping a wary eye on them, lest they attack.

With slow, strong beats of their wings, two angels lifted off and, in mid-air, kicked at each other, feet splayed in an almost comic fight. Their voices rose in tone and shrillness.

Then a third broke away from the cluster to come rushing toward her, wings outstretched, gait awkward and shifting from side to side. While she cowered, the beast fell upon her, took hold of her shoulders with the tips of the long fingers that spread the membranes of its wing apart, shrieking angrily in her face with horrible breath.

Deidre shouted, twisting, pulling the angel off balance. Clumsily, they rolled. The wings were like stinky warm sheets over her face; she was sure she could have snapped the light bones of the creature with her bare hands but the angel scrambled to its feet and suddenly backed off.

Then she saw the dirigible.

Still quite far away, under thin clouds and smoke lingering from the razed landscape, gleaming dully in the hazy sunlight, approached a ship. Not quite as high as the aerie, without a doubt the tan shape was an airship.

Deidre saw the wooden fuselage suspended from the oblong balloon, and the massive prop churning sluggishly behind it. Though she had only seen images of such a craft she imagined her rescuers standing within the cupola, all dressed neatly in uniforms identical to the one that the gram in her sanctum had been wearing yesterday. She imagined their waxed moustaches, their blue eyes. She imagined their resolve. Perhaps, she thought giddily, it was even the man himself, in the flesh, the man to whom she had listened, in her sketching room, presiding at the helm.

She sat up straight.

Obviously the angels had spotted this craft earlier, and when Deidre had fled Mingh straw's taunts, they'd been discussing a strategy, in their own way. Now they had resumed their dance, arguing among themselves, kicking and making their awful giggling noises.

"You're dead," she told her attacker, who remained standing over her, also watching approach of the slow-moving dirigible. It looked down at her with beady eyes. Its nostrils twitched. "You'll see, you filthy beast. You're all dead! You can't touch me any more!"

The angel blinked, hissed, and looked away.

Balloons were military crafts, under orders from—and in possession of—officials much higher in rank than her father. But was it possible that the Orchard Keeper had discovered her abduction and arranged for her rescue?

She waved vigorously, moving so she could see Mingh straw, who sat still, staring out into the clouds in the opposite direction, as if she remained unawares, unconcerned. Deidre scuttled back to the girl, calling to her, cutting through the crosswind. The angel that had accosted her shrieked once, but did not follow.

"They're coming," Deidre shouted. "Mingh straw, they're coming! We're getting help!"

The girl turned, very slowly.

Blood bubbled at the corners of her mouth. She smeared the blood with the back of one hand, marking her cheek and chin with demented crimson streaks. "Who is?" Voice thick, though the girl tried to smile. "Who's coming?"

"You're bleeding . . ."

"What makes you think, sister, that I need *another* sister? One more to take care of? The gods of fertility took care of *that*. Cut my tubes. I don't need another kid."

Deidre turned to pull apart nearby sticks, to better watch the airships' progress through the gap she made. "Can't you see it, Mingh straw? Look." She spoke as if Mingh straw was the child and she, Deidre, was the adult. She took the girl's hot arm. "Can't you see it? They're coming to save us. Everything is going to be all right."

Gleaming as it rose, turning flank toward her in ponderous yet graceful motion, the craft of the rescuers neared. An insignia, red and blue, almost impossible to make out from this distance—though she was sure she'd seen it before, and knew its detail, on sealed documents brought to Elegia—emblazoned the rudder.

In a very quiet voice, Deidre confided, "I only noticed their penises because I'm a scientist. That's all. A scientist."

At least three angels circled the airship out there, appearing in size and form as they had when Deidre had first seen them from the picnic site a lifetime ago, a world away.

Orbiting the dirigible, diving at it swiftly, pulling out at the last moment or occasionally holding place directly over the top of the craft, to hover uncertainly there, the angels clearly did not know how to deal with this threat.

And so, one by one, the creatures plummeted from sight, shot down, dead. Silently Deidre cheered, though she also felt a remote sadness, a surprising empathy for the angels whose source she could not understand; the beasts did not seem much smarter than moths.

Deidre's eyes narrowed. *It was a cruel world.* She knew that. Nature was impartial, reality harsh. Part of the order of things. But would she stick a pin through an insect again, if she had the luck to survive this ordeal, and again be given the choice? Would she ask Sam for the unfortunate owner of an archived spiral to be retrieved from the library, resurrected from extinction so she could kill it all over again? The idea of her specimen jar sickened her a little now and she wondered if ghosts of all the insects she had ever put into it were gathering together, watching her perils with grim satisfaction, siding with their winged brethren as they, too, succumbed to the nasty humans.

"Confession time, sweet ass?" Mingh straw's voice was slurred but insistent, as if Deidre's comment about the angels' genitalia had percolated down through layers of troubled perception to revive her. While Deidre watched the uneven battle, Mingh straw spoke once more:

"Is it time for true confessions? All right, then, sugar tits, all right. What I believe is that these monsters brought you here because they weren't happy with me. As a specimen. Because I'm broken and sick and they know it. They wanted another girl. A younger girl. A prettier girl. And I can— *Look out!*"

Something hit Deidre hard, from the side, lifting her completely off the nest and carrying her out into the open air. The landscape below suddenly filled her vision with a rush, and in the initial moment, winded, she wondered if an explosion had occurred, or if she were mortally hurt, about to plummet, but by the time her wits began to return to her she realized that she was dangling high over the ruined world, in excruciating pain, being carried off once more through the skies.

An angel—the black one—had her in its talons, and was flapping away from the aerie.

No pretence of being gentle this time. She was not gripped between the beast's knees; claws fully pierced the muscles of her shoulders, clinging to the bone beneath. She felt them scraping at her skeleton. From under her torn shirt, hot blood trickled, dripping down onto the land like a baptism. What came out of her mouth was not a scream. The talons tightened; the world grew dim.

She turned her head to see if the airship was changing course to come get her, but saw instead a white angel directly behind her, with Mingh straw hanging from its grip. The other girl was fighting, writhing, reaching up to hit the angel again and again and grab at its wiry thighs as the creature struggled to remain airborne with its load.

"Mingh straw!"

First one claw came free, then the other worked loose, talon by straining talon, as Deidre knew it would.

Liberated, Mingh straw floated for a moment, the suns' light playing through her hair. Suspended beneath the angel in a position that implied impending and beautiful somersaults, or some other motion defying any rule of cold physics or of nature, as if plunging down to meet death were an act of free will, a conscious decision she had decided not to take—not for this delicious instant—Mingh straw looked at Deidre, her blood-smeared face wild and flushed with ecstasy.

The inevitable plummet, the white angel, even the distant dirigible, all vanished as Deidre shut her eyes. Pain and horror mingled inside her, magnified by the image of the girl's tumbling body.

One last shriek made her jolt awake, disturbing her from that comforting place to which she'd been travelling, so she could glimpse, through rolling eyes before finally passing out, where they were headed. Oblivion did close in at last, leaving her unconscious, unfeeling, bleeding her life out, but the awful image of Mingh straw's death plunge had been replaced by another, an almost redeeming vision, for Deidre had seen, in that final instant, a hole piercing the sky, beyond which appeared pale and beautiful blues like none she could have ever imagined. Coming through that aperture, a calm shaft of light had enclosed her body, pulling her, with the black angel, upward along its axis. A luminous spear had been thrown down to pierce the world. Angel and girl rose towards an impossible, celestial opening.

MEREZIAH, L8-9

Gears within gears. Cogs and wheels. Whirling thick shafts, crooked, grinding, hissing steam, throwing off blue sparks as the din rose to a deafening pitch and then fell to a low, throaty moan. Sweat prickled Mereziah's face and ran down into the collar of his already damp uniform. On the catwalk's wobbly chain railing his palms were slick. His lungs ached from exertion. Needles of pain jabbed the length of his left arm. His knees creaked and cracked and knocked together.

In this ethereal place, the air was hot and pressing and he felt old, certainly, and out of shape, but truth be told the primary reason for his growing discomfort was the proximity of Crystal Max, who was walking, in all her tempting glory, directly behind him. Mereziah could no longer deny that he was suffering a ludicrous, juvenile crush. Crystal had become the manifestation of his illicit and suppressed desires. Physical want was another ache. He needed a companion. He *needed* her. In these strange, autumnal days, in this strange setting—before he fell dead to the bottom of the world—he needed to be with Crystal Max.

Where, he wondered, was the dignity in this?

A greasy piston, pumping heartily up and down in its housing, goading him rudely with its motion, loosed a burst of pressurized steam toward his face, and Crystal Max said loudly, directly into his hairy ear, her breath as hot as the steam, "Where the fuck are we, old timer? Any theories?"

For maybe the tenth time he wondered what her scent might be. Lingering on her skin, insinuating, burrowing deep into his dried out old sinuses; it made him dizzy. "I believe we are, in fact, *inside* the actual—"

"Do you know where you're going or don't you?" She pushed him between the shoulder blades, so hard that he stumbled. "Where are you taking us, old timer? Where the fuck are we?"

Us. Taking *us.* Crystal was right. He winced to be reminded of the plurality. There were twelve in the entourage, all following Mereziah at his own slow, pained pace, walking single file along the catwalk. A dozen people, suspended high above a roiling pit of steam and moving parts and mysterious machineries both seen and unseen, *following* him.

His stomach roiled.

These shaky catwalks had been underfoot, in some form or other, for hours now. For the love of his departed parents, Mereziah had never seen or imagined anything like this place. Not in his hundred years of living. Crystal was right again: where had he brought these people? Hissing and howling, misty, steamed, the environment was surely lifted right out of a fever-driven fugue. Wide areas opened, at times, big enough across for all of them to sit in a circle, if they so chose, or narrowed to skinny trails that forced them to turn sideways. Dead end paths, multiple junctions, drop offs. Catwalks twisting upon themselves so further passage was not possible. Catwalks gradually turning upside down.

At least he could see the exterior of the great shaft, still visible, serving as vortex to their travels. Pale, wrinkled, it seemed rather sickly looking from the outside as they corkscrewed slowly upwards around it. Once or twice, the group had no choice but to take a path that meandered some distance from the shaft—where he had lived his entire life—so to Mereziah it appeared as though the group were suspended above insubstance, with neither end nor beginning in sight, without anchor. These times, he felt like he was floating, utterly adrift.

Hurrying as fast as he could go, he hoped to escape both the girl and his thoughts, but whenever he glanced over his shoulder he saw those twelve faces, bobbing along after him . . .

Moments later, nudging him again, Crystal broke into his reverie by hissing, "I don't understand what this old bag is saying. Can't you get her to shut up?"

Sweating, pressing on, always pressing on, despite growing protest from his limbs and aching heart, despite his almost desperate mental state, Mereziah had never even heard the squalling. But he did now the noise rose above the general din in a wavering language of gibberish he could not understand or ignore again.

He turned to look. Ever since being carried down from the giant pod, the loud and rather round lady in question had been prone to these fits of hysteria. But old bag? Had Crystal really said that? The woman was elderly, certainly, but nowhere near as old as him. *I'm positively ancient by comparison. How old*, he wondered, *do I seem to her?*

Probably didn't help matters that after bringing Crystal out of the opening in the shaft wall, he had stood, bent at the waist, rasping and wheezing for a long time, trying to catch his breath while she rubbed at his back.

The others had to save themselves.

Crystal mentioned that the screamer was virtually silent when trapped inside the pod, so Mereziah was forced to consider that the lady must be having a breakdown. He also feared the outbursts might attract attentions of the mysterious giant soldiers, who he imagined were lurking out here, hiding in the thick steam or behind the next bank of toiling machinery.

Others in the group were grumbling now, pleading or demanding that the old lady fall silent. Mereziah's gaze fell upon Crystal's beautiful sneer, drawn to it. With effort, he looked away, at each of the scared, angry people in the dubious parade. Halfway back, the screaming lady—her own eyes pained and wild—had paused, at least, for now, to gather breath. Behind her stood the dark-skinned man who had carried most of the others to safety while Mereziah had been wheezing and coughing; at the very end of the line waited a half-dressed brute with narrow black eyes and a set of symmetrical scars on both cheeks.

Most of these people spoke a different language than Mereziah. One—a dusky woman in a veil—had not spoken a word the entire time. The array of faces caused Mereziah a stab of professional embarrassment, both from his ignorance of their cultural origins and from his now growing wish to rid himself of their dependence upon him; part of him wanted to learn about these people while another malicious part fantasized about pushing them all (except for Crystal Max) right off the damn catwalk.

He needed to rest. Honestly, where in the world were these ideas coming from? Unpleasant and meandering thoughts, the results of being in *love*? Were lust and want sicknesses to infect his brain?

The screaming, which had started up once more, didn't help matters.

On the move again, Crystal Max announced, "Lookie there, more moss."

And, suddenly, an idea occurred to Mereziah.

The moss. On Crystal's recommendation, they had all begun eating the strange growth—some gobbling more than others, for they were *hungry*—since first coming across some, shortly after emerging from the slit in the shaft.

"Be wary," Mereziah said, stopping in his tracks, looking down at the catwalk and mists far below. His belly rumbled. He cleared his throat. "Listen people, I cannot sanction consumption of this, uh, this matter." He tried to shout but his voice sounded feeble. He turned, arms out. "I think that eating this plant is the reason why some of us are in such distress. And perhaps it's the reason why I feel so . . ." He let his voice and the thought fade. Then to Crystal he urgently added, "Did she eat the most? When we found these plants previously? Crystal, is this some kind of *drug*?"

Crystal Max laughed. "Listen to yourself!" She bent to gather more of the tiny plants once more, which grew in dull green patches at the side of the catwalk. Though it looked like piles of damp dust, the moss, as Crystal had called it when she set eyes upon it, tasted surprisingly good. Still, consumption of the plant might just be the reason why his thoughts were so degraded, and why the large lady had gone insensate.

His gaze drifted across the smooth, inviting curves of Crystal's twin buttocks. Lingering there. Her pants were torn and he saw a grimy patch of her pinkish flesh.

"Please," he whined, squeezing his eyes shut to stave off temptation. "*Stop*." He reached out, to grab her arm.

Crystal shrugged him away. "Who the fuck are you to tell me what to do?" Licking the powder off her grubby digits, she looked at Mereziah with a defiance that set his heart pounding.

Several others in the group, he saw, were also stooping to scrape at the catwalk.

"Wait!" Mereziah shouted, lifting both hands high over his head. "Wait! I have reason to believe that these tiny plants are the source of delusional thinking, of madness, of, of unhealthy *arousal*!"

He was soundly ignored.

A quiver of anxiety ran through him and he drew a deep breath. "*Please!*"

The large woman answered him with a renewed scream, rising in tone and volume to drown out his own echo before all sound suddenly ceased. Abrupt, complete: the silence was tremendous. Save for the ringing in his head. He stood, stunned.

"What happened?" he said, but he could not hear his own voice.

Crystal frowned at him, and as the world resumed its crashing noise, she yelled, "You don't look so good!"

"Crystal," he said weakly, "please . . ."

She took him by the arm. "You better sit down. You look green. You're all worked up." Turning to the others—most of whom, glassy-eyed, were chewing—she said, "Listen up, people! We're taking a break. Pops here needs to sit down. He's not feeling well."

"Crystal, I'm . . . fine?" But a jab of pain ripped down his left side and, for a moment, breath caught on jagged peaks it made in his chest. Looking at the lovely, dirt-smeared face of Crystal Max, he imagined for a second that it might be the last image he would ever see in this life, so he let himself be directed to an area where he could fold himself into a sitting position and close his tired eyes. Even though he could no longer see the others he knew they were eating, licking, swallowing that moss. No one had taken heed of his warning. Was it possible they followed him solely out of pity? Or to keep an eye on him, since he was obviously the weakest of the group? His uniform, his position as lift attendant, was a sham. Pain and humiliation was the price he paid for his selfish dreams. His job had been to serve. For the betterment of the world. Now, he was an embarrassment to the memories of his dear parents, a burden to the living.

Crystal, crouching, shook Mereziah gently. "You okay, old man? You're breathing funny."

"Yes," he answered, opening his eyes. "I am all right." He tried to get to his feet but Crystal gently held him down.

"Rest, old man, rest."

Eventually, most of the discomfort ebbed from him. He began to feel marginally better.

The rest of the group had taken advantage of the break, resting, even lying supine on the platform they were stopped on. Only the veiled woman remained standing, her back to Mereziah as she leaned out over the railing, peering into the steam, towards the shaft they had fled. To Mereziah's left sat the dark-skinned man who had helped with the rescue: cross-legged, eyes closed, apparently oblivious. Though Mereziah's mouth was very dry, he wanted to talk, calculating that by asking intelligent questions, by interviewing these people and displaying his acumen, he could help regain the illusion that he was in control. He wanted his authority back, even if he had earlier desired to shrug it all off, because he realized he had little else.

"Black fellow," he said weakly, trembling, turning to the man who sat, humming softly. Mereziah tried to control his voice, the way his father had trained him to do. "So that, so we can better understand our, our predicament, may I ask you several pertinent questions? Black man?"

The eyes slowly opened. They were hazel and sparked in the dull light. "I have a name. It is Joseph."

Crystal Max said, "Old timer, I told you to relax. I don't need you getting into a fight."

Perplexed, Mereziah turned to her. "Fight? I have no intention of fighting. Why would you say that? There are some things I must know, Crystal. Things important to our survival."

"Like what? What do you want to know?" Joseph lowered his brows.

"What can you tell me about your abduction?"

"My what?"

"Abduction. When the soldiers came to take you."

Joseph stared for a long while before speaking. "I work at filter plant number seventy-two. Fixing filtration units that clean the air. All black fellows, as you say, work there. We all wear uniforms. Never seen anyone like me before? You never went there. But you sure breathe our air. All of you. My father worked at the filter plant. My son works there. My wife too."

"You have a family?" There was a touch of poignancy in these details. Mereziah appreciated Joseph's commitment to servicing systems of the world. At least they had that in common.

But Joseph seemed irritated. "My family is important to your plan? Important for our survival?"

"No," Mereziah admitted.

"Uh, do you have any kids, old man?" intervened Crystal.

"No. I have no children." A lump had formed in Mereziah's throat. He had never even *held* a child. "Continue, please," he told Joseph.

"Soldiers came." The man did not move when he spoke. His arms lay in his lap. "They didn't grab me, at first, or grab anyone around me. Like you, they ask lots of questions. We see others, like them? No. We see people from outside? No. They tell us that the sky is pierced, and that the world woke them up to find out why. They are *security*. But here in the world is too much chaos, too much mess." Joseph's lips tightened. "And they get no instructions, no guidance from the voice of the world."

"The sky? Did you mention the sky?" The words resonated inside Mereziah. Where had he heard this word before? Perhaps a client had mentioned it, a lifetime ago, in association with a story about the top of the world. For he knew that the sky *was* the very top of the world.

"All I've ever seen," Joseph said, "are ceilings and walls."

Crystal put her hand on Joseph's knee. "Me too," she said. "Where I come from, there's a ceiling overhead, so low we can touch it. I've never seen open space like this place."

Mereziah stared at her hand, pale on the other man's leg. Displeasure prickled at his own offended skin.

"You know," Crystal continued, recalling, "we have a car, where I'm from, an old car that sometimes talks about the sky, and about outside. But I don't know what they mean. No one does, not even Reena."

"Outside?" Mereziah did not know this word at all. He told himself to remember it, that it might be important, but all he could do was look at that hand, resting on that dark knee.

Joseph said, "The soldier looked me in the eye. It saw things there, or thought it did. And grabbed me. They have not found anyone who belongs here. No one. Only confusion in the world. Some men ran away. Me, I go with, so they don't take my son, or wife. They put me in that strange room, inside that tube. Where you came, large-eyed man. Skinny white man."

After a long pause, in what he hoped was a thoughtful manner— since parts of the story had drifted through him, like the mists— Mereziah said, "Thank you, Joseph," and he turned to Crystal Max. He wanted to tear her hand from Joseph's leg. "Did, did they look into your eyes too? To see if you belonged here? You didn't tell me anything about that."

Crystal batted her lashless lids, smiling coyly, and showed blackened gums. "My eyes? How could they not peer into them? Actually, old man, I did try my charm on the soldiers. But it didn't work. I thought I could sleep my way to freedom." She laughed. "Really, the soldiers didn't say much to me . . . I was taken long before Joseph here. For three days they kept me in that thing, tossing food down at first, then tossing *people* down. I was the first one in there . . . Except for two little freaks joined at the shoulder. I forget their names. Jan and Dean? Stan and Jim? I don't know. Anyways, me, I was walking down a hallway, down home, minding my own business. Having a good cry, actually, when they took me. From behind."

Feeling a twinge of arousal at the unfortunate turn of phrase in Crystal's story, Mereziah stammered, "I want you to know that we're going up. Towards the sky. Where the suns are. Have you heard of them? Where warmth and light and health is. We're going up." He felt his limbs quivering. "Do you hear me? We're going up."

Crystal said, "But I wanna go down. That's the other way. The soldiers told me I was from the bottom of the world, so I wanna go down."

"To where the dead fall? That's your home?" Mereziah was about to ask Crystal if she had ever seen his parents, waiting for him down there, waiting for him to join them, but he held his tongue.

Crystal said, "The dead? What the fuck? I don't know anything about the dead. There's no more corpses down there than there are up here. I only ever seen one my whole life, and that was some poor kid who died of the Red Plague when I was seven."

"Why were you, why were you crying?" Mereziah asked, as quietly as he could in the din.

"What? When?"

"You said you were crying when they found you. Why?"

"Why do you care?"

Mereziah glanced surreptitiously at Joseph, who had apparently lost all interest in the conversation. If he had ever had any. The man had regained his meditative pose. Crystal's hand, thankfully, was gone from his knee. "Why were you sad?"

"Shit, I was high. Like I am now. And I'd had a fight with my boyfriend."

"You have a boyfriend?"

"You're surprised?" Crystal's grin showed those dark gums again. "That's a little insulting. But I really don't see the point of this."

"Of course," Mereziah muttered. "I knew you would have a boyfriend. Of course you would." But daggers, once more, stabbed at his heart. He clenched his fists, best he could, picturing the boy: young—a mere teenager, perhaps—attractive, muscular. *Vapid*. How he hated that youth. How he wished the boy were dead, mangled. Had he kissed Crystal on the mouth? Put his hands inside her shirt? Been warmed by her flesh? Had he *touched* her? "Uh, what, what was the fight about? The fight between you and your lover?"

"Lover?" Now Crystal Max was no longer smiling. Her eyes had hardened. "You're getting a little nosy, aren't you, pops? I thought these questions were supposed to be about survival. The *fight*, if you must know, concerned another guy. It was about this little twerp called Phister who was always trailing after me, bugging me. We used to go out, me and him. But he probably doesn't remember that. Simpson Lang thought I still liked him. And I do. I do still like Young Phister. What do you think of that?"

Mereziah was unaware of the precise moment that he had

decided to lean in and kiss Crystal himself. All he knew was that he had finally transgressed everything he held dear, broken through that last barrier. Her open hand stung hard against his skull and snapped his head to one side, setting his ears to ringing even more. Attempting to sit upright, stunned by her quick defense and by his own inability to comprehend his motives, a second slap stung him and he raised his arms to ward off further blows.

Joseph grabbed Mereziah's arms and pinned them tight while Crystal Max managed to hit him again, and again, until a wiry man in a grey uniform rushed over, crab-like, to restrain her.

"You shit," Crystal said, panting. "You disgusting old bastard! Whydja kiss me?"

Mereziah tried to apologize but his upper lip was already swelling and he tasted blood on his tongue. One eye was beginning to shut.

"What the *fuck* did you think you were doing?!"

"I wanted . . . I thought . . ." He looked away, mortified. "I've never kissed a girl. I thought maybe you wanted . . . I've never kissed anyone." Not a lie, since he and Merezath had refrained from touching lips, all those years ago. He looked down at the catwalk, through which he saw mists below, and he wished he could fall through the grille, fall down to be with the dead forever.

But then he would have to face his parents.

He did not want to weep but tears stung his eyes. My goodness, he thought, I've lost my mind. "Look," he said. "I'm sorry, Crystal. I don't have an excuse."

He looked up.

No one was listening to him.

No one paid him any attention whatsoever.

His arms came free easily from Joseph's loosened grip. The entire group was looking in the same direction—

There were four. Two abreast, the soldiers filled the nearby bend in the catwalk. *Looming.* The catwalk creaked under them. Without a doubt, these huge humanoids were the captors Crystal

Max had told him about, standing silent in their dark uniforms, eyes glimmering red in their black faces. Their weapons were long, sinister, and raised.

"Hello," one said, in a bass voice.

The four of them seemed to exude chuckling.

"You people have crashed the wrong party. We're going to send you back through the hole you crawled out of."

Mereziah tried to get to his feet. "Do not harm these people. As representative—"

Flames erupted slowly, surreal, an upward curving tongue that made little noise, merely a popping sound at first. From the muzzle of a gun, the fire reached out to gently lick at the large lady—who was quiet now, of all times, as if at peace—and immediately burst from her clothing, engulfing her. Yet she remained silent, ironically, throughout this, until, with a groan, she pushed herself to her feet—showering sparks, ablaze—as if she'd just remembered a chore undone. Then, forced to reconsider, she sat back down again, in the roar of fire, to land on a pillow of sparks.

The stench of her death was horrific. Through those flames, which were already waning, Mereziah watched the woman's skin char and crack and seep forth all the boiling liquids that had once given her life.

When her corpse toppled, the soldiers advanced, perhaps to incinerate another victim, but they were too large for this narrow place of floating paths and steam. Too substantial. They jostled and rocked, out of their element. More flames arced up before them, glowing, throwing off intense heat.

Behind Mereziah, someone scrambled to their feet and started running but Mereziah did not have a chance to turn and see who it was because from beneath him came a terrific rending sound, the sound of the world tearing apart, and the catwalk snapped, spilling its contents.

With ancient reflexes, Mereziah threw his arms out to grab hold and cling to the chain railing as the entire catwalk swung down.

There was a sickening jolt, and it felt as though both his arms were torn from their sockets, but he found himself hanging painfully, swaying.

People plunged past him: the veiled woman; the burnt corpse of the silenced screamer; Joseph. As he searched in panic the chaotic and upended surroundings for Crystal, a giant fell from above, where it had somehow been holding on, making an awful racket as it passed him, clattering and flailing to be swallowed by the steam far below. It left a vaguely human-shaped hole in the mist that soon closed over.

Dangling, Mereziah grimaced. The fire lingered, but inside him now, destroying once and for all his old heart and lungs.

Detritus clanged, bounced noisily past, tumbling into the abyss.

The catwalk swung forwards and back. Everyone had vanished. Mists closed in.

Mereziah was alone again.

TRAN SO, L14

In circumference, the duct was hardly larger around than his torso, pressing up hard against ribs, shoulders, elbows, belly, knees. After the initial blind ascent, he'd calmed, and slowed, wormlike, and even had a quick, fitful sleep within the snug cocoon—though how long he lay inside, unmoving, he could not tell.

Now, on a horizontal stretch, the duct had narrowed—though that perception might have been an unpleasant trick Tran so's mind played on him. He was certainly starting to feel vestiges of primal fear nibbling.

The entire time he had been moving through these confines—all night? a full day?—he had seen only one dark glimpse of detail, when a wire of dull light shone straight up through an empty rivet hole. He had seen nothing else, nothing up ahead. None of the junctions, turns, dents that he slowly inched his way through. Only felt the cool, smooth surface, pressing against his body, smelled the metal and dust. Tran so had to trust that he could keep going. There was certainly no way to back up. He had little choice but to persevere, try to ignore the aches, the cramps, the onset of claustrophobia. Ignore the thoughts of, at some point soon, encountering a dead end.

Which, for him, would be literal.

He also needed to piss but could not bring himself to urinate in his own clothes and drag his body through the hot puddle.

Occasionally, stubborn animals squeezed past him, or tried to, forcing their way between his body and the walls of the duct; he felt fur a few times, scales twice, and, once, something slimy and foul rubbing against his cheek. He broke through many cobwebs. Breaths of warm, nasty air were exhaled into his face and sporadic, ambient sounds came at him from muffled locations unseen, beneath or above, from all around.

For now, everything was quiet.

He had stopped to rest.

Was he safer in here? Had it been a good idea to enter this labyrinth, scrambling in a panic up through an overhead panel, while the dark god clawed at him, trying, in its fury, to plunge in, those huge fingers inches behind his feet as Tran so frantically pushed himself forward? He had asked himself these two questions a hundred times as he wormed forward over the next many hours. No one could tell the future, no matter what they claimed. He was still alive, at least. *Maybe in an hour*, he told himself, *I will be in an open space, on my feet, eating, or emptying my bladder with great relief.*

Or perhaps I will be wedged tight, waiting for death.

Eventually, moving once more—as the dire thoughts became harder and harder to stave off—through the darkness of the tangy-smelling duct up ahead, he perceived, at last, a source of dim light. His eyes watered. He had to fight to remain calm. Anxiety might make him move too fast, get stuck, just metres from a possible exit.

Then he heard the muffled voices.

This new development gave him pause. What if he had come full circle? Was the angry dark god waiting for him to emerge? Were others there, about to cut off his passage? He tried to think of a plan but wanted so badly to stretch, to move with elbowroom, to breathe clean air, that frustration at the idea of being captured after all this caused surprising tears to sting his already bleary eyes.

Shimmying slower, he was soon able to confirm that the light ahead was coming up through a grille set in the bottom of the duct. This proved that, despite his earlier ascent, he was still travelling through a ceiling. One room's ceiling is another room's floor. He suspected he was a level above where he had started.

Increased illumination was becoming uncomfortable, but his eyes eventually adjusted somewhat, and he began to see dusty details: the cobwebs, the old grille, flakes of rust.

And now a rather pleasing aroma drifted into the duct, the likes of which he could not identify. He waited, a metre or so from the lip of the grille, listening, blinking, tingling all over. His muscles sung with tension. His elbows had been at his sides for an eternity.

The voices again. To his relief, one was a woman's. These were not dark gods, waiting to trap him. This woman was talking, in low, placid tones, with what sounded to be a child, though it became evident to Tran so that the child might be chastising or instructing the woman. Odder still, the younger voice rang with tones of familiarity. Unable to hear clearly any of the words, he shimmied a little closer to the grille, trying to be as silent as possible.

Soon he was able to peer over the lip:

He discerned little, except glare. He managed to rub the corners of his bleary eyes with dusty knuckles, one at a time, and, as his vision cleared further, he saw a room beneath him, a sleeping area, similar, yet more opulent and spacious than those he knew back in Hoffmann City. There was one large bed, covered by a thick red duvet and red fitted sheet. Plumped up by the ornate headboard, two red pillows. The entire structure of the bed was elevated off the floor, and the walls were decorated with designs that moved and undulated as he watched. How he wanted to bust out of the grille and lie supine on that bed, limbs outspread.

Despite the decadence, Tran so detected a general patina of age over everything down there, an overall yellowed tone of disuse and neglect.

Positioned directly over the bed, Tran so could not see the full extent of the room, nor could he see the persons—if they were indeed people—who had been speaking. He thought he heard them moving, but they were no longer talking.

The floor was a pale brown shag. Tran so had seldom seen carpeting before; it was a luxury where he came from, a sign of wealth and corruption—

The woman came into view. Bent over the opulent bed, she brushed at it with her hands. Looking down, Tran so could not see her face, but he knew immediately that she was young, and beautiful beyond words.

Just the cant of one arm, as she flattened the duvet, the shape of her leg as she placed it down to steady herself, was too much. Mingled with arousal was a familiar, bittersweet sadness: pining for Minnie sue, for vanished passion, for concepts as great as his own aging and mortality.

She was twenty years old, at most. Black skirt and black top, with a white apron over it all that had seen better days. A uniform of some kind? He thought at first she was also wearing a helmet but soon realized netting had been tied around her brown hair, containing it, holding it away from her breathtaking neck.

Tran so Phengh saw no one else in the room. Unprepared to move his head out too far over the opening for fear of being seen, or maybe moving dust or other debris forward with his body so that it rained down on the girl and gave his position away, he watched as best he could for a long while.

Her collarbone, exquisite, her smooth skin flawless and translucent. He imagined her body, lurking in the clothes that only hinted at its form.

Could she perceive him, he wondered, even if she did happen to look up from whatever strange toil it was she performed down there, to that soft bed?

He was getting a hard-on. He had not been aroused by a woman other than Minnie sue for a long time. He squeezed his eyes shut and mouthed a silent apology to his dying wife, yet grinding his own body against the ductwork all the while.

The woman below started to hum an innocent tune.

Scents he had earlier detected wafted up again. These were coming, he saw now, from a tube that the girl gripped in her left hand. He had not seen this apparatus at first but he regarded it clearly now as she raised it to spray, in a fine mist, the red linen of the bed. This dispensing hose led back to a tiny buggy on wheels, which she pulled now, and the buggy creaked farther into the room.

Tran so's eyebrows cocked upwards.

"Can you smell the mildew?" the girl asked, her voice throaty, oozing a sensuality that intensified Tran so Phengh's arousal. "I don't think it's much better. It only masks it, you know."

She straightened to push at her back with the palm of her free hand, so that Tran so finally saw her features: she *was* gorgeous. As he had sensed. So beautiful that he caught his breath and his eyes moistened with longing—

"Just you wait a minute," the trolley said. "Let me adjust the lavender ratio."

Evidently, the trolley was some form of minor god. Tran so had not seen the likes of it before. But the trolley was not the speaker he had heard earlier, the one with the child's voice. There was someone else in the room. Human, or god? He wished he could see more than just a rectangle of the chamber below, wished he could see more of the girl—

"Freeze, sir."

In that instant, with these two words, the mystery of the third voice, and of who—or what—owned it, was solved. And he comprehended, in that same instant, why the voice had sounded familiar. This time, it had not issued from beneath him. Before he looked up, across the grille, to the other side of the duct, he knew the voice belonged to a crawling god. Out of context, but unmistakable. Funny how his mind hadn't made the connection earlier. Preoccupied with the girl, perhaps.

He lifted his face.

There were two of them. Identical to gods of loose ends and traffic infringements, squatting there, in the duct opposite, they watched him intently with their compound eyes.

"Hello," he said.

"Who are you? What are you doing here?"

Deciding to tell the truth—or at least, the partial truth—Tran so Phengh said, "I am seeking answers to questions."

"Questions? What questions?" The crawling god on the left scuttled closer so that one pointed leg, glittering in the light rising up from the sleeping chamber, rested on the brink of the grille. "To me, friend, you appear to be spying on my staff."

"Your *staff*?" Again, Tran so Phengh looked down at the girl, whose face was upturned now, listening. His gaze fell into those eyes: beautiful and warm and brown.

When he reluctantly lifted his head again, to explain, the crawling gods had gone. Silently vanished. Squinting, he tried to locate the deities as they ran off down the dark tunnel—

There came a popping sound.

And the duct fell out from underneath him.

Tumbling once through the air, glancing off the softness of the bed, he crashed heavily onto the brown shag carpet. On his back, he lay in pain at the girl's feet in a settling cloud of dust and pattering debris.

She smiled at him.

He groaned. After a moment, he moved his arms, his legs. As he lay there, trying to breathe, reassured that no bones were broken, that incredible face kept looking down at him. *Smiling.*

Crawling gods came across the floor toward him, from an open doorway. At least six of them. They held position in a semi-circle around him as he managed to sit up.

"You could have killed me," Tran so wheezed, glancing toward the ceiling panel through which he had fallen: it swung, creaking, back and forth on its hinges. Another crawling god clung upside down to the tiled ceiling. As he watched, this deity vanished, moving swiftly into the hole and out of sight, dislodging detritus with its scrambling legs; something sharp landed painfully in Tran so's left eye and he groaned once more.

"You are trespassing," one of the crawling gods explained. "This area is for paid guests only. And staff, of course. But not just any staff. This is not a free-for-all. We run a tight ship here in the Department of Hospitality. Go tell your boss that."

Tran so rubbed at his injured eye. "Hospitality? You don't know the meaning of the word. And I don't have a boss."

"Renegade, eh? Well you are interrupting our new employee training. It sure seems you missed yours, in whatever third-rate department you skulked away from."

"I am not a *new* employee," the girl said, bemusement flickering across her face. She glanced coyly at Tran so. "There *are* no new employees, sir. I've been doing this job since I was born. I certainly don't need training."

Tran so got to his feet, brushing himself off. Crawling gods scuttled anxiously, as if he might bolt. His eye watered profusely. The same eye, he realized, the parasite had been in.

"I'd like to clarify something." He looked at the girl. "I wasn't spying."

Shrugging, and tugging at the hose she carried, so that the little trolley squeaked closer to her leg, she said, "If you'll excuse me, I have work to do."

"My name is Tran so," insisted Tran so.

"Sir," the crawling god called up to him, "you'll have to come with us."

He could have kicked them all aside, like crabs, and run away, but what would be the point? He wanted to stay in this room. He wanted to talk to the girl, to learn her name, to touch her hands and feel her neck, hot against his lips. He might never see her again if he fled.

But the damned gods would not let him stay.

"Where will you take me?" he asked them.

"Anywhere but here. We'll take you to our supervisor's office. He'll give you what for. And he'll contact your boss."

Tran so nodded. Most of what the little gods said made no sense, but the lake god had called itself a supervisor. If the supervisor of these lesser gods was a step further up their ladder of divinity, perhaps he had regained the trail he needed to be on. Mysterious ways, indeed. Would he get an audience with the god of all gods? Would he meet the network?

The girl, he saw, wore a nametag. *Hello. My name is Sandra.* Such a wonderful name. "Listen, Sandra, I can't help but think we were meant to meet."

The crawling gods actually laughed at his line. The girl, however, paid him no attention whatsoever. So he let his hand, which he'd held out, drop. He did not know what else to do. Should he actually touch her, hold her arm?

"Sir, please come with us."

At a loss, he let himself be escorted from the room.

Underfoot, the gods crossed his path hither and thither. He glanced back surreptitiously; Sandra was not looking at him, as he'd hoped. His ego withered.

They escorted him down a long hall.

Love had been so difficult, over the past months, to retain for Minnie sue. Ravaged by disease, she no longer really existed, outside of memories. Was he expected to remain at his wife's side the whole while she wasted away? When Minnie sue woke from her comatose sleeps, she called him atrocious names, hurt him in every conceivable way, screaming the Red Plague's obscenities at him. How many times had he knelt by Minnie sue's futon while she raved and cursed and spat at him?

They passed dozens of rooms. In most, busy women cleaned, dressed in black skirts with white aprons. None, of course, were as charming or as pretty as Sandra. But there sure were a *lot* of rooms. A *lot* of women.

And minor gods, too, dashing from doorway to doorway, giving out instructions as they went, barking out annoying orders, watching over the staff as Tran so was led past.

These hallways, like the sleeping chambers, were carpeted. A rich, decorative layer that altered tones of deep reds and burgundies covered the walls. Lights, mounted in the walls, set in sconces between each pair of doors, illuminated hemispheres of warm amber over the ruddy carpeting and over him as he followed the minor gods. It became apparent that the entire place was a series of similar halls and rooms. Difficult to find his way back to where Sandra worked. Nonetheless, he tried to memorize the layout.

But the vistas were confusing and the proximity of all these women distracting.

Secondary hallways led off, either side. These also were door-lined. Some doors open, some doors shut. More rooms, more women, more gods. He heard the various droning sounds of mingled voices and the laughter of people trying to deal with tedium, and an ambient humming overall. He thought about Sandra, her voice, her smile. He wondered what it would be like to fuck her, and he wondered what had happened to make him so obsessed. Had it been the spray? His heart pounded. He felt strong, alive; he had not felt like this in years.

"Who sleeps in all these rooms?" he demanded. "What are they for?" No response. "Why are all these women cleaning?"

Again, no answer.

At the end of this hall was a device about the same height as Tran so, a great block-shaped thing residing under a sign that said simply ICE. At first, he thought this block might be a primitive yet inert god, but as he neared he could tell it had never possessed sentience.

Beyond was an opening, a wide doorway into a large room.

Lined, on three walls, with plush couches. Tran so stopped at the threshold and the crawling gods bumped into his calves and scurried around his feet. There were pictures on the walls of this room, what looked to be lakes, and beaches, but these were so clean, reposed under blue ceilings set impossibly high, that he knew they were no location in this world.

Against the furthermost wall to his left ran an elongated counter behind which, waiting motionless—so he had not seen it at first—was a god on treads standing erect, almost exactly like a god of dispensing. Ludicrously, the deity was dressed in ill-fitting clothing. Tran so saw it blink, and knew it was activated; he immediately walked across the room. "Where is the network? I wish to speak to the network."

The god stared at him with tiny, cold eyes. One of the crawling deities quickly mounted the counter and scurried between them. "You are addressing a fulltime clerk," it said to Tran so. "This clerk is in need of repairs. Once again, you harass our staff. The supervisor is in the chamber beyond. Please cease all questions and do not leave our side again without clearance."

Tran so Phengh noted the door that the crawling god had indicated: large, green, unassuming.

The clerk said, in slow, affected tones, "Welcome to the nostalgia suites. Do you wish a room for one week? For two? Are you single? Do you have a family?"

"A *family*?" Tran so stared.

"Yes. Are you a family man?"

With one sweep of his arm, Tran so knocked a small bell from the counter to the carpet, where it rang dully. "I stayed with my wife longer than most people would have," he hissed. "And my son is dead. *That* is my family." The rage was whirling inside him, eddying, ebbing. He felt tension in his limbs—

Yet bending, nonplussed, to consult an open logbook, the big clerk said, "Then I take it you will not be needing two beds?"

"Listen to me, you piece of—"

The nearest crawling god jabbed at Tran so's hand with one sharp foreleg; the pain was tremendous and Tran so's knees buckled. Elbows out, splayed on the counter, he tried to support his sagging weight. He could not see clearly and his lungs laboured to fill.

"I told you this is no time to be insubordinate," the crawling god said, as if from a distance, while the clerk bobbled its head and remained quiet. "We've let you walk about of your own free will. We've given you chances. It's clear you don't take this situation seriously. I know you don't take us seriously. I know your type. Let me tell you, things are changing around here. Trust me, you don't want to lose the privilege of mobility. I'm so fucking tired of you yahoos coming down here, on a lark, big fucking joke, take a job just so you can fuck guests or party. Mocking us who believe in the glorious vision of this place!"

Tingling with pain, and taken aback by the tiny god's uncharacteristic rant, Tran so let himself be directed shakily around the counter to the green door of the supervisor's office. He could hardly walk.

The door opened inwards before he had a chance to knock. Within the dimly lit chamber there appeared to be a human male, seated behind a desk, with his feet up. The man was looking at Tran so Phengh, a small smile on his face. His round eyes were glazed and unfocussed. He was older—greying and overweight—dressed in a hound's-tooth suit just like the suit a dancer friend of Minnie sue's had used to wear during her act.

Tran so was about to introduce himself when he saw that the grey skin on the paunchy face and on the large, veined hands was oddly smooth and worn, and that an introduction was probably ridiculous. In some places—such as both cheeks and part of the high forehead—an underlying, woven structure showed through the dermis that was clearly non-organic. Tran so was in the company of another god. Another malfunctioning god.

"Are you the leader of these crawling deities?" Tran so said. "The *supervisor?*"

The man-god twitched and the smile widened, just an increment. "Gods?" Its voice was rough and deep.

"Yes. Like yourself."

"Me? A god? That's rich."

The eyes appeared humanlike, more human than any other god's eyes. To stare at them and know this was no man was unsettling.

"Sorry, all of us here, we're in the service industry. We're here to serve. There's no need to suck up. Please," —this, with an uneven movement of the head, addressed to the tiny subordinates that crowded the doorway—"leave us be."

The door shut quietly.

"They are creepy little spiders," said the man-god, rumbling what must have been laughter. "That's what they are!"

Now that the room was sealed, Tran so smelled the damp and mildew. Dim light came from a gooseneck lamp on the desk, which cast its greenish glow over the cream-coloured walls, the huge desktop, the crammed bookshelves. Over the god's ample paunch. The features of its face were underlit dramatically.

"Take a seat." Gesturing, with one of those plump, grey hands.

Tran so sat in a chair opposite. He was still reeling a little from whatever it was the crawling god had done to him. The chair creaked with his weight. There were pictures in golden frames on the desktop, turned so he could see them. The face of a homely woman; two homely children—boy and a girl. Tran so licked his lips. He would not say anything about the children or the ugly woman, though he was tempted; he would be cautious here.

"Call me Simon," the god said.

All this time, those eyes, though intense, had not really seemed to focus on Tran so, who even waved a hand between the two of them in a vain attempt to illicit reaction. "My name is Tran so Phengh," he said.

"And you're looking for a transfer?"

"Excuse me? A transfer?" Settling into the chair, stretching his legs. "Uh, that's right. I'm looking for a transfer."

"Good, good," Simon said. "What do you know about our

particular contribution to this grand facility?"

"Facility? I don't know what that word means, so I must say I know very little . . . Let me ask *you* a question. What do *you* know about dark gods—the giants who took me prisoner? What do you know about them? They attacked me at the bottom of Lake Seven as I talked to another supervisor, who was actually nothing like you, and then they apologized, and tried to attack me again. But I escaped."

"Ah ha! Giants? A sports fan? Me too, but the little lady isn't fond of me watching games. You know, chores to be done." Now one eye closed and opened slowly in a grotesque wink. "Sit back, young man, sit back and let me explain a little history of the nostalgia suites, and why they're such a popular destination with the guests."

"All right. Fine. But tell me what you know about the women who work here. Namely Sandra. I want to meet her again."

"Interesting." Simon chuckled. "I like applicants who ask me questions. As I said earlier, don't be shy, young man. My door is always open."

"Presently," Tran so said, "it is shut." He leaned forward. Simon's expression never changed. Was the strange deity blind? "I am married," Tran so said, "but my wife is very ill. Meeting Sandra has rekindled me. I am on a quest. Now I've met her, for the first time in ages, I feel alive. Do you know what that's like? I sincerely doubt it. And I'm not being unfaithful to my wife because the woman I loved died a long time ago . . . I don't know why I'm telling you this. Maybe it makes no sense to you . . . What do you think? Can I meet her? Do you understand what I'm saying?" He swivelled in his chair to get more comfortable. Most of the pain had faded to a dull, almost pleasant ache.

Simon, meanwhile, had apparently suffered some kind of lapse. Smiling, staring at nothing with its striking, blind eyes, a great deal of time passed before the body twitched and responded: "An interesting feature—" rumbling chuckles rose up and shook the ample belly "—are the windows. Have you heard about them? The first time I saw them I was blown away, I'll tell you."

"I know windows of time," said Tran so Phengh. "Windows of opportunity. Windows to the soul."

"Well, specifically," continued Simon, as a shiver ran down its length like maybe it was coming awake from a bad dream, if gods dreamt, or urinating, if gods pissed. "Specifically, we at the nostalgia suites are seven hundred metres beneath the crust. Yet each room has a window, we call them—that's patent pending—which can be activated, at will, to show dynamic, lifelike scenes, exactly as if the view were pumped in directly! There's a wide range of landscapes to choose from. We have the usual, of course: windswept beach; quiet glade with the occasional deer; water—"

Simon's feet suddenly slid sideways off the desk and he crashed loudly to the floor. Standing, lurching upright, like a drunk, the man-god resumed talking in the same tones—perhaps a little louder—as if nothing unusual had occurred:

"We have Fenton and Bellona! Sau Trenton in winter! Dozens to choose from! Truly astounding, truly! Surveys have told us that windows are the thing people love best about nostalgia suites. Our guests spend more time watching them than they do interacting with grams or sitting in front of plasma. Maybe they hope to see their grandfather crossing a street, or themselves, maybe, in younger days. But I *know* what they're really doing. They want to see if the images are on a loop! They can watch the windows for hours and never see the seam. The seam, my friend, doesn't exist! It does not exist!"

Tran so, who had initially been a little alarmed by Simon's movement and speech—wondering if he might be in danger of being assaulted—had relaxed once more. He said, "When I came in here and realized you were a broken god, my first thought was to rest for a while, and then, when I had a chance, smash you with something hard, maybe from behind, in the head. Now I'm not too sure why I wanted to do that. Vigor, I suppose. Hormones. But I think I can just walk out of here. You won't even raise an alarm, will you? I am not a man of violence. I seem to be slipping these past days."

Behind Tran so Phengh were bookshelves. He stood, took down a volume at random, opened it. Blank pages. He turned to Simon. "You can't help me. I do appreciate being able to hide out here for a while, and reflect, though I suppose it would have been better in the first place if you'd left me to my own devices. The dark gods that I mentioned were no longer on my trail." He dropped the book— *thud*—onto the desktop. "I think I'm in love!"

"Gods? Loves!" Simon turned, laughter wheezing now, almost obscenely. "Young man, are you aware of our health and safety policies? Are you aware of our *harassment* policies? They are paramount if you wish to work for us. Listen; take a temporary staff card from that box behind you. We can get your training started. I'll give you some brochures also. They're backordered. All the info you'll ever need to know about working for our little resort."

Simon faced the wall. There was an awkward silence.

"You know," Simon said at last, almost wistfully, "I had asked for someone to be sent up from management, to welcome new employees, but they have not responded. Budgets, I suspect. Board meetings and such."

From a box on the floor, Tran so took a badge. He placed the cord around his neck.

"So long," Simon said.

"So long," said Tran so. Carefully he pulled the door open, peeked out, and left. There were no crawling gods, only the broken clerk, waiting at the counter with its back to him.

"How do I get down?" Tran so asked.

"Down?" The clerk, who had been studying its logbook, looked around.

"Yes. To the boardrooms. To upper management."

"Simon told you to see someone? Down there?"

"Yes."

"That's *very* unusual."

"Simon says."

"Well, if you leave here, turn right, go down the hall outside—all the way to the end. Then turn left. You'll see an elevator. Past the washrooms. You can't miss it. Take it all the way to the bottom."

"An elevator?"

"That's what we like to call lift pods around here. Nostalgia suites, you see. Part of the whole package. The jargon. You'll get used to it."

"Thanks for the tip." Tran so started walking.

"Sir?"

"Yes?"

"Welcome to the team."

"Thanks . . . And sorry about the bell."

"Sir, you're going the wrong way! Elevators are to your right!"

Tran so, out in the hall, had started to trot. "I know," he shouted, over his shoulder, "but there's something I have to do first."

4. THE ANCESTORS

A steady trickle of people emerged from the smoke and slow-moving dust billows that rolled forward over the tiling. Dazed, they advanced, trancelike, towards the car. With his filthy shirt pulled up over his nose, Phister drove slowly around these refugees, in wide curves, drifting from one side of the hall to the other to avoid hitting them. Some limped, some left a trail of blood, some were so grievously wounded they should not even have been able to walk. Several sat with their backs to the wall, sleeping perhaps, too exhausted to continue. Maybe dead. Regardless of their state, all ignored him.

The air held a hint of acridity, even inhaled through the soiled fabric of his shirt. Smoke, naturally, but there was also a reek of underlying chemicals, a tangy bite at the back of his sinuses. This noxious brew was further compounded by the growing odour emanating from McCreedy's corpse, stiffening in the passenger's seat, where Phister had finally been able to wedge it. The old man's body turned greyer, curling further in on itself with each passing minute. McCreedy's cheeks were hollowed, his eyes yellow, glazed.

There was grit under the tires, grit on the walls, grit thick, hanging in the air. Unseen filtering machines hummed laboriously, sucking and blowing with little effect.

Under their patina of dust, the oncoming people were darker skinned than he, and generally taller. With black, almond-shaped eyes. And hair, of course: dark and straight. Teeth, too. Streaked and bloody and dusty, but teeth nonetheless. It was starting to seem that everyone had teeth and hair except for him and McCreedy.

Who were these people? Shades? They had continued to coalesce long after he was sure there could not possibly be more, materializing by the hundreds: families, pairs, stragglers. A father carried his child, draped limply in his arms. The child's eyes were open but unseeing. For that matter, so were the dad's. An elderly man, naked—as most were—had been splashed with blood or paint across his chest, streaked with white powder over his face.

Like all the others, he drifted quietly by.

Ghosts, Phister thought. These people are ghosts.

On this one, a horrid abdominal gash let slip a grey loop of intestine. Phister stared at the exposed innards in dismay as, stoic, the wounded man lifted red-rimmed eyes to peer beyond, down the hallway.

Phister almost attempted, for maybe the tenth time, a stab at communication, but that dusty dangling gizzard made useless words fail in his dry throat.

There were bizarre animals, too—the likes of which he could never have imagined (except in the recesses of his moss-fever dreams) that scurried, crawled, slithered, or swooped overhead, emerging, like their human counterparts, from the roiling smoke and dust. The beasts, however, met his eyes warily, and gave the car clearance.

They too were going in the opposite direction.

In the first desperate encounter with this unnerving parade— breathing fast, adrenaline coursing—Phister had shouted at the people to stop, to help him, help his friend. That was before he realized these hordes needed more help than he did, and that McCreedy was beyond all help.

But did these people not understand him? Could they not even *see* him?

Only when he heard one finally cough did he cease entertaining the uneasy idea that they all might be dead, himself included, and that he was in a new world, a necropolis, propelled there by his passenger or maybe by what the hunter had done to him.

Whatever this place was, it was certainly not home. And he told himself that he should continue, driving stubbornly onwards, deeper into the turmoil, against the flow, that turning around and driving in the same direction as the fractured humanity would be paramount to admitting time wasted, or the near-futility of his own passage, and recent decisions he had made. He remained lost. All anyone really ever sought was peace, and yesterdays that could no longer exist.

Or they were running away from something.

Perhaps the real reason he wouldn't turn the car around was that doing so would make him feel like he was heading back into a trap. Even though this level was a different one from where Cynthia's treacherous lair had been. Oh, there had been a mad flight—which was how all these adventures ended, it seemed—and he had driven, at top speed, arms around McCreedy, for a long time before frantically taking another lift pod. Down? Or had it been up? At least they had left their pursuers far behind.

Closing his eyes for a second, a whirl of blackness rushed over Phister like a vacuum, and he shuddered. Back there, on the level where McCreedy had died, there existed a monster composed of discarded and very unpleasant memories. This horrible beast, now threatening to rouse itself, licking its chops, opening one bloodstained eye, would not be as easily thrown off the trail as flesh and blood. Was it getting ready to stalk the car? The monster could only remain vague as long as Phister continued driving and did *not* turn around.

Who could have expected these silent, wounded people? These bizarre animals? Obviously fleeing a tragedy of huge proportions, one that Young Phister was, for all his illogic and inability to confront his own demons, driving straight into. From one disaster to another, Reena would have said. From the frying pan into the fire. And McCreedy? What would he have said, if he were alive?

But he wasn't. And Reena was so far away that he would never find her again.

Phister swerved the car gently past a dusty, vacant couple. The man had a headwound that should have stopped him in his tracks. The pair walked on.

No one tried to stop him. No one tried to warn him from going any farther. No one had even asked for his help. Could he run them down, if he was so inclined? Perhaps the refugees would not even try to step aside or meet his gaze as they disappeared, thudding under the tires or bouncing off the hood.

Wringing his sweaty hands on the steering wheel, Phister thought for another moment about McCreedy's sudden death, and of the nightmare fugue that had followed. He looked over at the inert body, unable to truly believe that McCreedy would never again speak, never move, never insult him.

Fumbling in the pocket of his shorts, Young Phister touched the strange brown rod he had taken from Cynthia's vest pocket. *The hunter.* Rubbing the textured surface with his thumb, he fervently hoped the ancient device might dispense advice or otherwise make him feel somewhat better; it did neither.

He had experienced no more visions—unless a blackout could be considered a vision—and he could not duplicate whatever it was that Cynthia had done to activate the device. There remained a tingling in his limbs, and he was fairly certain that the innocuous-looking tube was at least partially responsible for his current dizzied state of mind, and that it had lent him the superhuman abilities he had found inside himself to escape Cynthia's grasp—

His breath came in a great, sudden rush. He pushed his foot down on the accelerator.

"Get out of the way!" he shouted, voice muffled by his shirt. "Get out of the way!"

No one listened; he continued swerving.

Phister had told Cynthia he was not interested in being a victim of the hunter's power again, yet here he was desperate for answers that might possibly lay in that alternate place, or in that calm, resolute mind. He would put up with pain for just one more episode.

At least in that other place and mind there might be escape from the knowledge of McCreedy's death, escape from the disappearance of Crystal Max, escape from all that had happened after. From the growing reality that he would never reach home. From that bloody monster, trotting behind the car.

He shuddered again and stepped on the accelerator slightly more to gain a little distance. All he had left was his hope to one day revisit that pristine place, replace his thoughts by those in the mind he'd discovered there. He would leave crippled Young Phister behind. Leave these thoughts and doubts.

Taking his eyes off the hall to quickly study the cryptic engravings on the hunter, searching for assistance in the marks, or perhaps to learn how he had found that strength to get away from Cynthia's gang, a loud shout, from *very* nearby, startled him and he instinctively braked, pulling hard on the steering wheel and swerving, looking up just in time to see what appeared to be a small, extremely white toddler, naked, standing just a few metres in front of the wheels and waving its arms frantically as it vanished beyond the hood's line of sight.

"Shit!"

Moving sideways through the grit—McCreedy's body lurching forward in the seat—the car came to a stop.

"Not again," Phister muttered. "Not again . . ."

There had been no thump this time. Thankfully. No scream, no sickening sound of bones splintering under the wheels.

Young Phister, hands trembling, wondered if what he had seen was human, or even real.

"Hello?" Half rising from the driver's seat, he called out. The word, through the fabric of his shirt, was muted but echoed down the length of the dusty corridor. Ahead, from under a rolling tongue of thin smoke that was licking at the ceiling, materialized another dusty phantom. A man, this time. And then another. Marching, stoic, expressionless.

"Hello?" Phister's voice broke. "Hell—"

Clambering slowly up over the lip of the hood—real, but too pale, *too pale*—appeared first the small white hands, the domed head, the small torso of a young boy. Phister could only watch in horror as the naked child finally managed to pull his chubby legs up and, puffing, stood on the hood of the car. But when the toddler lifted his face to grin at Phister through the windshield, Young Phister's blood went cold: there were huge gashes on the child's neck, in three places. Flesh hung limp and grey.

"Hi yourself," the boy said. "We meet at last."

"Do I, do I know you?"

"Not really." When the boy grinned again, he showed tiny, sharp teeth. "But first let's talk about your inability to drive this thing. You should watch out, you know. You could have killed me." Those eyes were cold and green and now they turned towards McCreedy, slumped in the passenger seat. "What's up with your friend?"

Phister was dry-mouthed. He could not look away from the boy though he felt strong and growing repulsion. He said quietly, "That's McCreedy. He's dead."

"Funny." The boy's eyes flicked back towards Phister. "Me too."

There was a long pause. Fearful of what the answer might be, Phister asked, "Am I also dead?" For the idea that he was in a world of the deceased had never gone away, bursting to fruition again with the boy's sudden appearance and comments.

"Dead? You? What kind of dumbass question is that?" The gashes on the toddler's neck exposed raw gristle and dull bands of slack, lifeless muscle.

"I'm not? Then what about these people? Who are they? Are *they* dead?"

"What's the matter with you?"

"These others." With one arm Phister indicated the men, who were at that moment walking past the car. "Why are you the only one who can understand me?"

"Think I'm associated with these people? Is that what you're getting at?" The boy seemed offended. "I don't know who they are. Maybe they speak another language. How should I know?" He motioned. "What is that thing you're holding?"

Phister looked at the hunter. He had forgotten he was fondling it. He held it up.

"Can I see it?"

The boy came forward to lean against the windshield. On tiptoes he reached across to take the rod, which he turned over a few times before finally *harrumphing*. "It's empty," he said. "Who was in there?" Patches of the boy's skin were discolored, giving him a mottled look. His green eyes appeared without moisture and he did not blink nor waver his gaze.

"I beg your pardon?"

"Inside that thing. Who was inside?"

"What do you mean?"

"It's a sheath from the archives. It once contained a DNA pattern. No? A human's code was in there." The boy handed the hunter back to Phister. "Someone pretty important, too, by the looks of it. With an army of nanites, ready to roll. They were in there pretty recently, too . . . Sure you don't know who was in it?"

"Uh, no."

"Where did you get it?"

"I found it."

The boy stared for a while, not blinking. "Found it?" He tried to size Phister up. "So this dead guy, in the car. Did you bring him here so he could see a doctor? To get him fixed?"

"No. I came here by, well, by accident. I'm trying to get home. To bring him home, I guess. But I can't find my way back. What . . . *Who* are you?"

"An old friend of mine used to call me dead boy. You could call me that too."

"Dead boy?"

"Do you always repeat everything people say? It's pretty annoying. But yeah. Dead boy. 'Cause to tell the truth, I don't know what my name was when I was alive. Now I'm part of the world around you. You can call me what you want."

"How did you die?"

"I'm not sure. Gardening accident, maybe. Possibly murder."

"*Murder*?"

The leer on the boy's face was horrific. He had turned his head so that the gashes opened wide. Phister swallowed hard. *Murder.* Did the boy know what Young Phister had done to Cynthia and her cohorts? Had he been sent to make Phister answer for what had happened? But the true question was: what had really happened? Did Phister even know what he had done? Was there any way that carnage could have been real?

"Kidding," the dead boy said, and he chuckled. "Boy, you look like you could use a doctor yourself . . . I think the supervisor who reanimated me knew what had happened to the kid who owned this body, and maybe even what his name had been, but it never let me access that data."

"Reanimated?"

"Didn't I tell you that I was dead? Are you deaf? A supervisor made me into what I am today. How else do you think dead people get up and walk around? Nanites again, just like in your little tube. We might not be the same as we once were, and we might have different agendas—" that grin again "—but we can reach out and touch someone."

Phister recoiled from the pudgy hand.

"Of course, the main problem is we have to go for regular treatments to stop these damn corpses from falling apart. So now that the supervisor who sponsored me has stopped responding . . ." Seeing the expression on Phister's face, the dead boy said, "Look. I'll give you a crash course in reanimation. As an ex-person, I play host to an army of tiny machines that keep this body moving and working and stop it decaying too much. These tiny little machines do the bidding of, well, of the world. They're emissaries, you might say. So basically I work for the network. Understand?"

"No."

"I know what you're thinking. You're thinking: if he's being run by a million nanites, then why don't they do something about those big ugly cuts?"

"That's not what I was thinking."

"My supervisor used to call them *affectations*. And I guess they are. You see, I do have a *little* bit of free will. I like these gashes." With one hand he slapped at the flaps of skin. "What can I say? I like the effect they have on people. Anyhow, all those little guys inside me are starting to lose the battle now that Sam has powered down. So you see why I'm here."

"Uh . . . No. I don't."

"For goodness sake! You're on the medical level; I need a lift. It's perfect. And when we do find a doctor, we can get it to look at him too—your friend. If you want. Maybe even at you. Although it seems that now might not be the best time to become reliant upon the infrastructure, if you know what I mean." A knowing wink.

Everyone spoke in riddles. Phister was utterly baffled. "McCreedy doesn't need a doctor," he explained. "He needs a funeral."

"A funeral! That's a good one!" Chuckling, the dead boy reached up to take hold of the windshield's frame. As he tried to scale the sloped plastic, his feet found no purchase; they left twin, damp trails through the thick dust gathered there.

Again, Phister did not want to touch the boy's hand, at least not until it was waved right under his nose and the dead boy asked explicitly several times for help. So when Phister did grab the tiny extremity, to help hoist the boy up, he felt cold and undeniable proof that the dead boy had told the truth about his status. Phister pulled (half expecting to remove the arm from its socket), and the child managed to scramble up and over, leaping clumsily from the frame to land heavily next to Phister, nearly falling into McCreedy's lap. The dead boy had seemed much heavier than any toddler should ever be, and his stench was like the cleanser that periodically washed over the floors back home, seeping from tiny holes in the base of the walls.

Settling between McCreedy and Young Phister, the dead boy said, "Yeah, so, thanks for picking me up and finally getting the jist of what I was talking about. For a minute there, I was beginning to think you were a total idiot."

"No. But I'm kind of . . . I'm going through a lot right now."

"Who isn't? Seriously, you could have the doctor install a sense of humour in you."

Phister drove. Another person, up ahead. At least the smoke seemed to be thinning. After a moment, Phister said, "Really, though, who do you think these people are?"

"My guess? Probably escapees from a lab."

Which also made no sense to Phister.

They drove past this most recent addition to the macabre parade—a middle-aged woman this time. Phister saw a nasty cut over one of her eyes. Half her face was crusted with dried blood. She walked past as if the car did not exist—

The dead boy, meanwhile, poked at McCreedy with one finger. "Or, I don't know," he said, "maybe their city is gone. The dispossessed. Doesn't explain why they're so out of it."

"Please stop touching him."

Turning toward Phister, "There have been collapses." Up close, an odd timing to the boy's words, a twist to his bloodless lips that should have slurred the sounds he made but did not, as if they could have been uttered even if the dead boy kept his mouth closed the whole while. And his cold green stare, levelled from just a few centimetres away, was much more eerie and unsettling than it had been from the hood of the car. "I did learn that much about the collapses before I was cut off. Seems that parts of the world are folding in on themselves. Reacting to the wound. Shutting down."

"Wound? The world's wounded? It's *shutting down*?"

"Parts of it are, bud. That's what I think. There was a place I heard about, Tianna, that was virtually crushed between two levels when the levels above and below sort of, well, *merged*."

Tianna. That name was familiar. Phister recalled a fleeting image of a red-haired girl. He knew what her lips had felt like against his own, and how they had tasted. And he recalled her low, rough laugh and knew the way her neck smelled faintly of cloves when he buried his face in the warmth there. Softly, he said, "Tianna . . .?"

"Tianna. Yeah. It was a city."

"A city . . ."

The dead boy had become impatient. "What's a damned city? Is that what you're saying?"

"Uh . . ."

"What is the fucking matter with you? I'm supposed to be the dead one here."

Phister shook his head in an attempt to clear it. "I came up from the basement. Apparently. I left there just a few days ago, so all this is, uh, new to me."

"Are you from Public Works?"

Phister glanced over, frowning. "Yeah. I guess so. Because that's what the car says, anyhow, when it's plugged in. The Department of Public Works."

"You don't wear much of a uniform. You could pass for a guest. But no guest would ever go to the basement."

"Why not?" Phister was patriotically offended.

"Because there's nothing there. Just sewage that glows in the dark and pipes and flying rats." The dead boy touched his esophagus with two fingertips, as if adjusting it. "You know, you really shouldn't be afraid of me." He leaned in closer, his pale face right next to Phister's, and though there was no hint of breath from his mouth, his halitosis was enough to make Phister gag. "I'm your friend. We're on the same side."

"I'm not afraid of you," Phister said. "It's just that I did something recently. Something terrible. Something I can't quite remember and that I'm not really, well, not really capable of."

"You did something you're not capable of?"

"I'm pretty sure."

"How can anyone do anything they're not capable of?"

"I was being threatened, see? There was a group of people. They were the ones that, well, they told me they weren't going to let me go. So I got mad. I think I blacked out because I don't really remember what happened next, just little flashes. When I came to, they were hurt. Bad. One was a girl. But I think she was really something else. So yeah, there was a fight, and I—" Here came that monster, loping down the hall, slavering behind the car with claws out. Terrified, Phister could not continue his explanation; in the silence, the dead boy did not press the issue.

When he did speak again, his voice was soft, almost wistful. "Tianna," he said, "was once a place where a lot of people lived. And now it's gone. Just like that . . ."

"Are ceilings going to fall on our heads?"

"I don't know."

"Cynthia said—" Mentioning the name brought another quick image of blood pooling on the floor, and of an arm, bent in too many places. She had been face down, inert . . . But she had wanted to interfere. He could not let her do that. "Plus, uh, plus I actually saw soldiers. Several of them. Being made. I saw them. In the warehouse."

The dead boy rubbed at his cheek with one hand. Skin there moved like putty, and when he took his fingers away, the skin slowly resumed its place. "The warehouse, huh? You sure get around. You've seen stuff I only ever dreamed of. Literally." He laughed. "Now I wanna try and explain something to you. About what's going on. You know how a living body manufactures white blood cells when there's an infection, right? Or when there's a parasite?"

"No."

"Shit. You don't know that? Well it does. In self-defense. The world is reacting the same way. Because there was a breach, and something, or things, came in. So now it's trying to defend itself. Yeah, sure there's soldiers. They're security. White blood cells. But you see, without the network, everything has gone nuts—the process is not working very smoothly, to say the least. I guess this had to happen, sooner or later. Everything has a lifespan. The world is no exception." The boy continued to stare.

"Why you telling me this?"

"Oh come on. For your own interest, I guess." He smiled and, thankfully, faced front.

"What's going to happen now, dead boy?"

"I can't tell the future. Can you? I just want to be around long enough to see another morning. Maybe another one after that, if I'm lucky." Now the cold hand reached up to fall upon Phister's elbow, at the wheel. "We don't have too much time left. Personally, I'm starting to rot. I'm literally losing my mind."

"Sorry to hear that." Erupting directly between Phister's eyes came a sharp, throbbing pain. He groaned and shook free from the child's weak grip; the pain diminished.

"Now then," the boy said, "if we find a doctor, will you have your assistant reanimated?"

Phister managed to catch his breath. He was about to say that McCreedy was not his *assistant* but when he opened his mouth to speak he instead found himself mumbling, "Yes." Waning pain continued to twist and churn inside his head.

The dead boy chuckled. "That's good. Turn left here."

They turned. The hall narrowed and was much cleaner here; Phister lowered the wet dirty shirt from his mouth and breathed his aching lungs full. He picked dust from his clogged nostrils with a bitten thumbnail. Because there was less grit on the floor he realized how much rumbling sound the tires made previously, in the main corridor.

Several closed doors, either side. Red crosses on each.

The dead boy gave a few more directions. The car turned left, right, reversed once, turned some more corners. The hall continued to narrow, until it was hardly wider than the car itself. They encountered no more people. The smoke had gone, also, though the air still smelled of fire. Eventually the nose of the car came up against a barrier blocking further travel and Phister looked at the boy expectantly; there was no way to continue other than to back up and take another route. Phister suspected that the trap had been sprung, that the monster would catch up now, that the final resolution to his ills would kick in. The ride was over.

But the dead boy appeared genuinely baffled. "That's odd. I don't think this wall should be here. I consulted the online map just last night. That wall *really* should not be there."

"It looks new," Phister observed, feeling knowledge not his own creep into his mind and hide surreptitiously there. He turned to the dead boy and saw that the boy was staring at him again, but for the first time since meeting him, the boy appeared to be the frightened child he must once have been. So Phister said, "Everything will be all right, kid. I'm sure of it. Don't worry."

"We don't have time for this. Why don't we just come clean with each other? Just tell me why this damn wall grew here. Tell me!"

"I don't know," Phister said, and for the next moment he looked about the cul-de-sac, unable to understand where he was, or why, or how he had got there. When he at last dimly recalled his situation, he forgot who the people were with him in the vehicle, and why, of all things, they were both dead. Staring sidelong at the pair—comprised of a tiny, ambulatory toddler's corpse and the body of a very grey, puffy old man in cap and gloves—he dismounted slowly.

There was barely room to stand. As his feet touched the floor, power surged through his body and he knew he could have picked the car up and tossed it like a toy, if there had been room. Stepping forward, he laid his hands on the pristine wall of the dead end. Voices whispered, making him shudder, and briefly he closed his eyes so that the ghosts would leave him alone.

Cynthia had said she was going to kill him. Stop him. But he had so much work to do. He'd been asleep for a long time. The two little guys rushed him first while Cynthia watched, arms folded—

Some plans are bigger than lives. His arms came up of their own accord, powerful. A windpipe collapsed easily in each fist.

Seconds later, he sprinted after the fleeing girl, who seemed about to lift off—

He opened his eyes. There was a tiny panel, set within the pristine wall: creases delineated its presence. Touching the cool surface with his fingers—led to it by something other than his own will—he told the dead boy, "This wall is a safety feature. To deal with the fire."

Flicking open the tiny panel exposed a numbered keypad. Touch buttons, from one to sixteen. These he regarded for a moment before rapidly pressing out a combination. The wall rose up into the ceiling with a soft hiss.

Beyond lay exposed a large chamber, lit by a ruddy hue, which the smooth floor inside reflected. He blinked and, rubbing at the bridge of his nose—without another comment—got back into the car.

"I know how you did that," the dead boy whispered.

"Huh? Did what? Open that? It was a lucky guess."

The dead boy said, "Look. I know what's going on here. It's no accident that we met. Let me help you. Your friend's out of commission for a while."

Phister declined to comment and drove forward into the great chamber. Their reflections shimmered under them as if they were on a boat, crossing a river. On placid waters. The dead boy, who was not nearly as mesmerized by the wondrous sights as Phister—more intent was he upon Phister himself—shook Phister by the sleeve. "Listen. Are you listening to me? We've got more in common than you think. Do you realize that now? I know what's going on. I figured it out. Do you know who you are?"

This question he could not answer. Because he was busy dreaming. He shook his head. *No. I don't know. Who am I?* Was that the question? Well, Young Phister, that's all. Wasn't that right? Who else could he possibly be? Just Young Phister, lost in the world, trying to get home. Young Phister, who had recently fought a pair of identical dwarfs, tossing them aside as if they were dolls, and then fought a woman who was not a woman, so beautiful that he nearly wept at the elusive memory of hurling her aside as if she weighed nothing.

Just Young Phister, within whose head a layout of all these

rooms, corridors, and chambers was currently being mapped.

He muttered, "They wanted to stop me . . ."

Stretching along one entire wall of the chamber, as they drove adjacent to it—as far as he could see—was a series of bodies, each trapped inside its own coffin-like cabinet. Men and women both, naked, twined with tubes and wires, each resting inert under a translucent cover.

There were hundreds of them.

The car cruised silently past.

Immersed in a milky fluid, the bodies appeared to be sleeping. Next to each cabinet, a panel of dimly lit numerals pulsed. He caught a quick glimpse of a woman—slim, with great, floating red hair—so familiar that he nearly stopped the car, nearly called out to her, but her name did not come to his tongue.

Voices whispered. Were *these* people whispering to him? Moans blew like wind through his body, through his veins. *He knew these people*. He said, "You are my flesh . . ."

And the dead boy said, "I don't know about that, pal, but here comes the doc."

At first, when Phister looked to his right, across the open floor (more cabinets of bodies out there, against the far wall), he expected to see a man riding in the very strange car that was quickly approaching, but as the vehicle neared he could see no passenger within, nor even a place for one, and he came to understand that the speeding car was not a car at all—at least not like the one he was driving—but yet another sort of machine, one with numerous limbs and tools bristling out every which way. The oncoming car was, in fact, the doctor.

Frantic appendages flapped, clattering like a chime, and wheels slid on the tiled floor. The doctor blared in a tinny voice, "You can't be in here! Stop! Stop!"

Phister said, "My two friends here need to see you. They're both dead. It's quite urgent."

"Urgent? There are contaminants in the air! There is smoke, and a fire. How did you get in?" The doctor had slowed and was pacing them, wheels almost touching. Its motor pinged loudly and the numerous thin arms and spindly growths—the low-slung body had thirty or forty emaciated elbows poking up all over its back—moved and rang together almost hypnotically.

"You must present me with identification. We have been vandalized recently and—"

"Listen to me!" The dead boy stood up, holding onto the windshield's frame to steady himself. "Listen. What's left of the network has been fried. Understand? There was a breach in the sky. Do you understand me, doc? My supervisor and manager— SAM Fourteen—of Plantation Level, has gone offline. Like your boss probably has. I've been trying to tell this guy here but he's got problems of his own. He says he's from Public Works but he's in transition now. You have to help us."

"I'll need a work order."

"I'm giving you one!" The dead boy's shout was raspy and echoed down the length and breadth of the vast chamber. "Didn't you sign an oath or something? We need your help! The world needs your help! I just told you the supervisors have gone offline. And you're looking at your new boss anyhow. This guy right here! He's going to save all of us!"

Phister raised one eyebrow and glanced across at the doctor— who was still driving alongside—before turning his attention back to the faces trapped behind the curved covers. He was listening to their hissed and quiet tales of loves lost. Tales of children being born, of personal triumphs, of tragedies. He said, "These people are my ancestors. My descendants. They're my team."

The doctor replied, "I guess he should be my first priority." It gestured towards Phister. "You there, have you had those wounds looked at?"

"Wounds? What wounds?"

"You'd better stop. Let me take your temperature."

An appendage at the end of one of the multi-jointed limbs

clanked around within the others, knocking together with a sound like a sweet song and eventually emerging, extending towards Phister's car, toward Young Phister, who saw this coming in his peripheral vision.

"Sir," the doctor called. "You there, at the wheel, please stop driving."

But Phister was excited by the first clear thought he'd had in over a day. He said, "I know how to wake these people! I *do*. And I know why we came here— Hey, get that thing away from me!" Shoving aside the cantilevered arm was easy yet it came at him again and again and he had to deflect it each time. "Get out of my face!"

Phister accelerated; the doctor, for whatever reason, did not give chase, and soon dwindled behind.

"He was going to help us," the dead boy said. "I don't want to die again. Please turn this thing around."

They coasted for another few moments in the silence of the huge room. Although Phister still heard those whispering voices. Now he saw where several of the tanks had been smashed, their fluids released, bodies slumped and grey. He smelled decay. There was a panel where components had clearly been broken into. He said, "That's my archive . . ."

The dead boy had not heard him. He gestured toward the inert bodies rushing past. "You know, I once knew a girl obsessed with these people. She wanted to know what they were like, did they pull their pants on one leg at a time, what did they speak like, what did they think. She was always asking my boss questions. Me, I played dumb. Sam would answer as best he could, even though his memory was spotty. He had a crush on this girl, you see. She *was* pretty hot, I'll admit that. Then me and him came up with this plan . . . He did actually. Oh, it was a terrible idea, in retrospect. But we concocted this . . . aroma. Based it on what moths use to attract each other but then the breach happened and this stuff got into the air. And everything broke loose. You coming back, the security . . . That girl was my only friend and I deceived her. For which I feel eternally guilty." He made a snorting sound that echoed through the slices on his neck. "Hey, are you even listening to me?"

"I hear you."

"All right. So come on. Turn this car around, Phister. I've got about three hours left, tops, and I don't think you've got much more."

But now, truthfully, Young Phister was no longer able to hear the dead boy. And because he could no longer see where he was going either, he was forced to slow the car down to a crawl. But he did not turn the car around.

The last dim thought Young Phister had was that he had never introduced himself to the dead boy, so how did the dead boy know his name? But when his old name was repeated for a third time, he turned slowly, very slowly, to face the tiny passenger, who was still shaking him by the arm. He whispered, "Let go of me. I don't know anybody by that name."

DEIDRE, BEYOND

Variation on a recurring dream: caterpillars of several large species covering her, mostly those of moths. Writhing slowly over her legs, arms, belly, and chest. Tangled, struggling in her hair. They touched every conceivable place of her body except for her mouth, nose, and half-closed eyes. Larval insects surrounded her absolutely. Sometimes they were of glossy black scarabs, or blues and skippers and delicate fritillaries. Arachnids, even (though these were not truly insects).

Tiny, suctioned legs puckered, plucking at her skin. The rasp of mouthpieces grazed her flesh.

Under cover of the slowly seething mass, she was as naked as the day she'd been born. She smiled.

Actually, Deidre had never seen live caterpillars before. Not while awake. Only pictures of them, in illustrated printouts; Sam created all moths directly in their adult phase. So it was with great interest that she studied these dream-caterpillars. The majority of them—ranging vastly in size and colour, from pale greenish to a dull brown, some hairy, some with eyespots on the abdomen and, in a few cases, with tiny, erect tails quivering on the last segment—looked exactly like those in her pictures.

The moderately unpleasant sensation of caterpillars upon her flesh, when compared to the horrid emotions she'd experienced in the dreams preceding this one, were relatively benign. In other, nastier dreams, there had been blood, pain, and death.

A shudder passed through her.

Soon she would wake up. The carpet of caterpillars would vanish; the suns would come on; her beloved kin would be together, in Elegia. Like they were after any nightmare.

The first thing she would do upon waking would be embrace her father—who had surely just rushed into her bedchamber, after hearing her cries—and, maybe at breakfast, she would take the time to go around the table and kiss each of her sisters on the cheek, even if Miranda protested the unwarranted embrace and the older two scoffed and tried to turn away.

Imagining this in the dream, Deidre smiled again. Honestly, how could she have ever believed that the Orchard Keeper would send his family into exile? Or that a hole in the roof could open? That she alone, of all people, would be carried up *out of it*? By an angel, no less!

Absurd.

To blame for this disturbing series must have been the spicy stew Lady had prepared for dinner, and the reason for this particular sequence was that she had asked Sam about making Lunas, and the larger Sphinxes, and had thought, just before the gram's strange appearance, about metamorphic cycles. For everything there is a reason. Action, and reaction. Cause and effect.

Memories of her cozy canopy bed gave her the assurance she

needed to wait patiently for this intrusion of caterpillars to filter out of her mind. After all, dreams cannot hurt you.

Then a voice, quite like her father's, said something she did not catch.

"Pardon me?" Deidre's own words did not come out as clearly as she would have liked; more like a moan than anything intelligible; she felt her dry lips move.

"You're conscious. Good. And you can hear me? You understand what I'm saying?"

"Yes," Deidre said, twitching, because the caterpillar nuzzling her left nipple had begun to do something almost painful. Goodness, her mouth was very dry. "Is there a war coming, father? Please, is there another war coming?"

"Um." After a long moment—Deidre might have slipped back into sleep, if she was ever awake—the voice said, "I'm afraid I'm not your father . . . But I got the language right, and on the second attempt. Pretty good, eh? Of all the ancient tongues!"

Deidre was growing confused. But her smile slowly returned. This was more dream nonsense. Soon she would be awake for real. There would be sense and order. She felt herself rising up, right now, toward sanity, toward morning, toward her diurnal life and family. Again, this certainty gave her the confidence and ability to playfully indulge the dream voice. "If you're not my dad," she said, "then who are you?"

"That isn't important. An amalgam, a custodian. What's your name?"

"Deidre."

"That's a pretty name, Deidre. Exotic. Ancient. Listen, Deidre, I want to stress something to you. You're going to be *all right*."

"I know. I'm waking up." She licked her lips but her tongue caught on the hot skin.

"Yes. That's true . . . Though you were wounded in the retrieval operation. My little friends have almost finished their job. No permanent damage. And, like you said, you're almost awake. I'm *most* relieved."

Deidre became slightly concerned by these comments; the voice had referred to her being *wounded*, which had occurred in the exceedingly horrid *first* dream, the dream of angels, of Mingh straw's death.

Now the unpleasantness of what the larvae were doing to her became harder to ignore. She squirmed. Pinch yourself, Deidre thought, but the masses of caterpillars weighed down heavily upon her arms. Now the pain at her shoulder—where the angel's talons had gripped—was *tremendous*.

A scream bubbled up through her and she let it out— "Eeeeeeaghhhh . . ."—trying to thrash, to kick out.

"Calm down, Deidre, please! *Calm down!*"

She lay panting. Above her was a pale, lit ceiling.

"I'm dismissing them," the voice said, "it's all right, Deidre, you're going to be all right. They've done their job, it's over. Don't freak out."

Deidre had built up strength in her lungs to scream again but the larvae were on the move, leaving her flesh, marching off her body and onto the surrounding mattress. So she just drew a deep, shuddering breath.

This place was not her room. Here was no canopy bed.

She managed to sit up partially, propped on her elbows, watching in horrified fascination as the numerous creatures—still very much there, *real*, and alive—reached the rim of the platform she had been lying flat on and, with gentle plops, fell into numerous holes spaced around the perimeter.

She looked around. The room was small. That pale ceiling, just a few metres overhead. White, almost shimmering walls. A closed door to her left, no knob, an odd symbol embossed upon it.

Next to her hummed a delicate machine. Quivering, on an equally delicate stand. She regarded this device with growing fear; her father had a similar one in his private lab, where he sometimes tinkered and repaired staff. It was a gadget meant to keep the body alive and functioning while he operated, opening them up and poking around inside. Several attachments, resting in cradles or clips on the side. A cable, leading out of sight, reappearing to snake up over the platform, coil over her left leg, up her belly—

She yanked the cable away and when she touched the painful area above her ear where it had been taped, she felt warm liquid trickling. A patch, shaved on her head.

She whispered, "What have you done to me?"

And the spindly machine said, almost as quietly, "Not yet, girl, not yet. Now you've done it, silly."

There was no one else in the room. She looked at the wound in her shoulder. Where it should have been, the skin was covered by a light dusting of whitish fuzz. Her instinct was to rub the fuzz away but she shied from the agony that would most likely ensue. She did not want to confirm that she had been hurt. That would make it all real.

The caterpillars were gone.

Lifting her face, she detected an *absence* of smell in the air. This was the most unsettling thing so far. She filled her lungs with cleanliness and sterility and understood, without a doubt, that she had left the world and all she had known behind.

The dreams *had* been real.

Angels brought her to this place.

"Where am I?" she asked, horrified.

"A seed terminal." The disembodied voice came from all around, as if from the clean air itself. "But please, don't panic again. It's no good for either of us."

Initially, upon waking, Deidre had pictured a man speaking, but now, she realized, she was picturing a woman. Did the voice emanate from some form of free-floating gram? There appeared no light source to support this idea. And even if a drifting gram were possible, a beam of light would be needed to keep it going. So who or what was talking? *A ghost?* "What is a seed terminal?"

"Not just any seed terminal! *The* seed terminal! *Mine*. I'm the

201

one lucky enough to host you. All the others are fading away, right now, as we speak. Across the planet. All those little versions of myself, sad and disappointed, shrivelling up inside."

"How long have I been here?"

"Not too long, Deidre. A few hours. Those little worms are very efficient. Now, you need to get your strength up. You'll be leaving shortly."

Deidre said, "They're not worms. They're moth larvae."

"Moth larvae? Is that what they were? I'll have to take your word for it. I don't know much about these things."

She swung her legs off the bed, trying to ignore the pain that jolted up to her shoulder. Since the source of the voice and the tones it spoke in did not remain constant, all she could be sure of was that whatever spoke was invisible, intangible.

"Are you sure you feel well enough to get out of bed?"

"I'm leaving. Right now."

"Leaving? Ah, leaving . . . I see. Well, that might not be so simple. Nor is it advisable. Even if you could leave . . . Deidre, there's no place for you to go."

"I'm going *home*." But attempting to take a step, Deidre discovered she could not lift her tingling feet and that her knees were too weak to hold her weight. Grasping the edge of the platform, buttocks resting on it, she said, through gritted teeth, "What were those larvae doing to me anyhow? Working on my wounds?"

"Yes. Very astute, child. *Very*. But please, if you insist on moving about, let me assist. At least, let me help you into the courtyard."

The door before her slid open silently, letting in an organic yellow glow that fell over her, covering her body from head to toe with warmth. Subtly hinted scents also entered with it; she breathed them in, making her feel somewhat less tense. Blinking (and sneezing, which hurt like heck!), she did manage a faltering step.

Out there—if she could trust her senses—was a *garden*. She saw thin columns of light, moving through what looked like branches, and real leaves that winked in at her lasciviously.

"Where are my clothes?"

"They had to be cut away, Deidre."

"Then give me something else to wear."

"There's no one here to see you. There is no need for clothes."

"I *want clothes*."

"I might be able to conjure up a robe, I guess. I have very limited matter to work with."

"*Do it.*"

To retain the momentum of her decision to get up, she took a step, and another, breathing in sharply with each movement, walking forward gingerly until she had reached the doorway. Pausing, one hand on the smooth jamb, glancing about for any creatures that might be watching or hunting her, she saw that she was, indeed, at the threshold to a garden.

A path led between lush growths either side, ending at a nearby fountain, whose sparkling waters caught the light and chattered at her softly, as if laughing at her concern. The lawns were clipped, the bushes and trees all around well maintained. Her father would have been proud. In fact, this quiet place was so much like the gardens of Elegia that Deidre harboured a momentary hope she might actually be *home*, or that she might yet wake up from this final dream, but when she looked skyward and could not see the familiar suns, suspended from their cradles, nor the sky they hung from, her hopes were dashed.

Instead, overhead, a single reddish orb glared down at her, set against a pale cerulean that appeared infinite, with no visible walls or boundaries . . .

She looked away. Afterimages, burned onto her retinas, eventually faded from her vision. What she had also seen, just above the treetops, was unmistakably a shimmering barrier.

She was in a cage.

That voice, almost whispering in her ear now, said, "Do you like it, Deidre? We made this just for you."

"I do not," Deidre said. And then, because she could not help herself, "I want my mom. And I want to see my dad. He's an Orchard Keeper, you know. He can have your head on a platter, so you'd better arrange for me to go home. You better let me go. You'd better."

"Deidre, that isn't possible. Your biological, uh, parents, they remain inside."

"Inside? Inside what? Where are they?" Through the trees she saw two of the horrid angels now, flying high beyond the barrier, and she cowered. "Can they get in?"

"Who? Your mother and father? No, they . . . Oh, I see. Those creatures. No. They can't get in. You're safe here. And Deidre, I want to make this very clear. It was never our intention to harm you. The creatures were instructed to go in and retrieve you with *no* injuries whatsoever."

"They are monsters."

"I'm sorry to hear you say that, Deidre. They were all we had to work with. But you're here now, you're healthy, and you're perfect. That's all that counts."

"I've been kidnapped. I'm in a cage."

"No. The seed terminal is not a cage. It's here to *protect* you. It's large enough to roam around in freely. I'm sure the accommodations will meet your approval. Conditions outside are arid and hot, to say the least. All the provisions you'll ever want are in here. The water in the fountain is real, enriched, filtered. There is food, produced by a cabinet behind the bed . . .

"We have two days to kill, Deidre. All I ask in the interim is that you stay calm and hear me out. Will you do that? Please?"

"You really expect me to stay here for two days? With you? You're crazy." But the warmth of the odd red sun—if that single orb overhead could be considered a sun—made Deidre feel drowsy. And her feet throbbed. So she set off, hobbling down the path towards the fountain. A bench was shadowed there, under overhanging leaves. "All right, voice," she said, "here's your chance. Tell me why I'm here."

"You were hurt, Deidre."

"I *know* that! But *why*?" She took a deep breath to calm herself. "Anyhow, it was you that hurt me!"

"Not me, Deidre. *Them.* The locals. The monsters, as you called them."

"They work for you. You said that. Therefore you're responsible."

"We had to get you out. The operation was a success."

"What's become of Elegia? My family?"

"Everything you refer to still exists. There is trouble there, I'll grant you that. Trouble we didn't count on, but for now everything exists."

Deidre had reached the bench. Exhausted, she sat down carefully, feeling immediate relief. She closed her eyes briefly, then stood again to plunge both hands into the cold water, letting it run through her fingers and splash deliciously up her arms for a moment before bringing her hands to her face and wetting her skin. She drank deeply from her cupped palms and sat back down, dripping from her chin and hair and cheeks and feeling another fraction of a degree better.

"I'm still leaving," she said. "I'll sit for a while, get a little stronger, but I am getting out of this cage. Have you found anything for me to wear yet?"

"I'm working on it."

There were no birds to be seen or heard. No animals, no insects, no small mammals. Just like home. She would like to see a moth, or even a beetle, scurrying along the ground. If this place were truly just for her, as the voice had said, insects should have been added.

Maybe the larvae had been a concession in that direction? Had they only appeared to her as she'd seen them, because she was familiar with caterpillars?

Now that she thought about it, the layout of this place, down to the fountain and the bench she sat on, could have been lifted straight out of childhood memories.

What would Mingh straw's cage have looked like, had the girl lived, and been the one brought here? What did this place really look like under the veil of illusion she was sure the voice cast over it?

"Talk to me, voice." She tried to stave off the recalled image of Mingh straw's terrible fall. Light played through her lashes. "Explain everything to me."

"Okay. For the first part, you'll have to look. I'm going to show you something, if you can stay awake."

"I wasn't sleeping." She opened her eyes; before her was a crude gram. Through it, the fountain sparkled. Drops set the image quivering. Whatever the source might be of *this* illusion it was very high, somewhere above the treetops or even above the barrier itself. From the infinite blue? Deidre moved from side to side to focus better on the projection, but what the blurred gram depicted, or even what scale it might be, she could not tell. Some large lumpy growth? A convoluted mound? The reception was atrocious. A living thing? Yet there were hard edges, hints of construction. A tumourous machine, resting on a fairly smooth surface.

Was it a skin lesion, magnified by a million? The only visible result of a parasite, buried subcutaneously?

It bristled with numerous whiskers—some thin as threads, others fatter, hollow, emitting something that looked like smoke or steam or other gas—jutting up at various angles. Around the base, apertures slowly vomited forth slag or maybe pus that rolled glutinously and appeared to gradually harden. The configurations altered, adjusted, settled.

If this thing *was* a machine, it had a form of autonomy and had mutated in ways surely unfathomable to its inventor. Expanding in different, unpredicted directions of its own accord, the randomness of components betrayed no logic of singular design.

And if alive? Then its tortured shape had been created by a lunatic, in a lunatic's lab, and should be put to death immediately.

"What is it?" she whispered.

Movements glimmered like dull sparks. Detail was occluded. She squinted. Were there fans turning in there? Yes, those were fans. Hundreds of them.

"This is where you lived," the voice said. "The structure you lived in. This was taken over the past few weeks."

Indignant, Deidre said, *"That* is not my home. I never lived *there.*"

"Allow me to clarify, Deidre. Where you lived is being looked at here from, well, from high above. You've never seen your home from this perspective. Of course, we can't see the inside from this angle. But wait . . ."

As if suddenly diving, the vantage of the gram moved, swooping closer to the cancerous buboes and then rapidly among their folds, coming in to corkscrew dizzyingly between the stacks, past tense guy wires and massive sails that turned slowly in unfelt winds, past those fans she had spotted earlier and then through them too, between the blades, past other devices that looked like buildings and others that looked like creatures watching her, past growths that might have been heaped feces and past numerous other protrusions whose functions she could not imagine nor ever wished to, all whipping up at her so swiftly she had to grip the bench with both hands to fight the vertigo—

The rushing sensation slowed; the gram steadied; she could breathe again. Her grip relaxed.

"There," the voice said.

"What am I looking at?" These words leaked out of her, like a breath. She wanted to vomit. The unpleasant belief that truths were being presented to her, and that larger, even more profound truths were coming, had settled in.

"See the dark spot?" the voice asked, whispering in her ear from nowhere. "See it? Right beneath you, as it were?"

She did see it. There it was: dark spot against a field of static grey. Malignant. An ugly hole. She tried to peer beyond the darkness but vapour puffed out from the aperture, a quick burst that made her recoil, as if she might possibly catch a whiff of the gas or feel the exhalation on her skin. "I see it."

"That's where you came from. That's the hole we impelled the creatures to make. We brought you up, out of there."

Like a black fleck on a portion of exposed skull, she thought.

And through it? Inside that monstrosity? What? Her home? Her parents? Everything she had known and loved?

"Are you all right, Deidre? Your vitals show stress."

"No kidding." She leaned forward now, hoping again to change the perspective, to see the beauty in there that had once been her life. "You're telling me this is my world? This thing is my world?"

"You're looking at the uppermost part of where you lived. The part that lies *above*ground. Where you live—or where you lived, rather—is under the surface."

"Under?"

"Yes. Precisely. You lived inside an ancient artifact, under the crust of this planet. We learned of its existence recently. You see, we thought the entire planet was dead."

"This is the surface? Here? What's up here?"

"Not much. Mostly desert. And those flying creatures, of course. There are a few tribes of people trying to get by, but their genes are ruined, useless for our purposes. I don't even think you'd recognize them as your own species if you saw them. I dare say they could not tie their shoes, if they ever wore any, let alone make the staggering connections you've made since you've been here."

"Others? Like me?"

"Trust me, Deidre, they are nothing like you. You are *perfect*."

"Don't patronize me." She looked up at that bleary red orb, flickering through the leaves. The air seemed to make a slight humming sound. "Do you call that a sun?"

"It's a star. But yes, it is our sun."

"And my ancestors, the people who built my world, they came from up here? They all lived up here, once, on the surface?"

"Yes, Deidre . . . For the record, I'm not patronizing you. I truly am astounded by your observations . . . I have to admit that I was expecting a *much* more difficult time explaining things to you. I was ill prepared for your intelligence . . . And, frankly, Deidre, for your physical perfection."

Deidre chose to ignore the disturbing implications of this.

"I still don't understand. Where did they all go?"

"Who?"

"Everybody. My ancestors. Obviously, they must've been able to tie their shoes at one point."

After a moment, the voice replied: "Most of the people passed away. Fewer and fewer viable children. Ruination of the habitat. That sort of thing. Same old story. A few escaped. But the point is Deidre, humanity left behind a *refuge*. Buried under the surface, in a forgotten resort, of all places, they left behind a genetic gold mine."

"Why did you get angels to make the hole? Why didn't you do it yourself?"

"Angels?"

"The things that came in for me."

"Angels? That's an interesting name for them . . . Regardless, the question is another excellent one. And the answer is, in fact, quite simple. I have no hands, Deidre. At least, not here. Not *now*. You see, after discovering the underground trove, as it were, we seeded the planet from afar with these terminals, hundreds of programs, just like me, and we released, on a probe, the buds that eventually attached themselves to the, uh, angels, for training purposes. But, physically, my hands exist elsewhere. Else*when*. All we could do is wait for their signal, and get ready to activate the seed terminal that they brought you to.

"Angels are common here. They're able, with the proper amount of coaxing, to perform menial tasks. So they became our hands . . . Though I must say, I don't know what took them so long once they had broken through. We were frantic with concern. We thought we'd miss the window of opportunity."

"They built a nest."

"What? A *nest*?"

She looked away, into the trees, wondering if they were real or if she only imagined them to look like trees. "What are you planning to do to me?"

"Liberate you, Deidre! Destiny has deemed that we shall soon meet. In a mere two days, we shall be here—for a moment, against all odds, *together*, in time and in physical space. We'll meet, my dear. We'll meet. We're coming to collect you."

Impossible to ignore the undertone this time. Even the strange sun above her had suddenly chilled. "You let me out of here," she said. "You let me go home."

"I can't do that, Deidre."

The gram depicting her world crackled and vanished, only to reappear, for a second, clear and defined before fading again to a blur.

"I can't release you. Discovering you has assured our future, Deidre. The future of our species. We *need* you. You'll never know what you mean to us. To our future. As humans. You are the savior of our race."

Tears stung Deidre's eyes. She turned her head. "You can't be human. Please. Let me out of here. Let me see my family again. I'll do anything . . ."

"I'm so sorry to make you sad, Deidre."

After a long while, she asked, "Why me?"

"Luck," said the voice. "And I'm also sorry if the beasts have hurt you; they shall be reprimanded for those scars on your shoulder. They shall fly these barren skies no longer. Is that solace to you?"

"No." Weeping now, she understood that what was behind the voice was more frightening than the angels. *By far.* She wiped her tears away angrily. "It's not fair! I want to go back home! I want you to put me back inside! I demand it!"

"Please stop crying. *Please.* If I could hug you, I would. Perhaps you would like to get back onto the bed for a while? A small round of, uh, of larvae, of moth larvae, to lessen your pain? You *did* rise from the sickbed rather quickly—"

"No." Deidre looked around again; in the atmosphere of menace, the trees appeared suddenly sterile and so unmoving compared to those of Elegia. She thought for a second about poor Sam, and about the dead boy, and she wondered what it would be like to die twice, or to exist without really having ever lived. Sam had wanted life. The boy, too, had wanted life. *She* wanted it also.

But as she lifted her eyes skyward, towards that sun and bleached sky, everything reeked of death. "You can't keep me here. You can't." Sobbing, she wiped her nose on her forearm. "I hate you."

"If you ask me to go away, I will. We can talk later."

"Go away!"

She stood, bolting, crashing through the brush that grew behind the bench until she banged up against the translucent wall of the cage with her knee and forehead. She did not fall. Outside: endless, hostile sand, russet, undulating with heat.

Looking out, panting, her wounds hurting, her head throbbing where she'd hit it. When it became clear the voice had indeed gone away, she said, "Voice?"

The reply was immediate: "Yes?"

"You never answered my question. What's going to happen to me?"

"You're going to carry the torch, Deidre."

"What does that mean?"

"Try not to think of yourself. Think of your species. Deidre, I'm one of the ones that got away. We are your *real* ancestors. We lived here once, but we left. And we hit a brick wall, genetically speaking. Until a short time ago, we were facing slow doom. Then we discovered you. Stuck under the ground. There were rumours of the project, old news files of the habitat . . . So now we're coming. We're coming to get you!"

Tears streamed her face. Snot dripped from her nose. Nearly hysterical, she leaned against the barrier, pounding at it with her fists.

"Please," the voice whispered, "please, don't panic."

"Go away!" she screamed. "Leave me alone! Leave me alone!"

"I know this is a difficult time—"

"Stop talking!"

And for a time, at least, the voice did.

MEREZIAH, L1

Quick, clean pain woke him. He lay on his back. There was a stench in the air—wet coals, and something worse, something burning that had recently been alive. Had he smelled burnt flesh previously? That did not seem likely, but how else could he have identified it?

Damp mist nearly soothed him, but there was a disturbing, fluctuating susurrus of muffled moans and wails that grew louder now, nullifying the sensation. Mereziah opened his eyes—

Smoke, and sharp light. He moaned, wanting to rub at the irritation, but could not move his hands.

He coughed a moment later, and pain flared through him again. Some warm and damp membrane covered his mouth.

"Relax," a voice said, gently, from nearby. A large, blurred face peered down over him. "I've given you a shot. And you're in a mask. Try to relax." The face sported a red beard and had the soot-smeared features of a man who did not dwell in perpetual gloom. "Don't talk. You'll get your strength back soon."

Mereziah was about to disobey, and try to speak, when he realized it had begun to rain. A rare occurrence, but not entirely unheard of: he had experienced rain twice before in his life, falling down the length of the shaft.

What had happened to the world? And where was this place? He closed his eyes again. The pain was constant now, radiating out from his chest. Whatever was over his mouth was not easy to dislodge; he touched the substance with his tongue and found it to be resistant, like a layer of skin grown there. When he rolled onto his side to retch, the strange, pliable cover vanished to let out the hot bile but reformed quickly.

"Please, try not to move, sir, try not to move." The firm hand on his back rubbed. "You've had a coronary."

"My heart . . .? I'm . . . Who are you?" The covering over his mouth had not hindered his speech, and his throat felt raw, as if the fire he smelled in the air had burned inside him as well. But, as the voice had promised, he felt the pain lessening, in pulses, felt himself growing stronger. Soon his breathing came a little easier, and when he opened his eyes he could keep them open, though he blinked, squinted, and tears streamed his cheeks.

"My name is Steven," said the bleary face. "Please, lie still."

"Are we at the bottom?" Mereziah tried again to move his hands, wanting desperately to reach up and clear his mouth; whatever the thing was, it moved with his lips, conforming as he spoke. The sensation was horrible.

"I'm afraid I don't understand your question."

"At the bottom. Bottom of the world." Mereziah tried not to gag. His eyes were watering profusely. "With the dead."

"I brought you *upwards*, sir. Below us, there have been events. Of cataclysmic proportions."

"How far up are we?"

"Cataclysmic," Steven whispered, as if he had not heard Mereziah. Staring off into middle space, where a billow of grey rolled in as the thin rain attempted to slice through it, the bearded man said, "Most of the fires are out."

From within the haze just then came a swell of groans and cries: people were injured in there. Gravely injured. Wounded were all around Mereziah but he could not see them. Other sounds were urgent voices, people giving instruction, calling for assistance, trying to help in a helpless situation.

Steven said, "But there are fires burning below, on several levels." He looked at Mereziah again. "The air here is being cleaned. We've activated a small squall. It'll take a while but thank God the air conditioning is working."

"What . . . events?" Mereziah struggled to understand. "Did you say where we were? How high up we came?"

Now that Mereziah's senses were clearing, he saw that Steven looked exhausted, deflated, yet in an odd way seemed healthier than all the people he had ever known. Newer, skin uniform in tone, his body's lines less harsh.

Beyond the man's head was more smoke, more mist.

"A collapse, for starters," Steven said. "On level twenty-four, above the stasis tanks. We might still be there, if it wasn't for that fire.

"And apparently there's been a breach of some kind, in the outer structure. No one has been able to see the roof clearly yet and we have no data from outside. The suns are struggling to stay lit. I don't know how much time has gone by . . ." Letting his words fade, Steven looked up once more, as if for guidance, peering into the grey bank hanging over them both.

Finally Mereziah managed to move a hand, a foot. He tried to sit up. "I have to know where we are. I *insist*."

"There's fighting. And a thousand nasty viruses in the air. It's a wonder *any*one is alive."

Despite the small size of Steven's eyes, they held a powerful urgency, blazing with a power long-vanished from the old man—if it had ever resided in him.

A sudden wave of warm rain moved over, splattering loudly in the mud as the squall intensified. Dense veils of downpour consumed the landscape, then, just as suddenly, diminished.

"What is happening?" Mereziah whispered.

"I wanted to ask you that." Steven touched Mereziah's shoulder. "You have on an old uniform. I've never seen it before. I don't recognize it."

"I'm a lift attendant."

"The elevators?"

Mereziah was not sure how to respond.

"Listen, can you speak for the network? Were you in touch recently? Up until . . . until *this*?"

"I don't know." Water dripped from the red beard to Mereziah's face, mingling with the rain and the tears. "I don't recall a thing." Watching the falling droplets, Mereziah realized that Steven also wore a mask of some sort: a thin membrane covered the man's mouth, probably similar, or identical, to the one over his own.

"You have no insights at all?" Steven's voice verged on

desperation. "We were paid good money. But my God, how much time has passed?" His eyes implored. "You're the only person I've found wearing a uniform, the only staff member besides myself, so I thought . . ."

All Mereziah could say was, "You should have let me die," for now his memories had come back, triggered by the smell of charred meat in the air: yes, a woman had been burned, consumed by fire. He had watched her die. He had filled his lungs with her stench. But worse than the knowledge of how a human smells and looks when they are immolated, worse even than the fact that this knowledge was now integrated into him, never to leave, was the memory of the kiss he'd planted on the beautiful toothless mouth of Crystal Max. He recalled her indignity, her anger, her hatred of him. He recalled her subsequent demise.

Sheets of rain washed over.

He was responsible. For Crystal's death. For all of the deaths.

Right now, Crystal was probably telling his parents the truth.

Mereziah groaned, retching, wishing the mask or whatever it was over his mouth would suffocate him.

Steven's hand still rubbed at his back. As those fingers pressed firmly against his spine, Mereziah finally understood what the man had implied in their brief, confused conversation: cognition filtered down through the miasma of self-pity and pain exactly like a distant light overhead was now doing, filtering down through the haze of smoke and rain and grey vapour. *Suns*, Steven had said. So now Mereziah understood. He said, "We are at the top of the world."

"Yes." Steven nodded. "We're in a field, on the uppermost level."

Since there was already moisture on Mereziah's face, and his eyes had been watering for some time, it was hard for him to tell if more tears sprung from his ducts just then. *The top of the world . . .* How could this place—this muddy *disaster*—be the fabled upper reaches? Where were the fancy balls? Where were the green fields? Where were the children playing, laughing in the warm and welcoming light?

Both men, for a moment, were silent with their own disillusionments. Aside from the muted groans of the nearby wounded and the dripping of the dying rain, there was relative silence. Mereziah imagined that he might have shattered, with his own blatant disrespect for his position, with his bad decisions and addled capabilities, all bonds that held fragments of life, world, and reality together. Surely, it wasn't possible that the upper level had always been like this: corrupt, smoky, filled with pain. That his lifelong dreams to reach here were a bitter joke, revealed to him just now, in his last days, after everything else had turned to shit.

Or did he bring this misery here?

"Was there," Mereziah said carefully, "anybody else with me when you found me?"

"No, sir. There were no other people, I'm afraid. Are you searching for anyone in particular? A loved one?"

"I'm searching for someone, yes . . . These are fields?" He tried again, futilely, to sit up. "I'm in a *field*?"

"It used to be one, when this place first opened. We're near the easternmost part of Grant Park. But everything's changed . . . Listen to me, I tell you not to talk and then I ask you questions. Rest, sir, rest." Steven's hand remained on Mereziah's shoulder. "Try not to breathe too deeply. You've been given menzatane. More help will be here soon . . . Now I have to attend other people. I have to go back down."

"Look for a girl," Mereziah implored, words rasping out of his dry throat. "Look for a young girl . . ."

"Your granddaughter?"

Mereziah winced. He lay back down. Shame had succeeded in crushing him flat. These fields, he thought, are consumed with fire and drowned in water. There are no parties. No fresh air. No laughter or open grass. Because I have brought a plague upon the world. I am pestilence. I have killed a dozen people. I have killed an innocent girl.

A loud and violent disturbance from the fog jolted him from his unpleasant reveries: agitated shouts, the tremendous sound of something large and fundamental shifting under him, trembling the very ground. He tried to get up onto one elbow; pain, spreading through him, was once again exquisite.

The man, Steven, was nowhere to be seen.

Moans coming out from the bank of mists now were certainly from a living creature, but not from any human. Peering in the direction, touched all over by goosebumps, Mereziah could not see the source. Had he heard this sound before? Was that a shadow, moving? Silhouettes of some huge bulk?

Now two men burst from the fog and smoke, running straight at him, in a panic, stumbling past on the slick ground and splashing him with mud and rain—

A massive shape, massive shadow, lumbering closer but still obscured within the grey confines. Again and again the ground shook. Mereziah, to his astonishment, actually got unsteadily to his feet—holding his left arm cradled; it remained useless.

Then all the smoke and mists and fog blanketing the landscape suddenly swirled upward into a vortex, torn away in an instant.

He blinked.

Moisture, cold on his skin.

And stitches of pain, down his left side, but he was standing, staring incredulously into the near distance, where a handful people also stood, facing away from him.

The numerous wounded were laid out in rows and rows at their feet.

The apparition among them was a giant sloth.

It took a moment to register the creature as such; never before had Mereziah seen one of these beasts walking upright: it was massive, easily as tall as five men standing on one another's shoulders. Rocking slowly from side to side, the beast shambled toward him on giant, incurved claws. Gravity was unkind to the sloth but fires below had been crueler still: in places, the shaggy, matted coat smouldered and on the huge humped shoulder a patch of meat sizzled. Trails of smoke tried to tether the beast to the background yet it came on, relentless, blindly moaning.

Behind the creature, tented by a structure that once must have been tinted festive colours but was currently grim and damaged, a hole yawned so large it could only be the opening of a lift shaft.

Able-bodied rescuers tried to drag victims out of the creature's path; others attempted to distract the beast by waving, shouting, tossing clods of mud, wanting the sloth to veer away from the defenseless, but these objects bounced off of the scorched flanks as if they were nothing. The injured people alert enough and able to had begun to drag themselves away. The sloth swung its head toward Mereziah, as if seeing him there, and cried out an otherworldly roar.

"Stop," Mereziah shouted, stepping forward. His legs trembled. Did the beast know he was responsible for its painful burns, for the ruination of its home? "Stop!"

Waving one arm, croaking out calls, Mereziah hobbled. He strove to attract those huge claws, possibly lead the beast back toward the hole—from which now came a belch of black smoke, jetting straight upwards, and another sloth, emerging, claws hooking onto the edge as it came, moving slowly.

Notions of sacrifice and redemption blinded Mereziah as he stepped among the wounded. Some looked up with glazed eyes. A few reached out: a blackened child with weeping burns, making a thin, consistent whining sound; a young woman with a bandaged torso; a chubby man in a singed white suit who managed to touch Mereziah's leg—

Mereziah had no time to spare. He pulled free, his voice stronger than it had been in years, rising above the trumpeted pain of fellow man and tortured beast. He could not let his eyes waver from the rheumy gaze of the nearing sloth. Yet stepping among these wounded, how could he ignore the horrific nature of the injuries? People were bleeding their lives out into the mud, most so injured that they no longer seemed to have once been human. That sickening stench of burned flesh again, eroding his resolve. People were dying because of what he'd done. They would never return to life, nor cease to die, regardless of his attempts.

Surely, he might save a few? Wouldn't that make a difference? "Here!" he shouted, trying to keep his momentum. "Over here!"

Someone dressed in a brown uniform, with the same incomprehension in his eyes that Steven had, tried to stop Mereziah from getting any closer to the giant sloth; Mereziah wheeled. "That beast and I are from the same place! We must both go back!"

Uncertain, the man released Mereziah.

The sloth was perhaps a dozen metres or so from the nearest row of wounded, who had been arranged on coats and blankets by rescuers, filthy with mud and rain.

The second beast was fully emerged from the shaft, following its companion. Massive claws lifted, came down, slid slowly forward over wet grass and ichors.

A sudden whiff of wet, singed fur, as nauseating as the stench streaming up from Mereziah's own comrades, and the equally foul breath of the sloth, looming over him, cascaded like an ill and roaring wind.

Sounds of a body being stepped on were not what Mereziah had expected; the human form gave up its shape with veritable silence, not much different in tone than the sound those huge claws already made as they came down on nothing but mud and water and blood; it was the shouts of those lying helpless nearby—and who had watched this death, and were next to die—that raised hackles.

Mereziah screamed for the creature to stop, not sure what to expect next, or what to do—close enough now to the sloth to see his own lanky reflection trapped upside down in the tiny, fear-scarred eyes. He said, "Let's go back, where we belong . . . We've done enough damage here."

The creature stopped its advance, panting, one huge foot lifted over a man who, thankfully, was unconscious or already dead. The hot rancid breath fell all around Mereziah—

Then everything changed: a warm yellow light erupted, spreading out from above, falling over Mereziah, the beast, over the myriad wounded arranged at their feet. Mereziah's eyes watered anew. He felt his uniform and areas of his exposed skin instantly warm.

The sloth came no closer. Mereziah was close enough to lay a hand on the quivering, mucus-strung snout.

The second beast had also stopped, sniffing the air, blinking in the new light. Even the moans of those hurt in the fire and collapse of the world had stilled, poised in the new warmth, as if for resolution.

Mereziah waited for that big-clawed fist to finish its arc and smear him down into nothingness.

It did not move.

He broke contact with the animal's stare, looking up to see what could only be two shining suns, one almost directly overhead, another more distant, burning high against the roof of the world. All about him, the air was moist and steamy.

The light forced Mereziah to look away. But he had gazed upon the suns. He had seen their brilliance.

Perhaps his efforts to return himself and the beasts to the gloomy shaft from whence they had emerged were not futile. All he had to do was follow through, lead both creatures back to the hole, send them down, and vanish along with them. He might not be able to reverse time, or bring the dead back to life, but saving what lives he could was worthwhile, repair some damage, put a few things back where they belonged.

As if attempting to seek what small encouragements Mereziah had spotted in the clearing sky, the sloth lifted its head too, opening its mouth to show those grinding teeth, big enough across to be used as beds. Between the cuspids, in the fetid gape, a great black tongue rose and fell. The sloth took an awkward step backwards.

"Yes," Mereziah said. "Return."

With grace—the existence of which Mereziah had not previously suspected—the nearest sloth turned, shedding water and mud from its pelt.

There was a cheer, and other noises of relief, as if all breath had been held. No one was more shocked and elated than Mereziah.

"Wait for me, brothers! I'm coming with you! Wait for me!"

But as he took a step, his legs simply folded under him without warning, without any further pain, and he fell to splash on his side in the mud. He could not move. Despite the membrane, there was foul mud in his mouth. He lay there, between two wounded men, as if he had been part of their numbers all along, as if this spot had been reserved for him.

When the pain finally did return, it grew in great surges, coming up his left side. Yet he could do nothing but curl slightly in the mud, rocking like a helpless infant. As his vision darkened, he could not even see the retreating beasts, though the ground shook under him and he was dimly aware of their fading moans.

He focused on the face of the man lying next to him: handsome, middle-aged, with a neatly trimmed moustache and the pale green eyes of someone who had lived his life in the light. The face was alert, watching Mereziah. A very faint voice said, "You are brave . . ."

Mereziah remained silent, teeth grinding against each other as agonies whirled around and around inside his body and his vision grew darker still; whatever drug Steven had given him had clearly worn off.

All around, people were resuming efforts to assist the injured. Had both sloths gone back down? He could not raise his head to look. No one came to attend to him. For that he was grateful. On his wet skin and soiled uniform, which lay heavy on his body, the warm light still fell.

Blood crusted the man's forehead. More blood caked the dark hairline. And mud, of course, on the man's cheek, where it was pressed into the ground.

Mereziah said, "I betrayed my position, my family. I betrayed the *world*."

With his mouth grim and tight, the man responded: "You have saved lives. You saved my life. I am a good judge of character, if nothing else, and I know you are a good man. Qualities show, on your face."

"It is not true. But you are kind to say that."

"I would like to help you, as you helped me, would like to extend my hand, but I am unable to move." The man closed his eyes. After a long pause, he opened them again. "Your guilt cannot match mine. I sent my family away. My girls. I sent them all away."

Mereziah did not want to hear anything about family. Especially about girls. But perhaps this was part of his penance, to listen to this story as he lay dying. Not long ago he had lain his own confessions down, upon the madman, whom he'd then abandoned in the stalled pod. That unburdening had made him feel better, at the time. So now he would listen. He would listen . . .

"I don't even know if they're alive. The wound I've received—a spinal injury, I'm told—is nothing compared to that hurt.

"I came to understand information they were not aware of. I was caught up in events and I did not consider them. They were my family but I dismissed them. I thought they complicated matters. And so I sent them away . . . They trusted my judgement. Even my beautiful wife. Without question. She cut all her hair and took my kids in the wagon. They trusted me, and I sent them away."

"Maybe they are alive."

"It's also possible I sent them to their doom. Before you try to console me, I heard from several sources that my youngest daughter, my baby, was abducted. By beasts, no less, and taken away . . ." The man was quiet for a moment. Then he said, "All that matters is that my girls are not with me in these last moments, and that I failed them."

Mereziah stared. The voice had been fading, replaced by a thrumming sound from within his own skull. He thought: *I did love my brother, I did love Merezath.*

"—to create creatures for a living. Tortured, wretched beasts . . . I did not reflect upon their fates. Vivisections, tortures in the name of progress. We tried to *create* lives. We ended lives. When those two monsters appeared, I thought they might even have been made by me—"

Only the roaring in Mereziah's head now, going on for some while, before the man coughed dryly and continued: "I knew there was a hole in the sky. From the outside. And I knew that corrupt soldiers were being formed in the bottom of the world. My people told me. I also knew there was fighting and still I refused to go with my family. Because I was negotiating the sale of crops, holding out for more money, expecting food stocks would increase in value if there was a war . . ."

Overhead, the suns must have flared because the light intensified, became whiter, and hotter. And Mereziah saw it now, through the increasing nimbus of light; he saw the hole in the sky. Directly above him. The intense light was coming through, seeking him where he lay. And something else was happening up there, some activity, some struggle, but he could not look at it for long, could not be certain.

"Goodness," the man lying next to Mereziah said, squinting, and was then consumed by the glare.

But inside that growing light were other faces, coming to the fore. The faces of Mereziah's parents. They were not stern. Holding forgiveness in their eyes. They beckoned to him kindly, so Mereziah moved upwards, to be reunited with them at last.

TRAN 50, L32

Tran so Phengh stopped at a primitive canteen and drank three glasses of tepid water. He thought about the parasites the dark god had removed from his eye and he wondered if the giants were hunting him still. After eating most of a stale cake that the deity lurking behind the wall unit offered him, he bent to rinse his hands and face.

At his feet, the tiled floor was merely damp but in other places this long hall had been flooded to his knees. Almost totally dark, the ceiling was low enough to touch. Pipes clanged and howled. Some dripped on him. He had passed a few pipes torn completely from their moorings; these, spraying, had drenched him. He was now soaked to the skin, and his skin, irritated, tingled.

Dim lights flickered, brightened momentarily, became dimmer still.

Chewing, and licking at his teeth, Tran so opened his fly to piss into the dirty gutter. He looked both ways and muttered, "Management, my ass," for either he had been intentionally sent astray by the clerk or he had ended up in the wrong place by his own inability to follow directions: there certainly did not appear to be any form of higher god down here. In fact, the fetid place was deserted and crumbling before his eyes.

Soon, he told himself. If there was no change in the situation soon, he would turn back, re-ascend, and go home to Minnie sue.

For a second, he considered stopping off, apologizing to Sandra, but he could not trust himself to see her again and he was still somewhat stung by embarrassment.

He shook his penis dry. He did not tuck it away.

The air was thick here and the stench strong. Yet not altogether unpleasant.

Sandra. When he had finally found her, straightening the sheets on a bed, he had told her how he felt, what he wanted to do . . . The experience of being summarily rebuked had been a further blow to his ego, almost a physical slap. But how could the situation have ended any other way? Had he really expected Sandra to agree to his proposal? She had just stared at him. The look on her face, as she stepped back—the expression of disdain, and fear—had been answer enough.

Reflecting upon this now, in isolation, he felt that the rejection had a cathartic effect on him, seemed to have broken the spell he'd been put under. He felt closure, release.

What had possessed him? Had parasites of a more insidious nature than the ones from Lake Seven remained inside him, eating away at all he had held precious? How could he possibly have fallen for Sandra so completely and expected her to feel the same?

He was grateful that affection for his wife was rejuvenated. He had recaptured precious memories of Minnie sue, and put them back where they belonged.

Closing his eyes, he forced these images of his wife to remain in his mind. Slowly, he masturbated, tribute to Minnie sue, to their life together. He thought of her mouth, her breasts, her ass. His cock was hard and he came almost immediately, grunting and opening his eyes in time to see his jism falling in lumpy yellow streaks against the damp and mouldy wall. His seed trickled down to the water spigot.

And then the world shook, literally, and he just stood there, knees weak, grinning and panting.

He waited for his erection to subside. Love for his sick wife swelled and pulsed inside him.

He wiped his hands on his pants.

"Hello?"

Tran so wheeled at the voice.

"Excuse me, sir, sorry to be a bother . . ."

Coming hesitantly down the hall toward him was a trio of blond teenage boys, all dressed in clean, grey uniforms. Tran so tucked himself in and snapped up the fastening stud of his pants. The outfits these boys wore were different than either the Ensign's or the dark gods' had been, for these were well pressed, nearly pristine, as if they'd never before been worn (though they were damp and stained around the cuffs). Even the three faces had a fresh quality.

"Hello there yourself," Tran so replied. He held his hand out to shake but when he saw the reaction on all three faces, he decided against the gesture and let his hand fall to his side.

The boys had stopped several metres from Tran so, sizing him up with identical features.

Tran so had the feeling that if he turned his back he would never be able to recall any of their indistinct attributes.

Triplets?

Maybe fourteen, fifteen years old, tops.

"You understand what we're saying?" the one in the centre asked. "Because we met a girl, a bald girl, back there, who stared at us blankly and couldn't answer any of our questions."

"I understand what you're saying."

"Thank goodness." The teens glanced at each other; the effect was as if mirrors had suddenly appeared between them. They turned their wide eyes back to Tran so. The one in the middle spoke again, "Sir, we are *very* sorry to bother you, but . . ."

"Yes?" Tran so Phengh folded his arms. The boys were shorter than he, and slimmer. Though they had shown no signs of hostility so far, he did not trust their unease, their politeness, or their clean uniforms. If they wanted to fight, he was sure he could take all of them.

The one on the right spoke now, talking in the same tone and voice as his comrade: "We need help, sir. It's important. Crucial, in fact. *Crucial.*"

The one on the left said, "Do you know anything about what's happened to the floor plan? Or to the infrastructure? In general terms? Do you?"

"Slow down," Tran so said. "Explain."

"To the rest of the staff?"

"To management?"

"To anything?"

"Management?" Tran so nodded. "I'm also looking for management."

"You are?" This appeared to cheer the boys somewhat, for they became slightly animated. Certainly their interest was piqued. "Do you work for the network?"

"No . . ." *The network.* The god of all gods. Once again, maybe this strange place he found was on the path to getting answers. Just as he was ready to cease his search, and go home to Minnie sue, would he discover the truth? Could a hint come from such unlikely sources as these three lost souls? "I'm not from around here," Tran so said, cautious. "I just arrived. What can you tell me about this network?"

"It's broken."

"Kaput."

"And this is *really* not the scenario we were trained to expect."

"I have the growing feeling," Tran so said, "we have all been led astray."

"Pardon me?"

"Lied to."

"Lied to? I hardly see how, but . . ." There was a long pause during which the boy in the centre bit his lower lip and more looks were exchanged. "Sir, you may be right. Though it's not our place to speculate. And the word 'lie' has strong connotations . . . Something has certainly gone awry. We don't mean to alarm you, sir, but it looks like time is running out."

"Perhaps," the boy on the right said, "it already has."

They all agreed, nodding.

"Look here," the centre boy continued, "this hall—the hall we're in—isn't on our map." He held out a small, flat device, which rested inert in his pink, trembling palm, and exposed a meaningless picture of colour and lines.

Was this, Tran so wondered, proof of what the boy had said, about time running out? Tran so watched the image. Oily colours moved across each other, lines wavered. He had no clue what he was looking at.

"Our world," one of the boys whispered, returning the device to his pocket, "is falling apart."

Tran so Phengh replied that this information was not news to him, and, having arrived at the conclusion that the three boys were soft in their collective head, and that they would, in fact, be no help to him, walked away, heading in the direction he had been heading before he'd stopped for the snack. His back tingled in anticipation of an attack, for he still did not trust the youths; the only thing he heard were mumbled consultations.

He did not look back.

Another hour or so of more flooded corridors, slogging through more kilometres of muck, he decided that if Minnie sue had died in his absence, he would return to his fishing spot a humbled man, and sit there every day, as before, but never would he resume his attempt at forgetting his losses in life. They were integral to his being—

He saw the three boys again. Appearing from a wide opening in the wall, the trio bolted across, passing briefly from one side to the other, splashing in the shallow puddle there before vanishing into another archway. They looked as lost and scared as when they had first confronted him; they did not see him this time, staring down at their tiny device, arguing among themselves about whatever it was they saw there. Their voices, and the fall of their feet, soon echoed into silence.

As time progressed, the relentless uniformity of his surroundings was not only getting tedious but was also making him think that he might never find another elevating device, and that he was stuck in this limbo of darkness, water, and halls. The only way he could be certain he was moving on was the varying depths of fluids on the floor and the odd patterns it made, splashing up onto the walls either side.

The lights in the ceiling flickered. The floor shook. There was a distant rumbling far above, sending dust and other debris to patter down upon him, and by then he entertained the idea that somehow he had actually died in the ductwork, and had been given a test in the afterlife—temptation, by Sandra—which he'd promptly failed.

Was eternity in this place his punishment, his snide answer?

A hot gust of air embraced him and left him, cold.

Feeling twinges of disconcertion now, Tran so Phengh conceived of a plan to mark a trail as he went, perhaps scratched into the tiled wall, and was thinking about just what he might use to scratch the tiles with when he spotted yet another figure approaching, walking, head down.

He did not call out.

As the figure neared, he saw by the graceful, rolling gait that it was a woman. His heart raced. This might be the beginning of another test for him to mess up. He hoped the woman was unattractive. That would be easier for him.

Soon he saw more details: large, fleshy, bald. Dressed in threadbare rags. He began to feel a little better.

She finally looked up, and saw him. Her dark face, oddly pleasant, betrayed no surprise. She smiled with sad but welcoming trepidation; it was a toothless smile.

"Hello," he said.

Her skin was blotchy and dry, as if she were diseased, but her eyes, like her gappy smile, betrayed a humanity and warmth that almost made him forget about his concerns. Nonetheless, cautiously, in case he was falling under a spell similar to the one that Sandra's beauty had cast upon him, Tran so introduced himself. They shook hands. Her grip was cool, firm.

"You're from far away," the woman said. This was not a question.

"Yes." But looking into her glittering eyes, anxiety took a sudden, inexplicable leap inside him. He stammered, "I'm, uh, from, from Hoffmann City. It's where the water comes from. Above . . ."

Her smile widened. She continued to stare into his face. "I don't know where that is but we all appreciate the water. I suppose it has to come from *somewhere*. My name is Reena."

"Reena." The nervousness, which had stung his palms and roiled in his guts, now consumed him; he tried to force it away, to reason with himself, but to no avail. He took a deep breath. "I came here, came down here, searching for something called the network but now—" He shrugged and, to his mortification, uttered an awkward laugh that could only be described as part way between a honk and a titter. "I'll, uh, settle for the nearest exit."

"I'm afraid I don't know what the first thing is or where the second might be. An exit? From where? To where? Where can you go?"

"Up, of course."

"Up? Nothing but beasts up there." She might have been mocking him.

"There are some creatures up there," he conceded. "But no more than any other place."

"Is your hair a wig?" she asked. "And your teeth? They're real?"

"Yes . . ."

Reena seemed impressed. "The world is changing," she said. "*Rules* are changing. At the best of times I never knew what stories to believe. Then again, I didn't set out to find out which ones were true, either."

"I did," Tran so said. "I set out. That's exactly what I did!"

"And? Which stories are true?"

"None of them. Not one."

Reena smiled. "You know, I wasn't aware that these halls existed, going on and on like this. Maybe they never did before, not until now."

"Reena, listen, the network is sometimes called the god of all gods. Does that mean anything to you?"

She shook her head. "There are no gods down here. I think there once were, but not any more. But I have to keep moving. See, I'm also looking for something. For someone, to be precise."

"Who?"

"A friend. He was part of a search party, ironically. Looking for a young girl who had vanished. He set out in our car, three days ago. There's been no sign of him since. And now I suppose *I'll* be added to the list of missing people."

Tran so Phengh looked over her shoulder, where a sudden greenish flare in the distant hall had flickered, leaving red patches fluttering before his eyes. As he tried to rub these away, the lights immediately overhead sputtered and crackled and there was more remote, thunderous rumbling.

"Listen," he said, when the tremor had passed, "before you go, may I ask you a few quick questions?"

"Questions?"

"Yeah. I want to know . . . Do you think we're all lost? I mean, does anyone know where they are, in life?" Even as the words fell from his lips, they surprised Tran so; he hadn't been planning on steering the conversation to any topics metaphysical, no matter how ill-conceived or simple. He put his hand over his mouth and held it there, as if to stop further outbursts from escaping. He hoped Reena might look upon what he'd said in an amused light, but neither of them smiled. To attempt recovery, he stammered through his fingers, "I'm, uh, I'm sorry to hear about your friend . . ."

He found himself wanting to mention his lost son, and his dying wife, but there was no reason to burden this already sad woman with more gloomy news. He cautiously took his hand from his mouth and heard himself say: "To get down here I had to step into a tiny chamber, hardly bigger than my body . . . Just prior to this, I'd spent some time in another small confine, and was reluctant to enter."

Reena appeared to be growing increasingly suspicious of Tran so. He could not blame her. Wanting earnestly to dispel her notions, to be trusted by her, he continued:

"I had been assured that coming down here would bring me a few steps closer to fulfilling my quest. If I rode inside this strange device . . . Where I come from, in Hoffmann City, we believe that a giant tube, which some people, I've learnt, call a lift, or an elevator, accesses the god of all gods. This device I entered travels inside the tube." He wiped his palms on his pants and took a deep breath. "I think I might have been drugged, or infected. Once inside the device, I whispered my intentions to the walls and we began to move. For the longest time after there was silence. I thought about girls, to be blunt. I thought about Sandra, and about my wife, Minnie sue. The chamber, by this point, had begun to emit the scent of things growing in wet places, at the very cusp of decay. I was in there for a long time. Eventually, I curled on the floor and tried to sleep. Just as I was beginning to think I had trapped myself yet again, that I would never emerge alive from this chamber, it came to a complete stop."

Tran so still felt anxious. Why this anecdote was so important to relate he was not sure, yet it would make a huge difference, he knew, if he could tell the whole story to Reena.

But Reena, meanwhile, was looking downright wary by this

point. What if she walked away? Tran so could not be sure what he might do in that case. Making a motion with both hands, meant to indicate that the point was coming (though he himself was not convinced), he said, "This tiny elevating chamber did not open. I was not at my destination. There was no way to leave that I could see. I tried to get out at first, to force my way out, pushing downwards against the floor, pushing at the walls with my elbows, knees, and feet. Soon I gave up. I curled there, waiting."

Reena said, "Let me pass. I want to find my—"

"Wait. Listen." Tran so took another deep breath, braced himself to catch the woman, should she try to run. "I was preparing to sleep—I was so exhausted—when there came a light rapping on the outside wall. At first I thought I was dreaming but the knock was repeated. It came from a tiny window above my head that I had previously regarded but had not been able to open. Looking up, I saw an old, old man outside, with huge eyes, peeking in at me. I was shocked. He looked at me for a long time and then he said, 'Attendant here, how can I help you?'"

The look on Reena's face had momentarily returned to one more benign; evidently, Tran so had her interest again, if not her trust. He pressed on:

"I told this man my destination. 'All the way down', I said. And he asked me in his old man's voice if, when I was there, would I search for his brother? 'My brother,' he said, 'had been by my side for a hundred years and has now fallen to his death. Just two days ago.' He became emotional, saying he had always disliked his brother, disdained him, in fact, and that his brother was a prude, and a hindrance, but now that he was gone he missed him. He knew he should have said something to his brother when he was still alive but it was *too late*. So I'm . . ." Words faltered. What was he going on about? He tried to calm down but his heart raced in his chest.

"I would have loved my son," he said. "I'm sure I would have, when the boy was older. But all he did was cry. And take Minnie sue's attention." Tran so looked into Reena's eyes, searching them. "My boy never got a chance to get older. I want him to come *back*, Reena. I want to tell him . . ." He lowered his gaze. "I want him back."

"The dead don't come here," Reena said impatiently. "If that's what you're looking for. Dead don't come here and neither do gods. *People* live here. Regular people, like me. Living, breathing people."

"He was just fourteen days old when Minnie sue got sick."

"I'm going to keep looking for my friend now," Reena said. "I wish you luck."

Feeling heavy and cumbersome, Tran so Phengh stepped aside to let Reena pass. Telling her the story had not helped. He stumbled on, farther down the damp hallway. He would never find his way out of this place. What point did questions have? Quests?

Surely an infant understands that a father is tired and unsure?

The hall gently curved and, as he rounded the bend, he saw, for the third time, the trio of teenage boys. But they were no longer running. This time, they were hardly moving at all. One sat with his back against the wall while the other two knelt by him on either side. They did not notice Tran so approaching. The seated boy had his eyes closed, and glistened with sweat or was otherwise sheened, obviously in great pain. This understanding came as a shock, for Tran so realized he had come to associate the trio with harmless bumbling.

Directly across from the trio was an opened double door, revealing what appeared to be the foyer of a very large room. As Tran so got closer, he saw other boys inside, identical in dress and physique to the three (making Tran so wonder if the three were indeed the same boys he had previously met), moving about, bathed in a sick, green glow.

One of the kneeling boys turned. He must have heard Tran so. He stared for a second, eyes moist and wild. Then he exclaimed in a shaky voice, "Please, sir, stay away. It's not safe here. You shouldn't be in this area."

They had a layer of thin, translucent material over their uniforms. Like a mirage, this gossamer layer also covered their faces and hands, making the boys almost impossible to focus on. They seemed like figments, or ghosts. Glimmering shadows flashed.

"Is he all right?" But Tran so Phengh knew that the seated boy was not all right. Not at all.

The other two were administering a remedy of some sort: in their hands they clasped a small tube, as if it were a prayer card. A third tube dangled from the ill teen's neck to a tiny box on the floor, tethered to it by a thin and pulsing cord.

"Can I help?"

The nearest boy turned again. "Leave here. Please. It's not safe for guests here. There's been a calamity. You should not be here."

Tran so Phengh looked into the large room now, drawn to it. The area appeared to be even bigger than he had thought possible, as if space itself was distorted. The ceiling was hidden in a greenish haze. And the other boys—there were at least ten—were busy swarming the façade of a massive device that also vanished up into the same haze. Though they tinkered with the strange unit, none moved with any authority, and even as Tran so watched, they appeared to be slowing down, as if unwinding, their movements growing less and less certain.

Liquid pooled on the floor, which sank to a low point around the base of the device. More liquid dripped slowly from pipes overhead. The glow that Tran so saw in the room appeared to be rising up from the puddles themselves—

"Is that thing the network?" he whispered. "Is that the network, in there?"

"The network? Of course not," one of the boys answered curtly. "The network has been destroyed. In there is another disaster. A full meltdown."

Tran so took a step closer. The glow made him feel hot. The hairs on his arms were standing up. He shielded his eyes and took another step toward the door.

"Breeder," the sick boy hissed, opening his eyes and startling Tran so. "Are you a fucking idiot? Leave here! Get lost! You shouldn't be here unless you're made to *die* here. You think we were lied to? Oh, they fucking lied to us, all right."

"Already," one of the kneeling boys said, "you'll need medical attention. Don't even look in there."

"Is your friend going to be all right?" Tran so asked. "Maybe I can help you."

"Friend?" Under the membrane, there were tears on the smooth cheeks. "He's not my friend, *per se*. Now go. Please."

Tran so Phengh stood, useless, for a few seconds. A score of tiny flying animals, no bigger than the end joint of his thumb, came from nowhere to circle madly about his head, bumping into him gently before flying past, into the room, directly into the greenish light. As he watched, the animals fell, one by one, dead, to the wet floor.

He walked on.

Bodies, farther down the hall. Under the blisters and seeping buboes, the dead all had the identical features and stature of the boys he had deserted. One had apparently been tearing at his uniform and membranous cover, perhaps trying to breathe or otherwise reduce the pain he clearly must have felt as he died; the skin on the exposed chest was white and hairless. Like that of a child. Also exposed was an immature groin, the tiny testicles and penis of an infant. Of a newborn.

Tran so Phengh knelt, pulling the uniform back into place. He did not know what else to do. "I'm sorry," he whispered. "I'm so sorry . . ."

Adjacent to the body, an abandoned device, a tiny box, similar in appearance to the one he had seen being used on the dying teen. *Medicine*.

Tran so picked up the artifact. He would bring the medicine to the Hoff, to Minnie Sue.

Several more corpses, steaming in the cool hallway.

The lights flickered.

Looking back, he saw the glow, bathing the hall, but could no longer see the youths.

Further on, a junction; he turned.

A tube entrance, an elevator waiting.

He stepped inside.

Clutching the device, he went up.

ABOUT THE AUTHOR

Brent Hayward was born in London, England and raised in Montreal. His short fiction has appeared in several publications. *Filaria* is his first novel. Currently, he lives in Rzeszow, Poland, with his wife and two children.